It's Your Duty to Die

By

David R. Dye

MAPLE
PUBLISHERS

It's Your Duty to Die

Author: David R. Dye

First Published in 2026

ISBN 978-1-83538-875-4 (Paperback)
978-1-83538-876-1 (Hardback)
978-1-83538-877-8 (E-Book)

Book cover design and Book layout by:
White Magic Studios
www.whitemagicstudios.co.uk

Published by:
Maple Publishers
Fairbourne Drive, Atterbury,
Milton Keynes,
MK10 9RG, UK
www.maplepublishers.com

A CIP catalogue record for this title is available from the British Library.

Acknowledgement

I can't leave this book and, hopefully, move onto the next, without acknowledging the amazing work that Hospices do, throughout the UK.

I have seen first-hand, the altruistic care, comfort, and compassion they provide to their patients. And both it's day care and therapy provision, alongside loving care and pain relief for someone in their last days and hours.

They receive minimal financial Government assistance, so have to rely on us, the fabulously generous UK public. All I beg of you, is please keep giving generously. And if you've never given before, please consider it, and do your best.

Race, creed or colour; we will all experience the last days before we meet our maker. The dedicated Hospice professionals ease life through that valley. With them caring for us, there is nothing to fear!

CONTENTS

Chapter 1

Frank Junior's Aspirations

Anneliese and Matthew had spent more than fifteen years living in peace and tranquillity in a sleepy, caring and comforting community on the outskirts of Toronto, Canada. In the town of Oakville, on the edge of Lake Ontario, their lives had been completely fulfilled, watching Frank Junior grow and develop.

Some years had been interrupted by Anneliese's work for the CECD and the CIA, but they had learned to take that in their stride!

With Anneliese and Matthew leading the way, Frank Junior was turning out fine! He had excelled in his high school and was about to graduate with a Master's Degree from Duke University, Durham, North Carolina.

He had taken on a subject that had always fascinated Anneliese. And most of her Secret Service work had involved her in experiences that gave her the endless ability to help him. The subject, Political Science, was growing in importance, in the world they were living in.

Each day that passed saw global challenges spiralling out of control. Uncertainty and conflict appeared to be growing throughout the world. Anneliese's central focus had always been on two countries. The USA and the UK. Both had absorbed most of her time, over many years, in her position as a Secret Service Agent. However, as she was always on call, she kept a close eye on the dynamics as they developed; especially in Eastern Europe.

Anneliese and Matthew were extremely excited. They were expecting Frank Junior to arrive home late evening. Their best friend, Frank, another agent, would be arriving around the same time. They were busy preparing supper for everyone, and in between times, Anneliese and Matthew were constantly distracted, as they dusted and attempted to achieve housekeeping perfection!

Unlike Charles Dickens' opening paragraph in The Tale of Two Cities, this was not the best of times. It was beginning to appear the worst of times. And the season of darkness, particularly in the UK and USA was descending.

Frank Junior arrived about 10.30pm. Frank, his namesake, and Lucia, arrived ten minutes later. Supper was ready, but embraces were the priority. Matthew and Anneliese were amazed at how much Frank Junior had grown. He was now 6feet 4inches tall, but still one of the shortest in the Duke University basketball team!

After a torrent of love and affection from Mum and Dad, Lucia continued the outpouring of love. Frank then stepped forward with his usual reserved greeting; however the handshake, followed by a lengthy strong hug, meant the world to both of them! Frank Junior's respect and admiration for him would never be surpassed. His love for his Mum and Dad could never be challenged. But his feelings for Frank had been grafted into him from childhood, every day and in every way.

Matthew knew their drinks, and began to pour wine into the glasses on the table, as they all took their seats. Non-stop chatter continued for over half an hour. Bruschetta, and then a lasagne main course, were devoured with great appreciation. Wine flowed, but more slowly, as conversation transitioned into more serious topics.

Eventually, Frank Jr. talked about his friendships at university, his thoughts on different lecturers, and basketball team mates. He became visibly disturbed as he talked about a very good friend on the team. A power forward, who Frank Junior, as a small forward, seemed to have a strong intuitive link with. They always seemed to know where each other would be on the court, and therefore, had helped the team to many successful results!

Frank Junior slowly walked them through the story that had made such an impact on him. Apparently, his best friend was a baby when his Mother returned to her home, England, for the funeral of her Father. Immediately after the funeral she planned to return home in time for Christmas; his friend's first Christmas. She boarded a flight from Heathrow, longing to see her husband and little boy. It was a Pan-Am flight. A flight with a great, well respected airline. They had been in the air less than an hour, and were just reaching the cruising height of 30,000 feet, when a bomb, planted by terrorists, exploded; the Boeing 747 disintegrated. 243 people died, nobody survived; Pan Am Flight 103 was no more!

"My best friend never even got the chance to know his Mother. Never had that first Christmas!"

Frank swiftly moved the conversation on, before it became too morbid. Frank Junior had only six months left before he would graduate. He was confident he would achieve a Distinction in his Master's degree, Political Science. He was already sitting on a First Class degree in Economics, and his results had been so good his professor was pushing him to progress on to a Ph.D course after his Masters.

So that subject became the next conversation topic. Anneliese began to wax lyrical about how wonderful it would be to have a Ph.D in the family and how she thought he would sail through the course. Matthew was not quite so insistent, joking that three GCE's were enough in his life, but a Ph.D was not even heard of when he was a kid. Frank thought physical fitness, combined with a clever tactical mind, was the best thing to get you through life. Anneliese was beginning to scowl! Lucia giggled, saying, "I suppose a Ph.D is a cooking course? Do you learn to cook a Phud, or is it a Pud?" Her Mexican accent made it sound hilarious, and the men all laughed in chorus!

Anneliese, with a searching stare, questioned "What are you thinking of doing after you finish the Masters, Frank Junior, son of mine?"

Frank Jr. first glanced at his Dad and slowly moved his eyes to Frank. He stood, put his wine glass on the table and walked round behind Frank and Lucia, placing a hand on each of them. Their faces turned to stare up into his. Now he was faced with letting the genie out of the bottle!

With an expression that spoke volumes, his eyes met Anneliese's. "Mum, I really don't want to disappoint you, but you can't blame me for wanting to be like you, or indeed, Dad and Frank. There is only one career that my head and heart will accept. I am going to follow in your footsteps! I am going to work for the CECD or CIA. I have approached both organisations, and they are more than receptive. Tentatively, I have accepted a position with the CECD and will commence training in April next year."

Matthew and Frank stood, slowly stretching to offer hands of congratulation. Anneliese dropped her face into her hands. Both men sat down again. As Anneliese looked up, she tearfully stuttered, "Why oh why oh why? I have spent my life trying to protect you and make the world a place of peace. Now, in a heartbeat, you tell me you want to step out into a world that is balancing on the edge of a precipice." Frank Jr. was about to reply, but Matthew turned to Anneliese. "Darling, you know and I know that Frank Jr. is an intrepid character. He has analysed this to death in his own mind. He knew he would be sailing against the wind with you, and I am certain he has had sleepless nights knowing his intentions would be difficult for us to accept. But let's hear him out. In his mind, the reasons will seem David size, whilst the obstacles, you, Anneliese in particular, Goliath size! But his character, his personality, the mind he inherited from you and I, has driven him to conclude he has to take this route."

Anneliese's eyes opened wide as her face showed some relief. Frank Junior sat back in his chair, and slowly sipped his full glass of Cabernet Sauvignon. Seeing a more relaxed expression on Anneliese's beautiful face, Frank Jr, opened.

"Mum, Dad, Frank and Lucia. I love you more than I could even attempt to describe. But I want to do this more than anything! The early learning period through my life instilled in me what wonderful people you all are. I want to be the same. I want to be remembered as the same sort of person. One who cares. One who attempts to make a difference. If I can come close to the achievements of any of you, I will be happy!"

"You will recall the story I told you earlier about my best friend, Ryan. The impact on him, losing his Mum, has scorched a mark into me. The different episodes and events that I heard about through the years. That difficult day when the US President was attacked. The stories about your influence Mum, on the dismantling of the Berlin Wall. Those things will never leave my mind. And I don't want them to! Those events prove what endless wonders you all are. The recent stories about Istanbul and how you helped the President avert Civil War. He sat and told me that, as if it was a bedtime story. Mum, I want to emulate you. I may not be as good, but I will try my very best! And I promise I will not be a reckless idiot!"

The rest of that evening and the next few days were a gloriously happy time. Anneliese came to terms with Frank Junior's wishes and intended career. Matthew and Frank strutted around with pride in every ageing step!

Frank Jr. applied himself to his Masters Degree, every minute of every day, throughout the next six months. He was determined to achieve a distinction to ensure he captured the CECD position.

The final result, a 3.9, was outstanding. The next hurdles were his second interview, and then six months slogging through gruelling training…. Both physical and psychological.

He flew into Brussels on October 14, 2017, to attend the interview. He caught a taxi to Interpol's National Central Bureau. The person he was due to meet was only using an office in the building for this interview day. He did not have a person's name as it was classified. All he required was the appointment letter!

He sat, unflustered and confident, in the lobby for about ten minutes. Then an elegant young lady approached. "Are you Frank… Frank Teer, here for an interview?" "Yes, Mam," replied Frank as he stood and shook her small silky hand. She smiled, turned and gestured him to follow. She found him a seat in the 3rd floor corridor and said "He will not be long," as she disappeared through an office door.

Just a couple of minutes later, the same office door opened, and a rather stout man strode up to Frank Jr. He stood, peering down at Frank Jr. as he offered his hand. Frank Jr. stood, and as they shook hands, this person said, "Frank,

I am Commander Farrell. Well, I have to say you have grown quite a bit since I saw you last. Come in, come in!"

They sat opposite one another in comfortable armchairs. "Before we get to you Frank, I'm dying to ask how your mum, Anneliese, and Dad, are faring. And that clandestine character, Frank?"

Frank Jr. was at ease. He liked the vibes emanating from the Commander. Frank Junior spoke about them with great affection, told a few anecdotes, as he described where they lived on the edge of Lake Ontario. Some reminiscing about family visits to Niagara Falls, and the great times he had experienced at Duke University.

Eventually, the Commander, with a growing grin, said, "Frank, I'm not going to speak or question you about your academic results. Nobody could ask for more. And I won't waste time on your background. I know and respect your family and Frank more than I can say. So the only things I want to touch on are these. First, are you physically fit?" Frank Junior, attempting not to appear pretentious, said he had played for the Duke Basketball team throughout his time there. And had recently been offered the chance to join the Philadelphia 76ers.

"Frank, that's more than enough for me. And from that, I assume there are no medical conditions you are exhibiting or are concerned about." "No, Sir," was the reply. The Commander took a very deep breath as he stood up from his armchair. He moved to a corner cabinet, and took out a couple of glasses and a cut glass decanter. His neck strained to turn to look at Frank Jr. "Would you like a drink with me?" Frank Jr. with a mischievous smile asked, "Commander, do I need one to handle this last question?" Commander Farrell coughed, then laughed. "Yes, you probably do, but also I would love you to tell your Mum and Dad that we had a drink together."

"Well, in that case, Commander, I would greatly appreciate a drink with you." They both settled back in their comfortable armchairs, slowly sipping Napoleon Brandy.

"The last question is this." Commander Farrell wrinkled his nose as he spoke those words. "And this question is not just so I can tick a box. It's because I owe so much to your Mum and Dad, and Frank as well. I almost feel as responsible for you as they do. This last question, if you convince me with your answer, will take you into the most gruelling time of your life. Why you would want to do that, God only knows!"

"So, here we go. Why do you want such a dangerous career? A job so intense that you live and sleep it every moment, every hour, every day of your life?"

Frank Junior leaned back in his armchair, took a sip of his Napoleon Brandy, then placed his glass carefully, on the side table. As he sat forward in the chair, he said, "Commander, that's an easy question for me! Mum, Dad and Frank have helped prevent this world sinking deep into the quagmire, to the point where we would not be able to take another breath. I watched them playing their part. I want to carry on their work. I want to make a difference and I know I can. Humans in this world will need to continue combating the evil forces that attack continually. I will use everything in my power to resist and triumph over evil."

"I want to help prevent that Iron Curtain being raised again. I want to fight for freedom for everyone in this world. I want to battle the scourges of addiction. I want to help build a secure, productive, rewarding and peaceful future for everyone. But most of all, I want to help build a future that respects and protects the vulnerable. Children, the elderly, the disabled, the infirm, the sick and the homeless."

"Sorry, Commander, if I'm droning on. But this means more than anything to me. I am fit, healthy and fearless. I will give you my all on every assignment!"

Frank Junior stopped, took a deep breath, then gulped his brandy. The Commander, with his glass hovering close to his lips seemed overcome! "Frank, the words you spoke, the passion, the sense of purpose in your demeanour, have astounded me. The only thing I can say is that you are your Mother! Anneliese, in the body of a man. And obviously a very competent person with exemplary objectives for humanity. I will always treasure having talked with you today. I will be enormously proud to have worked with both Anneliese, and her son Frank. So Frank, yes, with my grateful thanks, I offer you the positon of Secret Service Agent with my organisation, CECD."

They stood and slowly moved toward the door. The Commander said details of the training course would be provided shortly. As he began to open the door, Frank Jr. turned and shook the Commander's hand. "I know you and Mum have been through a lot together, and I'm so happy that I will be able to continue to enjoy that legacy. But, Sir, could I make a request?" Commander Farrell, with a questioning gaze, squinted as he searched Frank Jr.'s expression. "Oh, it's nothing serious, Sir. It's just that I would prefer to be referred to as Frank Junior. Frank is his own person. A very special person to me! Mum and Dad gave me his name, but I am not Frank. If I ever get close to being like him, I will be ecstatic. He has mentored me my whole life. He is my closest friend. So, it would be heresy for me to pretend to be him."

Training was next on the agenda. It was scheduled to commence on April1, 2018. Not a particularly encouraging day to start on, however, this guy was out to prove he was no fool.

The programme would begin with a month of firearms practice, building to firearms combat of several types. Open warfare, buildings incursion and attack and jungle warfare, all supervised by senior CECD Agents and SAS operatives.

The following month would involve survival, defence and attack training on Dartmoor. The last training element had been scheduled with the US Navy SEALs in their training camp at Shaver Lake, California. This was the toughest part. Two months of non-stop stamina training, use of almost every type of military equipment and water craft on the lake.

Chapter 2

Top Class Training

At the end of this physically and mentally demanding period, a Navy Seal Lieutenant arrived at the Camp to meet the trainees and award those that had successfully completed the programme. There had been 42 on the course, including eight female secret service and military personnel. Most of these people were Marines or SEALs.

On an extravagantly blue sky, sunny September day, the trainees paraded in the main courtyard, in front of the Senior Officers building. They had practised this part on several occasions. Their lines were perfectly straight. Every person was spic and span. They stood proudly to attention. No uniforms, just gym kit, joggers and pure white t-shirts.

The lieutenant, in full dress uniform, read out names, one after the other. But only names of those that had graduated. Those that were unsuccessful would be allowed a second attempt in a year's time.

It was Frank Jr's time. He was number 33 in the list. Until then, only about 40% had been successful. But with enduring respect for discipline, the unsuccessful remained, proudly, standing in line to attention!

The lieutenant, in a loud, but calm voice, shouted Frank Junior's name. "Frank Teer, one pace forward!" Frank Jr. immediately responded but wondered why. The lieutenant with a proud expression, continued, "I want the whole class to hear this! Mr Teer achieved the best rating of this class. Indeed, he achieved the highest rating that we can find in our history books. So, Ladies and Gentlemen, please join me. Three cheers for our British colleague, Mr Frank Teer!" The cheers were loud; then, they broke ranks and surrounded him with congratulations ongoing!

At that point, a Chrysler limousine arrived. It was a SEAL's Commander, here to join the evening celebrations and pay tribute to the new recruits.

Gradually, everyone ambled off to dress for the evening. All except the lieutenant and Commander, who were deep in conversation, with constant sideways glances at Frank Junior as he strode off to his bunkhouse.

They all returned, suited and booted, for the soirée. They had only had an hour to preen, polish and prepare. The eight females amongst them looked divine, sensational, and received immediate attention from every man in the place.

Frank Junior was amongst the last group of arrivals. His appearance, his tall statuesque physique, his hand tailored Worsted suit, indeed, everything about his persona, was captivating. As he began to mingle and chat with his colleagues, his strikingly strong jawline, blonde hair and overall presence attracted enamoured glances from every one of the ladies.

But before any of them had the chance to gain a foothold, the SEAL Commander and his lieutenant approached and cornered him at the edge of the bar.

The Commander and his lieutenant were both very personable characters. Initially, the Commander offered Frank Junior his congratulations. He smiled up into Junior's face as the lieutenant asked what they would like to drink. Frank Junior responded, saying, "A Red Dog beer, sir, if they have it." As he spoke, his blue/green eyes never left the Commander's face. This was a behaviour tactic that Anneliese had instilled in him as he grew up!

The drinks arrived, they clinked glasses and the Commander uttered "Cheers!" As his Jack Daniels hit the spot, the commander blurted out, "Frank, you are so much like your mother, Anneliese. Both in looks and prowess. She must be so proud of you, as you must be of her! When I saw your name, it didn't immediately connect. But it did when I saw you in the flesh."

"I worked with your Mum on several occasions. She is superb at her job. And a guy, another agent, who was also called Frank." Junior was now feeling at ease and at home with his superiors.

With an expression that indicated the Commander was searching through his memory bank, he slowly removed his cap and scratched the front of his crown. His eyes came alive as he swivelled to eyeball Frank Junior. "Someone else just clambered into my recollections" said the Commander. The lieutenant showed eagerness to listen.

"Your Dad was here for training with us! It's rather misty, but I think his name was Matthew." With a surprised expression, Frank Junior replied, "Yes, that's my Dad. I didn't know he'd been through this! He's never talked about it!"

"Oh yes, it's all coming back! He was a short-term agent assisting Anneliese. He will be so proud of you, because he never came close to your results. But he did give it everything, especially the last exercise with boat training. He had six or seven attempts and nearly drowned. But your Mum rescued him. She was not going to let the love of her life drown in Shaver Lake. He was asked to come back in six months, but I suppose he was distracted by his assignments!" "Please give my very best wishes to your Mum and Dad."

Before he continued, Frank Junior leant on the bar and ordered another round. He had been surprised by these revelations and the Commander's kind words, but as the drinks were arriving, he gathered himself and batted the emotion away.

Turning to face the Commander and Lieutenant, Frank Junior, with an assertive tone, said, "In that case Commander, and you also, Lieutenant, I am offering you a sincere apology." Both began to develop concerned expressions. Frank Junior, with a mischievous glint in his eye, said, "You have worked with, and experienced, the best of the best!" He let out a short giggle. "But now you look as though you are saddled with me, for many years yet! So Sirs, best of luck!"

The rest of the evening was spectacular. Female attention was constant. Wonderful music, dancing, banter and humour with the successful, and encouragement for those that had not found success. They all knew they would meet again with Frank Junior sometime in the future.

Anneliese and Matthew were overcome with emotion when Frank Junior arrived home. They had a splendid two weeks together, enjoying friendship with Frank and Lucia, neighbours and the local church community. Several barbeque parties and nostalgic lunches, and dinners at restaurants along the edge of Lake Ontario. The two weeks ended far too quickly. Frank Junior was scheduled to meet with the ageing Commander Farrell in Brussels, and subsequently, again, in London. He was looking forward to meeting Anneliese's old friend, Jerome, now Director of GCHQ.

Chapter 3

On The Starting Line

The meeting with Commander Farrell was in the Belgium Parliament Building, the "Paleis der Natie", smack bang in the centre of Brussels. He had been allowed to commandeer a small spare office on the first floor.

Frank Junior eventually located him and the meeting was time limited. The Commander was on a very short fuse as he had been requested to attend a meeting in the Cabinet office with the UK Prime Minister, later that day.

His instructions to Frank Junior were to scurry to GCHQ to meet with Jerome. The Commander would join them later that evening. He could not stipulate a time as it depended on the length of the meeting with the Prime Minister. Frank Junior would be given his first assignment, after they had talked with Jerome!

It took until 5.30pm for Junior to arrive at GCHQ. The traffic from Heathrow had been diabolical. As he sat in the back of the taxi, watching the clock ticking as they travelled nowhere, he mused that terrorists had designed the M25 and one day would fly over the lines of stationary traffic, strafing every vehicle into oblivion!

The security guard inside the entrance door viewed Junior's papers then escorted him to reception. Following a phone call, Jerome rushed across the reception area to greet Frank Junior. Jerome stood back for several seconds, peering at Junior. "Oh, my dear Frank Junior, looking at you, all grown up, is making my life pass before my eyes. Well, you managed to find us in the Doughnut." Junior stopped! But before he could speak Jerome said, "Oh that's what this building is known as. It's a circular building with four floors. I will take you around and then you are scheduled to meet James Bond. I'm only joking!"

After a quick tour, smiling at clusters of Intelligence Analysts, working away on their computers, they entered Jerome's office. His secretary circumvented her desk and as she shook hands and welcomed Junior, Jerome introduced her as Miss Money, but really just Penny! A gorgeous strawberry blonde, she giggled then asked, "Would you both like coffees?" They both nodded and smiled.

Initially, all Jerome wanted to talk about was Anneliese. Then Matthew and Frank. Jerome's eyes glistened as his emotions weakened. As he regained total control, he said, "Frank, before the Commander gets here, I need to brief you on a few things!"

"You probably realise that the Commander is planning to talk with you about your first assignment. When he does, try not to look disappointed or bored! Junior, you don't mind if I call you Junior, do you?" Frank Junior's face became expressive. "If I can come close to matching Frank's ability, I will be ecstatic. So no, I prefer to be called Junior."

Jerome developed a parental gaze. "Well, the thinking is you should stay here with me for a few weeks. Meet the Intelligence Analysts, the ones you will be relying on in the future. The individuals that will be your lifeline when you need assistance!"

Frank Junior's mind began to race on. "So, Jerome, what do you think he has in his mind for me after I have learned the basics from you, and hopefully Penny!"

Jerome's eyes widened, followed by his smile, "Frank Junior, you have only been here five minutes and already are starting to sound like James Bond. I'm going to drag you into a more serious thought pattern. It is essential because I have promised your Mother that I will watch your every movement, and take every step with you, to keep you on the right road, and totally safe!"

"The easy part will be here, working with me. I am not at liberty to tell you where the follow-on assignment will take you. However, I am sure it will take you into a very dangerous world, as a field operative."

Jerome ventured to search Junior's face, whose eyes began to sparkle with excitement.

There was a loud knock on the door, which distracted both of them. Penny opened the door, announcing that Commander Farrell had arrived. Jerome and Frank Junior smiled at one another and adjusted their seating around Jerome's large walnut office desk.

The Commander waltzed in as if he was floating on cloud 9. Obviously in an exceptionally good mood, he strangled Junior's and then Jerome's hand. Jerome stood and said, "Commander, please take my desk chair. You are in the driving seat in this meeting."

As he sat, he gently eased his glasses out of the case and took a couple of seconds to focus on first Jerome, and then Junior.

Peering at Frank Junior, the Commander decided to get straight into the detail. "Frank Junior, initially I would like you to remain here for a few weeks to learn about, and get some experience of, the GCHQ work. It is our bedrock so take this element of the assignment very seriously and conscientiously." Frank Junior smiled. He already knew this part. Frank Junior, now trying not to appear impatient, slowly lifted his eyes to the Commander's questioning gaze. Frank Junior concluded he needed to appear accepting. "Well, that sounds fine. Sir, I need to learn the basics, and there is no person better equipped to teach me than Jerome!"

The Commander was pleased with the progress so far. But now he needed to tackle the more difficult phase.

He stood, took a deep breath, and then circled the room. "Frank Junior, how are Anneliese and your Dad? Are they ok with you doing this work?" This was a repeat of his earlier question, designed to allow thinking time before the serious business.

"Yes, sir," replied Junior. "It took a while to get them to see that this meant everything to me. But you know Mum and Dad! Once they got their mind around it, they were totally committed to helping me, every step of the way."

The Commander, with an unsettled expression, first glanced at Jerome, whose lips arched for a second or two, as if he was coaxing them to speak. As the Commander turned his gaze to Frank Junior, Jerome's lips decided to move. "Commander" he said, "Whatever you have in mind for Junior, will not faze him. Forget all the formal interviews, all the research and analysis that has been applied to his history. I have talked at length, with both Anneliese and Frank about him. I know he's the new kid on the block, and you are just being careful."

Jerome's eyes swivelled to look at Junior. Jerome now became passionately committed to continue. "Sir, some people may view Junior as a cocky pretty boy! Envy would have played a part in that. If I were you, I would prefer to listen to Frank and Anneliese. They know Junior inside out, and are both convinced he will give his all on any assignment he is given. One thing that Frank said to me keeps ringing in my ears. His comment to me was that Junior never showboats, has the intellect of his parents, is fearless, and will probably be the game changer this world needs!"

Jerome glanced at Junior saying, "I'm sorry if I've caused you any embarrassment." His face smiled as it turned to the Commander. "And I also apologise to you, Sir, for meddling in your business; but I believe there are times when one needs to deliver a sincere opinion."

Commander Farrell developed a grin, and smiling eyes. "Jerome, you have blown away all my concerns. So now, Junior, what was it Jerome said people may think about you? Well Junior, you cocky pretty boy, I am just going to get straight to the point, and ignore my concerns for you or your family"

"We have masses of intelligence regarding events in Afghanistan. You may recall the Russians withdrew in 1989. Muslim rebels, the Mujahideen, took control. Armed conflict escalated in 1994. An Islamic fundamentalist group, the Taliban, eventually emerged and seized control of Kabul."

"In 1996, a terrorist organisation called Al-Qaeda was welcomed by the Taliban and established its headquarters there. Their leader, Osama bin Laden, was killed by US SEALs in an operation in Pakistan in 2011."

"He was the Satan that instigated, planned and coordinated the September11, 2001 attacks on the US. These were the worst atrocities ever experienced since World War II. And things have continued to go downhill since then. Afghanistan continues to be the melting pot for terrorist activity, particularly Al-Qaeda, who now seem to have a new terrorist ally, a fanatical Islamic fundamentalist group, ISIS."

Chapter 4

First Assignment

"After all that background information, your assignment, once you finish here with Jerome, is in Pakistan and, subsequently, Afghanistan. We have many agents there trying to work out what the terrorists' next move will be. Your partner in Pakistan will be a woman named Kainaat. She is very experienced and excellent at her job. Depending on what develops, you may be required to do front-line undercover work in Afghanistan. A worrying factor is your height. You are too tall, however, there are a few tall Afghans and our people will do their damnedest to make you inconspicuous."

Exactly three weeks later, mid-day, Frank Junior's commercial flight landed in Lahore. He was extremely excited by his naïve feeling of adventure. He only had a small brown leather travel bag and a suitcase to extract from the carousel. The throng and bustle of the multitude of Pakistanis' further stimulated his spirit of adventure. As he stared at the whirling carousel, his mind recoiled, reminding him of the need for his presence to exude calmness and unobtrusive behaviour.

Having found his luggage, he reminded himself to appear calm and collected; as if this was nothing new to him. Once immigration accepted him and he smiled his way through Passport Control, he sauntered through Customs. He slowly exited into the melee of people surrounding the Arrivals Gate.

Wearing casual clothes, he came to a halt, a few yards beyond the gate. In a light blue Tee shirt emblazoned with a Red Cardinal, and Phoenix in bold letters, he appeared as an American tourist or globe trotter. He stared at the crowd before him, searching for any sign of a colleague. The temperature, up around 35C, was beginning to have an impact. He was glad he had worn knee length denim shorts and ignored socks. All based on advice from the guys in GCHQ.

His eyes traversed the waiting hordes, from right to left. He picked out a card, held high, by a young lady. As he peered at the card, which read "Kookie from Phoenix," she pulled her scarf away from her face, and began to wave. It was Kainaat, his Pakistani partner.

Frank Junior ambled towards the exit area. Kainaat shoved and pushed her way through the crowd to meet him. They shook hands as she whispered, "Junior, let's get out of here! But before we go, this is our colleague, Abid. He is accompanying us for added protection."

Their car was close, and they were soon on the road to Islamabad. Kainaat explained it would take about 5 hours to reach the CIA Headquarters in Islamabad. Junior replied that he had been given briefings, in meticulous detail, about the journey, and so far everything, well almost everything, had been accurate.

Kainaat, with a slight questioning frown asked, "Junior, what was not completely correct?" Frank Junior casually replied, "Well, the only thing was that they showed me many photographs of your exquisite features. But none of them did you justice."

Abid, driving the battered Jeep, began to chuckle. Then he loudly said, "Junior, you are going to fit in well here. Well, at least with the ladies!" Kainaat's eyes looked into Junior's.

Blushing as she eased her words out, she said, "Junior take no notice of Abid. I understand the scarf made it more difficult for you, and I do appreciate your compliment. Although I have to say I think it is somewhat misguided!"

As they continued talking, throughout the journey, Junior asked, "So what is a ladies attire called?" Kainaat, her eyes fixed on Junior's, replied "It's our national dress, Called Shalwar Kameez. I think the word Kameez is used in English but I'm not sure what it refers to. Our dress is a long tunic, paired with loose pants to help us cope with heat. And, of course, the scarf that, traditionally, is pulled over the head and across the face. But we can pull it away when we need to, or want to!"

The conversation gradually became relaxed and, in consequence, constant. Kainaat was born in Peshawar, close to the border with Afghanistan. She had done very well, exceptionally well, in her local school. Her results were beyond belief. Indeed, she had been considered a child prodigy. Kainaat stopped talking and peered into Junior's eyes. "How did you manage to get me talking like this? I am embarrassed. I am sounding like I am a pretentious person, but I'm not! You, Junior, seem to have some power that makes people open their hearts to you."

As she recovered her confidence, and Junior's kind expression comforted her, Kainaat bravely continued. "My Pakistan Government publicly declared my results in news articles around the world. Soon, my parents were inundated with offers of financial support. Finally, due to some UK and American benefactors, I was invited to Princeton University in New Jersey, USA. Initially I was not enamoured. Leaving my home, my family, my country. Sleepless, confused nights were the norm. I was distraught for weeks. Just the thought of attending the interview terrified me!"

"I was rescued by my Father. One evening, as I was sitting at the kitchen table, probably exhibiting a morbid stupor, he came and sat opposite me. He leaned towards me and held my hand. Then he said, "Kainaat, may I talk with you?" This was unusual. We never really had conversation." It had always seemed he was there to lead by instruction! His first words were, "You are a very clever girl, academically gifted, so all I've ever needed to do was to watch over you. But I suppose I'm doing that now. Here and now our relationship is changing. You are no longer a child. You are a woman. A woman in turmoil, struggling with a decision that may change your life, your future!"

"I am so proud that you are academically gifted. But opportunities give us the chance to grow those strong seeds that are already bursting to gain the light. As every day goes by, we have the chance to grow wisdom. A clever mind, enhanced with wisdom, is a formidable combination! And, in my mind, a fast track to wisdom is to see and experience other cultures, different worlds, and new relationships. This is your chance. You can always change your mind and come home. We will always be here for you!"

"I only want to say one more thing." He continued, "I am captivated by American swing music. There is a song with lyrics that I listened to earlier. The words, as I listened, made me realise that this was the time I had to speak to you! Not to instruct, not to lead you, but to help you think your way to a decision. The words were "for once in my life I have someone that needs me.""

Frank Junior had listened intently. He had found listening to Kaimaat's story a moving experience. Shuffling closer, he embraced her saying, "Your Dad was right! You are proving it every day. And I am so glad we are going to be working together. You are already my buddy. Now I need you to help with my education and wisdom in this new world."

They arrived at the CIA HQ in Islamabad. An old factory building, obviously chosen for its nondescript dilapidated appearance.

Over the next few weeks, he was taught some Pakistani language. He was a quick learner. Kainaat was seriously impressed. Some of the CIA professional make-up artists and clothing experts transformed his appearance. He was told to sun bathe, two hours every day, and make-up was also applied rigorously. His face, now with a beard, appeared older and almost the colour of a pint of English bitter; his overall appearance, with Pakistani tunic and loose pants, a wide male draped scarf, and very flat sandals, resulted in a masterly transformation.

It was now the beginning of September 2018. The next week was scheduled to take Junior out into the local community; shopping in markets, drinking in bars, eating in cafes' and restaurants. Generally testing local acceptance of his appearance, listening to conversations and acclimatizing him to the surroundings. Kainaat accompanied him every step of the way. Only for about three or four hours every day, then back to HQ to read through all the intelligence input from agents in Afghanistan, and a few local operatives.

Frank Junior and Kainaat, sitting in front of a computer, were reading and deciphering a list of encrypted messages. Junior thought for a moment then questioned Kainaat. "You never said what degree you got!" Kainaat pushed back on her office chair. Turning to face Junior, with a twinkle in her dark brown eyes, she replied, "My degree is in East Asian Studies. I chose to stay a further two years to tackle a Master's degree in Computer Science. I loved my time at Princeton, but decided that was enough academic life. It was time to step into a world where I could use my education and God given talents to try to make a difference in this difficult world!"

"I returned to my home in Peshawar, close to the Afghanistan border, intent on enjoying a few months with my family and friends. However, after two weeks, in the town, one day, I was approached by an American and his wife, asking directions. They took me aside, into a quiet area by one of our monuments, then he became direct. He worked for the CIA and quietly explained they wanted to offer me a position. All the while his wife, although I now know she was another agent, held my hand, appearing comforting and sincere. They would be in touch to arrange a formal meeting. That occurred only a week later, at the CIA HQ in Islamabad. That was two years ago. And I am so pleased to be here with my colleagues, and now you, Junior."

The next week had been scheduled as intense training. Mostly, it involved work on intelligence reports. Kainaat's knowledge and teaching ability was superb. After three days, she had Junior reciting every key area along the border, and throughout Afghanistan. This geographical training incorporated describing the terrain around Kabul and a two hundred mile circumference surrounding the capital city.

Kainaat had provided Frank Junior with a list of eight informants, as well as safe houses and establishments, mainly cafes, which would welcome and protect him. Now his next milestone in his undercover journey would be to work along with the Afghan community. He also had a code that, in an emergency, could be used with the British troops based in Afghanistan. However, he was directed to keep his distance from them in order to assure his cover was maintained.

Frank Junior was a very quick learner. He was a natural, quickly gaining acceptance amongst the local community, and began to slowly, but carefully, gather intelligence.

Within eight weeks, Kainaat recalled him to headquarters. With Pakistani thick black coffee steaming in front of them, her eyes explored his Asian attire and cosmetically dressed features. Kainaat had taught him how to transform his facial presentation, and he had become an excellent make-up artist.

Kainaat, with a sombre tone, slowly began to explain why he had been recalled. "The UK remaining troops are being withdrawn in the next couple of months. Our lifeline to them will disintegrate. We will have continued support from the Americans, however, not as accessible as with the Brits. The Americans are constantly at battle stations, in combat with the Taliban and now their new ally, Al-Qaeda. ISIS also are beginning to rattle their sabres. So the future looks pretty bleak!"

"Your job, for the time being, will be to provide intelligence to the Brits in their withdrawal process. You will be required to constantly monitor Kabul and the surrounding area. Collect intelligence, and if you have even a sniff of an attack, let us and the Brits know!"

Kainaat stared with a tender expression into Frank Junior's eyes. "Any questions so far, Junior?" Frank Junior's face became mischievously thoughtful. His cheeks drew in, then speech emitted from pursed lips. "Yes, just one question. Would you accompany me to dinner tonight? I will make it very special because I have been stuck out in Kabul on my own, and longed to see you again!"

As Kainaat's eyes met his, she attempted to become assertive. "Junior, are you taking this seriously? You should, you really should; you are on a very dangerous assignment, so please, don't treat it like child's play!"

After a long dangling eloquent pause, Frank Junior began to chuckle. Kainaat, at the point of exasperation, exclaimed, "Junior, please listen carefully to me. This is my parlous proposition. If you convince me you can take this assignment seriously, I will give you more detail!"

"Ok", said Frank Junior, "I'm been enjoying myself in your world. I know it can be scary but that is what I've always expected and wanted. I promise you, I always take my assignments seriously. I would never risk compromising any assignment!"

The look in Kainaat's eyes told the story. "Junior", she said, "I am going to praise the day, before the evening." "You should know that as you have convinced me, I will be your partner in this field operation. You will need to introduce me, wherever we go, as your wife. And to get things off on the right foot, I would love to have dinner with you tonight!"

Later that evening, Kainaat picked Frank Junior up from his hotel. In her battered, well-worn Citroen 2CV, she drove them to a restaurant in a quiet back street of Islamabad. On the way, she explained she was a regular and well known by the proprietors and staff.

Frank Junior could not take his eyes off Kainaat. Her make-up, an entrancing lavender above her eyes, was bewitching! Her long eye lashes fluttered like butterfly wings, landing on a gorgeous orchid. Her silk purple sari swished as they entered the restaurant. These sights and sounds would be engraved on Junior's memory forever!

The evening was better than anything Junior had ever experienced before. The restaurant staff were happy, attentive and seemed exhilarated, seeing Kainaat in the company of a young man.

Frank Junior could not resist flirting with Kainaat. The food and wine gradually inflamed the spirit of romance. Kainaat moved closer to Junior, took his hand and with intense emotion in her eyes, she whispered, "Junior is it ok for us to feel like this, when we have to work together. It's a difficult, important job, and I am feeling guilty. I have had feelings for you from the moment I saw you, but is this going to be too complicated?"

Junior pulled her even closer. As he exhaled sharply, the feeling of her, so close, consumed him. As the seconds ticked by, the silence was deafening. Kainaat angled her face up to his, searching for an answer.

His hand reached to her soft, silky face, and turned her lips to his. He gently kissed her lips. He had never felt like this before. He wanted it to go on forever. But he knew he had to convince her it would be fine.

"Kainaat, we will work on this thing together. We are great together. We will take care of one another. You are smart and dedicated, and so am I, I think!" And with a mischievous giggle, he added," Best of all, I love complicated!"

They spent the next few weeks together, researching every nook and cranny in and around Kabul. Every smoky dive, markets, cafés, street traders, gradually gaining acquaintances and acceptance in many difficult community and tribal areas. Kainaat took the lead, using the CIA network to assess all individuals in their vicinity. Every day they spent time quietly discussing everything they had seen, and learned, and its importance.

They had been directed to a small flat in a downtrodden, dilapidated area in eastern Kabul. An area where they were learning to become Afghan streetwise. Kainaat was fluent in both Dari and Pashtu, but in Kabul, Dari was the primary tongue. Frank Junior dedicated himself to learning Dari , and within a few weeks, was confidently approaching fluency. However, in difficult scenarios he would rely on Kainaat to take the lead.

Late at night, they increasingly submitted encrypted intelligence reports. Their input, after several months, was providing invaluable information to the CIA HQ, and subsequently, to the UK and US Forces.

Prior to the withdrawal of UK troops in October, they worked frantically behind the scenes. Their level of vigilance and, consequently, contact with CIA administration, became intense. There were concerns about the possibility of attacks on the departing UK troop transporters, but Junior and Kainaat dispelled each and every rumour. Their intelligence input now had respect throughout the CIA organisation and had reached the ears of the CECD hierarchy.

The war in Afghanistan continued to rage on. The Islamic fundamentalist group, ISIS, over the last several months, had become brutally active everywhere in the world. They were developing into a fearsome terrorist army, gaining control of large slices of Iraq and Syria and reinforcing the efforts of the Taliban in Afghanistan. They began to use tactics, aimed at striking fear and disgust into the whole world. Evil, brutal videos were constantly shown on social media. Journalists from the Western World; British, American, French were shown being beheaded. How much further could evil depravity invade into a world that deserved to find the perfect peace!

Chapter 5

Memories of Terror

Anneliese, tormented by anguish and concern for the world, and in particular, her son Frank Junior, viewed every detail of world news every day. World leaders; the US President, the UK Prime Minister, had to face up to some terrorist attack, almost every day. She talked with both of these world leaders every day. They respected her views, and she theirs.

Many years earlier, in the middle of a flaming hot summer, August 2001, Anneliese, Matthew and Frank Jr. had driven down from Oakville, Toronto, to Buffalo in New York State to watch the American football match between the Buffalo Bills and Chicago Bears. They arrived in Buffalo around mid-day. All roads to the stadium were jam packed. Every house driveway, grass verge and vacant space had been commandeered by groups of families and friends; all enjoying the fabulous weather, drinks from makeshift bars, and barbeques sizzling everywhere, delivering salivating aromas, and succulent food to everyone.

Matthew stopped the car about a quarter of a mile from the stadium, and parked close to a constant line of barbeques. Then as they stepped out of the car, a young mid-twenties Buffalos' supporter spied Anneliese. He rushed from their camp and invited them to join the fun and food. Matthew turned to Anneliese as her eyes and smile agreed!

They had a glorious time with those American people, who had been so welcoming. By 2pm everything had been packed away and they all continued enjoying the company, as they strolled to the stadium.

After an exciting spectacle, Frank Junior was breathless. He and Matthew had screamed, shouted and applauded throughout a knife edge game, with the Buffalo Bills finally achieving a deserved victory. Frank Junior would remain a fan forever!

They enjoyed an overnight stay in a Buffalo hotel, then returned to Oakville on the Sunday morning. They arrived just in time for the Eucharist service at their local church. As they arrived home after a heart and soul warming service, Anneliese heard the phone ringing; she put the key in the lock. The boys had been left to unpack, as Anneliese rushed to the phone.

Frank Junior, in a nostalgic melancholy mood, sat in their Kabul abode recalling every detail of that very special day with his Mum and Dad. His surroundings now were a world apart. But then, Kainaat walked into the room. His expression gave it away. "Junior, what is going on in that mind of yours? I can see that you are confused between happiness and memories that bring sadness."

Kainaat poured Junior a glass of red wine, then sat beside him. "Please tell me where your thoughts were heading?" Junior took a few large sips then turned to look into Kainaat's eyes. "I was remembering a glorious trip with Mum and Dad. That weekend is indelibly printed on my heart! Or, at least, the first part of the weekend. We arrived home on Sunday. We had spent Saturday at a Buffalo Bills football game. I was about eight years old and recollect it as an overwhelmingly happy occasion."

"As we pulled into the driveway, we could hear the house phone ringing. Mum rushed into the hallway whilst Dad and I began to unload the car. When we got in the house, Mum, with a glorious smile, said it was the President; President Hayden."

"I usually called him Uncle Bruce!" Kainaat interrupted. Her voice moved up in pitch. "What, the President of the United States of America; you called him Uncle Bruce?" Frank Junior's eyes peered at Kainaat's astonished expression which caused him to chuckle uncontrollably. As he gradually calmed, he emphasised, "Well I was only eight! I wouldn't speak like that now!"

Kainaat, enjoying the story, reached for Junior's hand as she continued to smile. As Junior began to move the story on, his face became strained. Kainaat's smile weakened, as her grip strengthened.

Mum said, "Tomorrow we are all invited to the White House. William Webster, my favourite CIA Director is now fully recovered and the President wants us to attend a celebration in Mr Webster's honour. As President Hayden expressed, William has been through a very difficult time and had served his country loyally for many years!"

Kainaat's gaze at Junior became questioning. "So why do you appear so disturbed?" "We never got to the airport! Mum and Dad were up first, preparing for the trip. The day is a sort of haze. Mum was getting me up and into the shower, but the phone started ringing; non-stop! From that moment, it was utter mayhem. This should have been an exhilarating, wonderful day. One day before my Dad's birthday. I had packed his presents in my case the night before. But now that fucking phone first seemed to capture Mum, then Dad, then me. Then Frank and Lucia tore in. The TV was turned on. Frank was listening on a small hand-held field radio telephone. Someone was screaming at him! Mum was answering one call after another. This was becoming the most intensely grotesque and scariest day of my life. This was 11 September, 2001!"

"By about 9.45am, all planes in North America had been grounded. On TV I had seen some of the horrific, barbaric acts of terrorism. Planes crashing into the World Trade Centre. The building on fire, people jumping out of windows from 30, 40, 50 stories up. Mum did her best to drag me away from the TV but that bastard phone would not stop! That tragedy; that depraved, barbaric tragedy will stay in my minds-eye forever. Those insidious maniacs were inhuman. And in this world today, their numbers are growing. Demented fanatics that need to be cauterised and eliminated from this world. We have to confront this evil. My Mum has devoted her life to preventing the ever-growing threat of wickedness, and defeating the contagion of evil. And I swear I will continue!"

"But Kainaat, we both know that, as every day passes, these evil monsters' numbers are growing. You probably know better than most because you are seeing it here and now! The Taliban are treating women like animals. Not allowing them education. Beating and raping them whenever they want to. And committing atrocious, violent acts, mindless acts, everywhere!"

Kainaat's expression saddened. Sitting close, on their badly worn couch, Kainaat took Junior's hand. Wiping a tear trickling down her cheek, she spoke, attempting to convince herself. "Junior, together we are as hard as nails. Together we will, at the very least, subvert, or even prevent these monsters from torturing young girls and women. I have lost several friends and informants. We must work hard to alert every woman in this area to be careful. Then we must find the ones that have been abducted and bring them back to safety. It's time for us to go on the offensive."

Junior swigged half his glass of wine. He closed his eyes, as his mind rattled through the options. Junior's eyes opened to embrace Kainaat's stare. With an assertive tone, he blasted out his thoughts. "Kainaat, maybe it's time we should get into some field action. All this intelligence gathering has been worthwhile, but, perhaps the time has come to use it! I think we should talk with the CIA. Ask them to underwrite an operation in conjunction with US Special Forces. Either RECON or SEALs or both. We can work our informants to find the women that have been abducted. And join the Special Forces team to rescue them. That would be a real one in the eye for the Taliban."

In Washington DC the President and his team were all for the idea. They had already planned a complete withdrawal the next year, 2020, and strategic thinkers had convinced the President, now President Fleming, that this strike would provide a cloud of propaganda which would soften the focus on the withdrawal of US troops. Rather than a defeat, the rescue of oppressed Afghan women and girls was expected to generate accolades across the world and, therefore, receive greater publicity than the US withdrawal!

For the US troops, it was Christmas in Afghanistan. Although always having to maintain constant vigilance, they made the best of it, with festive food and drink, flown in for the occasion.

The operation was planned for the third week of January 2020. Kainaat and Junior received encrypted communications from CIA headquarters two days before the planned execution of "Operation Taboo". They had previously, using ratified informants intelligence, identified the target location in a remote area, 30 miles north of Kabul.

The orders from CIA HQ said Kainaat and Junior would join the assault teams, supporting the troops with their local knowledge.

Chapter 6

The Rescue

J unior and Kainaat travelled, in a four-wheel drive pickup to a secret location between Peshawar and the Afghan border. Their driver, once again, was the local CIA colleague, Abid. Only he knew the location. They sat, shivering in the pickup, parked in an arid flat landscape.

Abid looked at his Omega military watch several times. Junior and Kainaat sat quietly in the freezing darkness. They knew not to question; and in any case, had worked out why!

At precisely 10.30pm, the distant sound of an engine could be heard. Abid started the Toyota pickup's engine and flicked on the headlamps. Over some sparse trees, and out of the dark sky, an even darker silhouette began to descend. A black painted Chinook troop carrier helicopter landed about 50 yards away from their pickup. Kainaat and Junior, already dressed in dark RECON Special Forces battle dress, began to exit the pickup, as a trooper ran towards them. Abid muttered, "Good luck, see you soon." The night air was freezing, about -4c.

But with troops pulling them through the hatch they were soon sitting in the warm, among the attack team. As they took off, the troops around them all began to welcome them with loud voices so as to be heard over the engine and rotor noise. Junior looked along the line of troopers and counted 20. By the uniforms, he saw it was 50/50 SEALs and RECONS.

10 minutes into the flight, a lieutenant, Lieutenant Fowler came to them.

"We will be landing about a mile from the target coordinates. Then we will hike that last mile, which should take about 15 minutes. As soon as we have successfully completed the assault, we will radio coordinates for the pickup. Where that will be, depends on the women's condition. You two have I-phones linked to our tracker devices. Follow our progress and sit with the pilots to assist them. This last part is extremely important to conclude the operation, so please keep your focus. Are you OK with that?"

Junior glanced at Kainaat, then replied, "Well, no Sir, we're not! Kainaat and I are coming with you. It was our idea, our suggestion to the President. We want to see it through."

The lieutenant pulled his beret off, closed his eyes as he rubbed his forehead. Peering into Junior's eyes he said, "With respect, are you two fucking mad?" Straightening and inhaling sharply' he loudly exclaimed, "These guys." He stopped to stare down the row of troopers. He continued, "These guys are highly trained specialist troops. They are battle hardened! But, even so, most of them are sweating, nerves are jangling, and pressure is building!"

Once again, Junior glanced at Kainaat, who had remained composed. Junior's expression hardened as he turned back to the lieutenant. "Sir, with the greatest respect we are highly trained for this type of operation. And we are not fucking sweating! We will get those poor women and girls out!"

"You guys think we are pussies that only take aim on a computer screen. That's a long way from the truth. We are field operatives! Undercover agents that have been working in Kabul for a very long time!"

"The only thing we need from you is assault weapons, because you guys didn't even consider that we might be going along with you. And a couple more things. These human beings we are rescuing are all females. They will be traumatised. They will be inconsolable! Kainaat here is a local woman who can relate to them. She will make all the difference! My last point is this. Your pilots have I-phones and can track us as well as anyone. So, you don't need us sitting here like superfluous idiots."

Slowly, a wide grin settled on the lieutenant's face. "Well, I never expected that! You make some very good arguments. My Commander is up front. I will go and talk with him. But his decision will have to be final, because we are only minutes away from landing!" Junior smiled as, 2 minutes later, the lieutenant returned with two Glock 19 pistols and two MK48 machine guns. He then handed them cross-body ammunition belts. Turning away, he shouted, "they are loaded."

They soon completed the trek and the troops prepared to attack. Commandos' crawling around the target, in two's and three's, they took cover behind scrub land and bushes. Three SEALs, crouching low, sprinted to the door of the first shack and pressed against the wall, either side of the door. Another three SEALs did exactly the same manoeuvre at the second shack door.

Both doors were flimsy wooden structures that had suffered years of rotting and erosion. They signalled. At both doors, the troopers simultaneously took two steps back, then crashed forward, kicking the doors off their hinges. All the SEALs rushed across, and with helmet torches, followed the first three in. Junior and Kainaat were among this wave.

The RECON Special Forces immediately followed. Before they reached the door, constant gunfire began. At least 40 rounds were heard! Initially, women were screaming, but then the gunfire stopped, the screams subsided, and the first shack became silent.

Junior and the SEALs searched using powerful flashlights. At the end of the shack, they found women and girls locked in several small crates. Behind the crates was a wooden cell structure made from thick wooden planks. Inside they found more women and girls.

Meanwhile Junior searched around for Kainaat. He had lost her once they were inside the dark shack. As he headed toward the door, shouting her name, she, quietly and painfully responded, "Junior, I am here."

He found her lying in the corner, behind the door. She had been hit by a stray bullet as they entered the shack. Junior kneeled beside her. The bullet had entered high on her thigh, close to the femoral artery. The blood loss, initially, had caused her to lose consciousness.

The RECON forces had entered the second shack. No resistance; the place seemed empty, until they moved to the rear of the building. They found two women, two dead women! They were totally naked, and were hanging with lashes on their wrists up to the roof beams. They could not be helped!

Whilst the SEALs released all the women and girls in the first shack, Junior was giving aid to Kainaat. He pulled off his maroon neckerchief and applied a tourniquet to her thigh. She whimpered as he twisted it using a small piece of wood that had fallen from the door. The women and girls began to pass them. Mostly they had been naked, in those freezing temperatures. They had been given some sheets and rat eaten blankets by the Taliban, but now the SEALs had brought them warm, thick blankets.

As the SEALs were assisting the women out, Lieutenant Fowler found Junior and Kainaat. In the torchlight he kneeled beside them. "Kainaat, what happened?" he asked. "Think I was hit by a stray bullet, Sir," she replied. Lieutenant Fowler turned to Junior. "We must get her out of here now, and onto the chopper." Junior stood, and with a caring voice asked Kainaat, "Will you be able to cope with me giving you a fireman's lift?" "Yes, Junior," she replied, "Just get on with it!"

The Lieutenant radioed the Chinook to land close, then helped Junior lift Kainaat onto his shoulders. She never even murmured. As they stepped over Taliban bodies, lying all around the shack entrance, the Lieutenant followed behind Junior, holding Kainaat's legs to steady him as he moved carefully, but quickly, towards the Chinook.

They were the last to leave, and last to board the helicopter. The blades were beginning to turn as they helped one another to gently pass Kainaat to two of the RECONs.

Once aboard, the chopper was away. Kainaat had been placed on a stretcher, which was now being pulled along the gangway to the centre of the fuselage. Junior dropped to his knees alongside Kainaat. No words were spoken as they both looked around. The chopper was full to the brim, 20 military, 18 women and girls, Kainaat and Junior. With the pilot and co-pilot they totalled 42; close to the maximum of 44.

Junior knew he had to keep Kainaat talking; keep her brain alive and kicking. Kneeling by her side, a trooper arrived and stood with them. But then, slowly dropped into a kneeling position beside both of them. He was a tall thick set, strong looking man with a sincere expression. He asked, "Kainaat, how are you feeling? I am the Commander on this operation, and I am not going to let anything happen to you!"

Kainaat's response was slow but lucid. "Sir, I am fine, and thank you for caring. You have had a lot to deal with tonight, but I will be OK!"

Junior grabbed the Commander's arm. "Sir, what is your name please?" His response was slow and deliberate, as he peered into Junior's eyes. "I am Commander Wyatt. Why is it important to you?" "Well, Sir, because I always feel I need to know who I am working with, especially when I need help. And I need help right now! That tourniquet can't stay on longer than 2 hours, so we must get Kainaat to hospital as fast as possible."

The Commander nodded to Junior and with a smile at Kainaat said, "I'll just go to the cockpit. We will fly to our camp in Lahore. There is a field hospital there!"

When he'd gone, Kainaat pushed up on her elbows. "Junior, drag me down the end to the women. I want to check on them, talk to them; tell them they will be OK with us."

Junior lifted one end of the stretcher and dragged it 15 feet into the midst of the women and girls, seated either side of the fuselage. Again, Kainaat pushed up on her elbows, looking around at all the sad, terrified faces. She began to speak as she peered around into the eyes of each and every female. Her words and tone were comforting. Junior knew she was speaking Dari; which he mostly understood. She then repeated her words in the second Afghan language, Pashtu.

These brave females, that had suffered such a terrifying, horrific ordeal, began to spark into life. First one knelt beside Kainaat, held her hand and kissed her cheek. Twinkles were returning to all their eyes, as their bruising, abhorrent, abusive treatment was smothered with the stardust of kindness.

Another woman, clutching her blanket stood and, with genuine affection, shook Junior's hand. Speaking in her Afghan language, over and over, she repeated, "Thank you Sir, thank you Sir, you saved our lives!"

Now followed a wonderful surprise. A third woman, a beautiful young woman, knelt beside Kainaat. With tears running down her cheeks, she screamed "Kainaat, it's me! Asha!"

Kainaat, leaning on one elbow, tried to get close to Asha's face. Asha helped, pulling Kainaat close, both arms around her neck and back. They embraced for what seemed an eternity. Both began sobbing, with Junior watching, with disbelief!

Junior guessed this was a really special moment. His curiosity became dominant. He now dropped to his knees as he held a hand out to Asha. He had to know! He blurted out, "Asha, how do you know my Kainaat?" There was a momentary silence, which Kainaat broke! Grabbing his forearm, Kainaat whispered, "Junior, she is one of us. She was my partner before you descended on us."

Now began a replay of the embraces, which, this time, included Junior.

Soon after, they landed at the Lahore military base; Kainaat was rushed out first. Everybody else was told to stay put until they got her on the way to the field hospital. Junior was accompanying her. As they began to move down the Chopper, all the rescued women, led by Asha, stood, clapped and waved.

Asha wasn't going to leave it at that. She caught them up. Junior asked the troopers' that were helping, to wait a second. Asha whispered, "Kainaat you know the procedure. We will have to go through debriefing and that could be a couple of days. But then, could we meet and have a nice time together. My time recently has been, well you know!" Kainaat smiled and replied, "I would really love us to get together!" "And if it's ok, I will bring my partner, Junior." He smiled at Asha. Then Kainaat said, "contact the hospital, as I don't know how long this will take;" as she pointed to her thigh!

Frank Junior was desperately trying to stay calm as he waited outside the operating theatre. Kainaat had been wheeled off the Chinook, straight into a modern, well-equipped, field medical facility; prepared, and given pre-medication. Then directly into the operating theatre. The surgeon described the operation to Junior, confidently stating it would be relatively straightforward.

"It won't take more than an hour, Frank!" As he shuffled away in his surgical Scholls, the surgeon remarked, "Frank, sit and relax. Get a coffee; we'll have her up dancing in a week or so!"

Over two hours later, Frank Jr was fighting stress. Chewing his lips, his mind was suffering from a worsening negative imagination. The door opened and the surgeon, with a tired lazy lope, eventually faced Junior.

"I'm so sorry, Frank." Junior gasped, thinking it had all gone wrong. "No Frank, it's ok! She'll be ok in a week or two! I was just about to say sorry it took so long." Junior smiled as he leant back, trying to relax his stiffened shoulders.

Heartened by Junior's warming expression, the surgeon began to explain the operation. "Frank, the shell was embedded deep in Kainaat's thigh, close to the femoral artery. It didn't appear that close, but it was!"

"We got to it pretty quickly. Normally, we would have just eased it out and then patched her up. But as I started to do that, all hell broke loose. The bullet was at an angle and had nicked the artery. As we started to ease it out, we were drowning in a blood spout. The bullet had been damming the nick. So now it exploded! We were prepared and pumped blood into Kainaat for half-an-hour. The femoral artery is a massive blood vessel in the body. I was covered and had to change most of my clothing. As did most of my colleagues! Once we controlled the fountain, we got in and quickly repaired the tear in her artery. At one stage, I wondered if I should throw three coins into the fountain for a wish!" Junior laughed.

The surgeon, as he inhaled, grinned at Junior. "She will be ok, old son! And I don't know what we would do without you brave folks." Searching in his pocket, he grasped Junior's hand. "This is an AK47 bullet, probably fired by the Taliban. Give it to Kainaat. To have forever, as a keepsake." As the surgeon turned to walk away, Junior said, "Sir, what is your name?" He swivelled and smiled. "Well Frank, it's an historic English name. In the US it's an unusual name. But I'm stuck with it! I am Jake Gubbins. In the UK there is a saying, it's a lot of old Gubbins." Junior stopped him. "Well, Sir, I am so pleased we had your lot of old Gubbins here today! You have patched Kainaat up and I am so grateful! And explaining your work puts you at the top of my brilliant surgeon list. Thank you, Sir! We will never forget Mr Gubbins."

Over the next two weeks, Kainaat put her heart and soul into recovery. The first stage was physio in her bed. Next came painful walking on crutches. Then a satisfying progression to physio in the hospital gym, and walking on sticks. Whenever Junior had a chance, he was at the hospital, working with Kainaat in the gym. By the end of the second week, Kainaat was receiving encouragement from the other patients in her ward, as she took slow, tentative walking steps, up and down the aisle way.

Asha contacted Kainaat, and dinner at a local restaurant was arranged for the middle of the third week.

Frank Junior, driving Kainaat's battered Citroen, arrived to escort her to the restaurant in the hospitality area in the centre of Lahore.

As Junior and Kainaat reached the hospital double-doors, they were pushed open by a uniformed trooper. He stood back, holding the doors open for them. Junior and Kainaat were concentrating; attempting to get Kainaat through carefully. The trooper exclaimed, "Kainaat! Junior! Great to see you doing so well!" His focus had been on the hobbling Kainaat, but now his eyes moved to Junior.

Standing at the entrance, Junior said, "Great to see you Lieutenant Fowler! "I didn't recognise you in full dress uniform!" Lieutenant Fowler developed a wide grin. "Yes I'm attending a presentation later on. A presentation ceremony led by Commander Wyatt, to recognise some of the troopers that excelled in Operation Taboo!"

The lieutenant's voice quietened as he moved closer. "I probably shouldn't tell you this, but I'm going to! Some of our troopers will be told today that they have been mentioned in dispatches! I know that can't apply to you, Frank Junior, due to secrecy requirements. But what you will be pleased to hear, is that the Commander has personally spoken with both the CECD and CIA hierarchy. He let them know, in the strongest terms, that he believed you, Junior, deserved recognition!"

Junior glanced at Kainaat, then with a surprised expression, whispered "why?" "Junior, I applaud your modesty, but my report incorporated input from two of my sergeants. We all agreed your combat achievements, in that operation, were above and beyond. If it hadn't been for your quick thinking and bravery, we probably would have lost several troopers. The bottom line is that there were 12 Taliban in that shack. You shot and killed four of them, and in the middle of that assault, overcame three in hand-to-hand combat. And, by the way Kainaat, you have also received a mention for your outstanding calming, care and attention to the females. Made our job a whole lot easier! I've got to run now, but great to see you both looking well! Keep smiling!"

Kainaat and Junior both inhaled as their eyes moved up to the sky. With that news, they were both in very high spirits. Together, they ambled to the Citroen.

Arriving a little late at Arcadian Café Packages, apparently a favourite of Asha and Kainaat when they worked together, they were met by a white jacketed parking valet. First, he escorted them to their table, then excused himself to go park the Citroen.

The three of them spent the first half-hour, embracing, followed by small talk and ordering. Junior was impressed with the modern décor and glittering lights in the ceiling, flickering on the dark blue furniture. The Manager, Shalid, welcomed their return, and then set-off to fulfil their order.

As he left, Asha stopped talking and peered around the room. There were not too many customers as it was early evening. Asha bent double to peer under the table, lifted the table lamp for a check, then, once again, her eyes searched around the whole room. She whispered, "We're ok to talk, but keep it soft!"

After a few sentences, as the wine arrived, Asha explained that in her early years working with Kainaat, their work had involved intrusive surveillance; but then progressed to equipment interference. Subsequently, they had both been promoted to field operatives. They had been separated when Kainaat was assigned to Pakistan and Afghanistan.

Asha had been deployed to Hungary, to work on intelligence gathering, in view of an anticipated threat to countries in Eastern Europe. The suspect, indeed the only suspect, was Russia. Intelligence analyses indicated that President Putin's key objective, indeed, his fixation, centred on re-establishing a totalitarian USSR. The analyses were strongly supported by intelligence provided by some of the best CIA agents in Jackson.

Asha, obviously a very experienced CIA agent, went on to explain that she had been recalled to assist with the safety of US troops during their withdrawal.

Junior and Kainaat had been listening intently. Asha needed to sip some of the glorious Chianti that had been sitting in front of her. Having had two or three sips, she slowly eased away from the tension that had been building in her mind.

As she prepared to speak again, Kainaat interjected. Glancing first at Asha, then Frank Junior, she said, "Then Asha disappeared and all I knew was that I would get a new partner." Her smile was so strong it engulfed Asha and, especially Junior. "I was getting a new partner. Some kid from Canada. His Mum was extraordinarily accomplished, and so he had got the job. It was you, Junior!" She giggled! "I was landed with you!"

Junior chuckled then reached across the table to clasp Kainaat's hand. Asha leaned back in her chair then exclaimed, "Oh, my God, are you two an item? I'm sorry, I had no idea!"

Kainaat, with a wry smile, inhaled as she said, "No Asha, we're not. We agreed to be fervent friends and colleagues. We work well together, and so far, we have stuck with that agreement." Junior, with a reluctant expression, nodded.

Asha took a gulp of her Chianti! She thought for a moment about what to say and how to say it. "Well, it is absolutely accurate to say that you two make a cracking team. I need to explain how I got to be abducted; it was like this. I was in the Kabul market, searching out some of my recently acquired informants. In the middle of a large group of women I was asking if they knew the lady I was trying to find. Suddenly, we were surrounded by Taliban. They herded us all into trucks. Abusing us on the way. We were driven for miles. Once we reached those shacks, they mistreated women that were not, in their opinion, wearing appropriate clothing. Some women and girls were sexually abused in those shacks."

"I kept quiet and kept my face covered, but I saw them behaving brutally to some of the women. Two were dragged out to the other shack. I am still seeing that in my mind's eye. They were brutal animals!"

"I will never forget you two for saving us, rescuing us from that hell."

Frank Junior, Kainaat and Asha were now one very close team. They did extraordinary work, gathering intelligence in and around Kabul. Frank Junior rearranged their small apartment to allow Asha to move in with them. The three of them agreed schedules for cooking, cleaning and showering. It worked well because they stuck to the schedule!

However, it wasn't long before the powers that be decided to reorganise their lives! At first the UK, and then the US troops, had been withdrawn; CECD and CIA Directors decided to re-assign most of their Agents to areas of the world where they could make more of a difference.

⸺◆⸺

Chapter 7

New Orders

First to receive new orders were Kainaat and Asha. These two, now very experienced Agents, were requested to travel to Washington DC immediately. They would be given details of their new assignments within one week, and had been given assurances that their under-cover work would be decided in the USA.

Both young ladies had mixed feelings. They would be leaving their homelands. Asha, from India, had never lived in the western world. However, that made this new adventure more exciting than anything before. And, to crown it all, they would experience this new life journey, initially, together.

That evening, Frank Junior sat thinking how to re-configure his work life after the girls had gone. He was a stoic character that never let deviations in his present circumstances throw him off balance. His Mother had always instilled in him, not to let incidental changes in life, throw him off the road he was travelling on. At least, not without convincing argument!

Asha and Kainaat had been preparing dinner. In view of the news, Junior had been let off the hook.

Dinner was served! As they sat with delectable Indian dishes in front of them, Kainaat and Asha quietly sipped their red wine. Suffering a tinge of sadness, Junior took several large gulps of the Cabernet Sauvignon to quell this emotion. Then several deep breaths. Another couple of gulps, as he leaned back in the thread bare, winged back chair.

Staring at his two flat mates, he slowly and softly began to hum. His volume gradually increased, and the hum transitioned into tuneful lyrics. "Born in the USA"; the headline was repeated three times. He stood, imitating Bruce Springsteen. His vocal intensity increased when he began to hip-thrust his way behind an air guitar. The song softened and the end was close; he sat, with a glorious smile eyeballing the girls.

Kainaat and Asha had been silent throughout. Kainaat first broke into laughter, then asked Junior "Is everything ok?" Junior, as he began to tuck into his Tandoori, glanced up at them. In a woosy, inebriated voice he replied, "Yes, it's superb! I am so pleased for you! You will love it in America, and the bonus is, you are going together. Of course, I will miss you both dreadfully, but we will be together again soon. I've absolutely no doubt on that score. My Mum is a short distance away from you in Toronto, Canada. I will give you her number and if you need help with anything, she will always be your failsafe!"

Two days later, as the girls were finishing their packing, Junior received his encrypted e-mail. It was short and sweet. He was recalled to London and would receive detailed instructions on arrival.

His first port of call was to be the Foreign Office, to meet with Commander Farrell.

Frank Junior was elated. He rushed out of his room, back to the dinner table, to give the girls his news. As he sat, he poured himself a large glass of Bordeaux that he had been saving for a special occasion. The girls watched and wondered. Two gulps, and a strained grin, as he attempted to suppress his excitement.

Pushing his hair back off his forehead, his grin widened as he focused on the girls quizzical gazes. "Kainaat, what time is your flight tomorrow?" he asked. "It's 7.55am, why are you asking?" "Well, I'm going to try to get a flight around that time, and then we can all travel to the airport together!"

Kainaat glanced at Asha, then asked, "So where are you going?" Junior stood, poured Bordeaux into all their glasses, then bent as he slapped his thigh. "I've been recalled as well! I'm going back to London, but don't know where from there." "I'm so pleased, I thought I was going to be alone, stuck in this dustbowl."

Kainaat and Asha both leaned across the table and grabbed his hands. Their squealing, giggling and laughter came to a halt when Asha asked, "But what about your packing, and you need to get a flight." Junior now began relaxing, sipping his glass of wine. "Asha, they are not things to worry about. I've got less than nothing to pack. Rent on this place is fully paid up. And I'm certain I will get a flight. We will take Kainaat's Ugly Duckling Citroen Diane to the airport and just leave it in the car park. Someone may, sooner or later, find it attractive." Kainaat giggled, causing her to splutter as she drank the wine!

"Let's spend the rest of this evening celebrating our new adventures." As Junior said those words, he stood and drifted to their CD player. High volume Taylor Swift, the girls' favourite, blasted into the walls. The girls quickly sauntered into the centre of the room and began twisting, twirling and sensually wiggling every part of their slim erotic bodies. It was only a few minutes before Junior joined them, with continuous laughter; drinks and food through to midnight.

The evening ended with close, slow dancing, to a George Benson CD; both girls, semi-inebriated, were clasping Junior as they all danced together, close with him. They were so slim, Junior's hands clasped around both their waists. Junior then took his leave to try to organise his flight. His was slightly earlier than the girls, at 7.25am.

Only a few hours' sleep before the drive to Islamabad airport. They dumped the Citroen ugly duckling in the car park and wearily entered departures. For a couple of minutes, the girls sat on their cases, recovering slowly from their hangovers. In contrast, Junior was sparking; running on adrenalin fuelled excitement. He would be first to leave, and that moment came.

He first pulled Kainaat up off her case. Hands clasped behind her head, his kiss was tender then passionate. He leant to pull Asha close; caressing her with a gentle kiss. As both girls stood mesmerised, staring into his eyes, he pulled them both close and together; they hugged for a full ten seconds.

Junior pulled away and inhaled. As he pushed his hair back off his face, he quietly uttered, "I love you two so much, and will miss you. But wherever we go, I will keep in touch. And I will insist we arrange a get-together as soon as possible." His flight was now being called! Junior gathered his single case and travel bag. All three of them hugged again, then Junior sprinted across the departures hall into immigration. Kainaat and Asha tearfully meandered through behind him!

Bleary eyed, they slowly trudged out of Washington Dulles International Airport. The flight had been uneventful, but both of them had consumed more alcohol, which was now wreaking its revenge!

Two local Washington CIA operatives had met them, and would now deliver them to the CIA headquarters in Jackson, Virginia. As they drove, Asha's mind recorded every famous building, statue and fountain. She was ecstatic to be in Washington DC. Kainaat's appreciation was dissimilar. She was fast asleep with her head resting on the rear-seat arm rest!

Frank Junior's journey had been several thousand miles less. So now, mid-day, he was sitting in that same corridor in the Foreign Office, where he had attended his second interview.

A door opened, and out strode the fabulous Penny to greet him. The mutual admiration seemed to warm the whole corridor. Frank Junior allowed his emotions to dominate. He stood, hugged Penny, and kissed both her cheeks. As they broke apart, Penny stepped back, with a surprised but delighted expression. Then rapidly stepped forward, clutching Junior close and kissing both his cheeks. "I am so pleased to see you, and know you are safe!"

As they peered into one another's eyes, that door opened again. Out stepped Commander Farrell. Standing in front of the doorway, he beckoned, and said, "Frank Junior, please come in. I'm so glad to see you!"

Junior stood back and with an outstretched arm, invited Penny to lead. As they entered the office, Frank Jr leant forward and whispered in Penny's ear. "Can we meet later?" Her head turned slightly, as she muttered a singular "yes."

The meeting with the CECD Director General gradually got underway. As they had known each other for so many years, the initial courtesies were sincere, but fast.

The Commander commenced saying, with a stressed expression, "I need you to help with an unusual assignment.

The USA and also the UK are under threat from a virus. Our initial analysis assessed the likelihood of it being a man-made virus as 50/50. But that assessment indicates that if it is, the culprit is China. The outbreak is worsening day by day, so you need to be careful. Take all the necessary precautions that you are advised to take. We do not know yet, how deadly this may turn out to be. But we need someone, and that's you, who can communicate with our scientists, and medical people. And then, if necessary, get over to China, undetected, to gather intelligence."

The meeting was close to ending. Commander Farrell stood and began to pace the room. He came to a halt in front of his desk, slowly turned and sat on its edge. Peering down into Junior's eyes, he said, "There is one other thing I am going to tell you, in confidence! You must keep it to yourself for now, only because it has not been formally announced yet. I will be retiring at the end of next month. I have loved this job, but now my age and some health issues are restricting my performance."

Frank Junior's jaw dropped. His eyes searched around the room for a moment, as he untangled his bewilderment. "No Sir, your ability and execution of your duties has always been superb.... Beyond reproach!"

The Commander leant forward and placed his hand on Junior's shoulder. "Thanks Junior, those kind words mean a lot. However, my resignation has been accepted, and today the position was offered to an excellent candidate; and she has accepted."

The Commander peered at Frank Junior, waiting for him to ask the question. After a deafening silence, the Commander continued, "It was a tight contest. The selected candidate required support from the main Agencies in Western Europe; Germany, France, Italy, Spain and of course, Great Britain. All the Director Generals of those five countries voted for.... Your Mother!"

Another dramatic pause followed. Junior inhaled as he leaned back in his seat. "You knew that I was about to tell you Anneliese had got the job. But you didn't say a word, Junior. Why? Don't you want her to take the position?"

Chapter 8

CECD Director General – Anneliese

Frank Junior's eyes peered back at Commander Farrell, and as Junior scoffed, his expression saddened. "You're right Sir, I am concerned" said Junior. "I guessed from what you explained, and because she is the very best! But she has put her heart and soul into her job, despite pressure and stress every day. And for my dad also."

"But, in truth, I suppose I knew this day would come sooner or later. And I'm certain she is delighted, because she has dedicated her life to this job, almost every minute since she left University." As Junior was speaking, his face brightened and smile widened. "Well, now it's a certainty, I am also delighted. And Commander, I will work my balls off to support her and prove you guys could not have selected a better person for the job!"

Commander Farrell lent forward and grasped Junior's hand. He stood and as the Commander shook his hand, they swift-hugged. Moving toward the door, the Commander said, "Anneliese will be here tomorrow to talk with the staff, including you, Junior. We have taken the liberty of arranging for you both to stay at the Trafalgar Boutique Hotel, just along the road." Junior, with smiling eyes, replied "Thank you, Sir. Well, I'll see you tomorrow." "Yes, 10am, here," replied Commander Farrell. As Junior began to step away, the Commander uttered, "You and Anneliese together in this business will make a formidable team!"

As the door closed behind him, Junior lent forward and whispered to Penny, "Trafalgar Boutique for dinner. Is 8pm ok?" She smiled and nodded as her hand stroked his.

At 7.55pm Junior wandered out of the hotel and stood waiting for Penny to arrive. Standing opposite Canada House, watching the Canadian Maple Leaf flag fluttering in the wind, his mind began to reminisce, remembering the great times he had, playing ice hockey, and modelling his game on some of the Toronto Maple Leaf professionals. Pictures of his home tracked through his mind. Wonderfully happy times with Mum and Dad, walking along the edge of Lake Ontario.

As he stared up at the fluttering flags, his mind was thoroughly enjoying the picture playback; so much so, he was oblivious to all around him. The silence was shattered by a voice that exclaimed, "I can see you are in a pleasant place; or are you just thinking about me?" Junior's mind snapped back into the real world. He looked down as Penny gripped him around the waist and laid her head on his chest. She looked up into his eyes saying, "Are you going to greet me with a kiss?"

Junior arched forward and kissed Penny on both cheeks. "I'm so sorry, Penny, seeing those Canadian flags, my mind had drifted back to my days with my family in Oakville."

"Well Junior, by the expression on your face, your thoughts were enjoyable. Let's see if I can bring that same look back during our evening together." Penny giggled and Junior chuckled, as he took her hand and they entered the hotel.

Their table was ready! The Maître D'Hotel took Penny's coat to the cloakroom, then escorted them to their table, in the corner of the restaurant, near a window looking across to Canada House. Trafalgar Square, the fountains, and Nelson's Column could be seen, just across the way!

As they sat in their booth; Penny chose to sit opposite Junior. "This is fabulous, the décor, the ambience, the lighting, and our position. I can even see Nelson lit up by the arc lights. Thank you, Junior for inviting me!"

They were just about to embark on get-to-know-you chat as the wine waiter arrived with the wine menu. "Penny, white or red, and do you have a favourite?" "It's red please," replied Penny. "Me also, " said Junior as he perused the wine card. Chuckling, Junior asked "shall we go for the most expensive." His voice softened as he quietly said, "we are on expenses". Penny gave a grateful nod. Junior's eyes returned to the waiter, who was wearing a red and blue pristine uniform embellished with gold brocade and epaulettes.

"We would like a 1955 Chateau Neuf du Pape." Penny had taken the wine card and immediately stuttered, "But Junior that is over £280!" The wine waiter hesitated!

Junior developed a widening grin. "Yes Penny, but I've been away for a long while. If I'd been here, we would have consumed at least 100 bottles of cheap plonk. This just gets us even!" The wine waiter puffed out his chest, smiled, then marched off to the wine vaults!

The wine arrived. Frank Junior obliged with tasting, saying it was excellent. Penny and Junior now had the chance to chat. But only for about 10 minutes. The Head Waitress arrived to take their order. Junior asked if they could have another 15 minutes, as they had not seen one another for several years.

The Head Waitress replied, "Of course, Sir, there is no rush. Please take as long as you require." Junior was sensitised by her accent. Then as his eyes moved to hers, he needed to keep her at his table. She was very beautiful. Dark hair, dark piercing eyes and a genuine smile. "Would you mind telling us your name?" "Of course not sir, I am the Head Waitress and my name is Csenge. Any wish you have, please ask me!" Junior's eyes devoured her!

"I have travelled the world Csenge, but I've never come across such a beautiful name. Where are you from originally?" "Sir, I am from Hungary, but I have been living in London for 15 years." "Csenge, I have some friends, two female work colleagues, who are moving to live in your country. Would you mind if I put them in touch with you." "No sir, not at all! But now I will leave you for 15 minutes or so."

Penny and Junior both took their glasses and sipped the wine for a minute or two. Penny had now decided to say exactly what she was thinking. "Junior, we are just here as colleagues tonight, and we have been friends for many years. But I have to ask! Were you sitting here with me whilst you chatted that waitress up? Or, is it that you never stop working and really believe she may be able to help your colleagues?"

Frank Junior smiled at Penny and said, "You have always intrigued me! You are so perceptive!" he waved his right hand in the air as he explained, "Yes, I was working! I have two very good friends that may be heading out to the Russian/Ukraine border. That is just my suspicion as it's not confirmed yet. And so, I saw a possible chink of light and was following it."

Penny relaxed, and shuffled her bottom around the booth to sit close to Junior. "Ok, so who are these colleagues you worked with; and tell me some general stuff about what you've been up to for the last few years."

A few seconds later Csenge arrived to take their order. She listened and wrote the order, but all the time, her mind was fixated by Junior's looks. His blonde hair, blue/green eyes, strong chin and seductive smile. As she swayed away, Penny and Junior resumed talking. Junior said "Penny, you know I can't give you details about our work in Afghanistan! Those colleagues are now in Washington awaiting assignment."

During their dinner, Junior ordered a second bottle of wine. Once dinner was over, Penny gradually moved closer, her breast brushing his arm. She gently stroked his thigh.

Junior's eyes scanned every delicious feature of this beautiful female that had captured his mind several years before. Her pouting lips with slightly upturned corners, wide sparkling eyes under fluttering dark, long eyelashes. Strawberry blond hair draping over her cheeks down to her shoulders.

Although a few years older than Junior, the ageing process had enhanced her curvaceous body. Junior's hand slowly slid around her tiny waist. He now sensed the voluptuous contrasting curve, out and over her bottom. Like a swan's neck, as it gently drifted down into that sensuous expansion.

Penny eased closer, her eyes blinking, as her questioning gaze met his. Now, easing away again, Penny whispered, "No Junior! We must not get romantic. I know we both want to; we've always wanted to, but this is completely the wrong time. Your Mother is coming here as my boss. This would complicate everything. I don't want to risk losing my job. I love my job! In fact, the only reason I came tonight was to find out more about her, so take a breath, then tell me all about Anneliese!"

Without a word, he grasped Penny tighter and pulled her close. It seemed an almost involuntary action, responding to his craving. His right hand slid down to Penny's buttocks as he tugged her even closer. Their lips glided forward, but before they could meet, Csenge, the head waitress appeared. With a mischievous grin, she uttered, "You seem to be enjoying our fabulous restaurant. Can I get you anything else? Perhaps some sorbet to cool your mouths?"

Penny shuffled away, as Junior smiled and replied, "No thank you, Csenge, we'll just finish our wine, then we will have to leave. Perhaps you would put the bill on my room." "Certainly, Sir. Please come back again soon!"

Csenge departed, smiling at them as she left. Junior's eyes peered into Penny's. "Please stay with me tonight" he pleaded. "No Junior, I would love to accept your invitation, but I can't. I have explained why! We must just remain friends." Junior leaned across and kissed Penny's cheek, then whispered, "But you know, and I know, that we are destined to find romance eventually!"

As they strolled out to reception, the Maître De met them, saying he would retrieve Penny's coat from the cloakroom. Junior excused himself, to go to the Restroom. About to step away, he turned to say, "Sorry Penny, I've spent too much time in Canada. I should have said the toilet."

As he swiftly moved down the corridor, Csenge approached. "Bon nuit Sir, hope to see you sometime in the future." "That's for sure," replied Junior. "I will be back again tomorrow evening. Will you be here?" With a twinkle in her eyes, she answered, "Oh yes, Sir, I will look forward to it."

After choosing and thoroughly enjoying a sumptuous American breakfast, the main feature being magnificent pancakes, maple syrup and crispy streaky bacon, Frank Junior strolled along to the Foreign Office. By 10am, the staff that had received an invitation were assembled in the large Victorian conference room. Possibly around 40 people were noisily mingling and networking. A handsome, meticulously dressed man, standing with an arm draped over the white Adams fireplace mantel, was the centre of a group's attention.

Frank Junior, standing just inside the entrance door, scanned the assembled company. His eyes met several, and then Penny's. She gave him a witheringly sad smile. He returned the smile, with pursed lips! His eyes moved to the man hovering by the Adams fireplace. It was Jerome! As their eyes met, Jerome loudly exclaimed to his group, "It's Frank Junior, he's made it here!" Placing his coffee carefully on the mantel, he minced across to Junior.

With everybody in the room, now engrossed, Jerome and Frank Junior grasped each other in a forever hug. It appeared they were stepping apart, but then Jerome stood on tip toe and kissed Junior's cheek. He swivelled and shouted to the room, "Please excuse me, this is my wonderful Godson. He's been on assignment in Afghanistan for years, and now he's back home safe!"

Commander Farrell entered the room, just in time to savour those last few words. He turned as Anneliese followed him, clasped her hand and led her into the centre of the room.

Standing side by side, Commander Farrell inhaled deeply. His head dropped for a second, then lifted. His voice crackled as he began to speak. "By now, you have all probably heard on the grapevine that I will be retiring at the end of the month. Working with you, and your predecessors, has been a privilege and a blessing. And now the time has come! A time to introduce you to a person that has been a blessing to this world for as long as I can remember. Today is not about an ending, it's about a new beginning. This world deserves it, you all deserve it! As you all work, every day of your lives, to protect us from the cruelty that conflict and terrorism brings!"

Commander Farrell turned to Anneliese, shook her hand and embraced her. Speaking again, he gently grasped Anneliese's hand;" I would like to introduce you all to the new Director General of CECD, and I am sure she would like to say a few words to you all." The Commander held out his arm indicating the floor was hers.

Anneliese's usual trait surfaced. She left the Commander and slowly paced around the large conference room. Although now over 60, her poise, elegance and beauty were captivating. The room became extremely quiet.

She returned to the centre of the room. In a gentle but commanding magnetic voice she said, "We only have one job to apply ourselves to constantly. Every minute of every waking hour. The job we all signed up for is to keep people safe, eradicate cruelty and abuse, and prevent, or end, conflict. You guys have done an extraordinary job on this over the years. But evil is gaining ground. So that's where we come in!"

"We are not going to be beaten. Every one of you must apply every minute of your working day to find ways to keep our world safe. And I don't mean just in Europe. Our work with the United States has always brought amazing success, and so that's how we will continue. Commander Farrell and I can tell you hundreds of stories about our work with the Americans, but that's for later."

"In the meantime, I am going to put my trust in you, and I hope you will do the same with me." Anneliese took a breath, stood straight and glanced around the room. The applause slowly began, then raised to a deafening crescendo!

Anneliese needed to stay at the Foreign Office until about 7pm, to start the process of handover with Commander Farrell. She discreetly chatted with Jerome and then Frank

Junior, not wishing to immediately encourage tongues to wag about a secret service agent being her son. But she would meet with Junior for dinner at the hotel.

They met in the restaurant at 8pm. Junior was there first and had already ordered wine. Anneliese arrived and stood in the restaurant reception area, glancing around, trying to spot Junior. Very soon, they spied one another, and walked toward the centre of the aisle-way.

Anneliese had changed from her navy blazer and grey trousers business attire into a cream low cut dress, with matching over-jacket. As she strode down the aisle, her swaying, lithe frame, and stunning appearance, drew attention from every quarter. As they met, with a wondrous embrace, Junior's memory was captured by the Chanel No 5 fragrance and the feel of her soft, smooth, velvety skin against his. All around, customers watched and wondered!

Once seated in their booth, Anneliese sat close, clasped his face and kissed both cheeks. Junior, his eyes fighting back tears, uttered "Mum, I've missed you and Dad so much." "And we miss you every minute of every day." She sighed and blinked back her tears. They both leaned back, inhaled then exhaled sharply. Their exuberance calmed, allowing Junior to speak first.

"Mum, congratulations. How fantastic that you are now in charge of the CECD." Anneliese's proud smile became hidden as she brought her wine glass to her lips. She sipped for a few seconds, then edged a napkin to the corners of her mouth. A slight cough to clear her throat, then she quietly uttered, "to be honest Junior, I didn't have to give it much thought. I have been in this work almost all my life. Now you are in it! There have only been three things in my life that have given me fulfilment. You, my work and Matthew! And when I sought your dad's advice, he was absolutely clear.

"You don't need my advice! This is something you have no choice in. You have been chosen by powers that know far more about what's going on in this ugly world than we do! They know, I know, and Junior will know, that you are the one to make a difference." Anneliese turned in her seat and peered into Junior's eyes. Continuing she said, "Just at that point, Frank walked in and heard those last few words. His steely eyes reached into my soul, as he exclaimed, yes and I know you are the only person for the job; your track record has always indicated you would be offered it sooner or later, and I know your heart is crying out for you to say yes! One more thing! We were all crying out for you to say yes. Me, Matthew, Lucia and the whole world! And Junior will work with you every step of the way. So go get them, Anneliese! You will make so much difference; in 10 years it will be a better place for all!"

They quietly enjoyed dinner and a couple more glasses of wine. Junior, throughout the meal, kept replaying the words Frank had uttered to Anneliese and Matthew. Frank's encouragement and blessing meant everything to Junior!

Anneliese now announced that she needed her bed. It had been a long day, and jet lag was taking its toll. She had a late morning meeting with the Prime Minister, which may become protracted due to the number of conflicts and recent terrorist attacks. Junior interrupted her explanation saying, "Mum, I have kept up with all the world news. One area of concern for me is the growing conflict between Russia and Ukraine. What's your view on where it's heading?"

Leaning closer, Anneliese whispered, "This afternoon I was given sight of all the intelligence reports. If you had seen them, I think you would bet your house on Russia going to war with Ukraine. They will invade in the next year or not long after." Junior scowled, uttering, "What a diabolical waste of life, and most of it will be civilians."

Anneliese stood, clasped Junior's hand as they slowly wandered to the exit together. They embraced on the hotel steps as Anneliese asked, "Will I see you tomorrow?" "Not sure about during the day, but could we meet for dinner again tomorrow evening, about 8pm?" Brushing her hair back, she smiled as she floated to the lift.

Chapter 9

Csenge – Wide-eyed and Excited

Junior, returning to the restaurant, met Csenge. She looked even more ravishing than the previous evening. She stood close and he held her hands. "Csenge, what time do you finish?" "About 10pm" she replied. "Please, meet me in reception, I need you to help me with something!" Csenge frowned. "Oh, no, nothing to worry you, just some advice." Csenge, with a quizzical look, chuckled saying, "You want advice from me?" Looking back, over her shoulder, she trundled back towards the kitchens.

They met in reception, just after 10pm. Csenge, wearing a hoody, appeared as if she didn't want to be seen with a patron of the hotel.

Junior, recognised this and hustled her outside, where the first objective became a taxi. In Trafalgar Square, he soon managed to flag one down. Once in the rear seat, he directed the driver to the Gaucho Restaurant in Mayfair. He turned to look at Csenge. Her eyes were sparkling. Reaching for her hand as they arrived at the restaurant, he helped her out of the taxi.

They found a table in the corner of the almost empty restaurant. Junior asked, "Red or white?" "Gin and tonic please," replied Csenge. They began some small talk, with

Csenge asking his name. Junior explained why he preferred Junior to Frank. The conversation began to move on, as the waiter arrived to take their food order. Junior asked with a sharp tone, "For now, could we just have the drinks, and then have some time alone?" Csenge's brow furrowed, wondering why Junior appeared so fraught. "You seem anxious, Junior. Is something troubling you?"

Junior stretched back in his seat, then slowly leaned forward across the table. Getting as near to Csenge as possible he uttered, "Oh, I am so sorry Csenge. I have some worrying business on my mind. In fact, that's what I want to talk to you about. That's the subject I need your advice on."

Peering into Csenge's eyes, he sipped his red wine. Leaning forward again he continued! "Before I explain, may I ask how you spell your name?" "Junior, to you it will seem a strange spelling. It's CSENGE" Junior with a wide smile, exclaimed, "I would never have guessed that!" "However, you pronounce it CHENGER? Is that correct?" "Yes, absolutely" she replied. It was now her turn to sip her gin and tonic. With a wry smile, Csenge quizzed, "So what is this concerning work stuff all about?"

Csenge developed a look of surprise as Junior pushed his chair back, bent to look under the table, then grabbed the table lamp, turned it upside down, then placed it back on the table. Peering around the restaurant, his eyes gradually returned to Csenge's. As he was about to speak, Csenge asked, "What job do you do? What is your profession? Are you a restaurant critic or something?" She began to giggle. Junior, seeing her frivolous gaze, also started to chuckle!

Then, first taking a deep breath, Junior said, "Ok, Csenge, I will start at the beginning." Once again Csenge cheekily giggled, "It's a good place to begin!" Junior's smile widened, as he whispered "You remember I mentioned I have two colleagues that will be moving to live in Hungary."

Csenge's expression showed intense interest. "So what is their work? And you have not yet said what you do!" With a mischievous grin, Junior softly muttered, "I am an operative, and so are my friends." "What is this operative?" Csenge questioned. "Possibly, the best way to describe it is to ask you if you know what a surgeon is and what he does?" "Of course," she replied. "He performs operations. Removes things that may be hurting us, and repairs our bodies." "That's a wonderfully accurate description of his work," Junior replied.

Another swig of his red wine, as he focused on Csenge's searching expression. His voice softened as he began to explain. "Csenge, we do the same type of work." Csenge needed her drink and took a large gulp. She thought for a couple of seconds, then said, "So you are all surgeons?" Junior continued in a whispering quiet tone. "Not exactly. We work for governments. I work for European governments. My friends work for the American government. We work to prevent pain and suffering. We spend every waking hour finding ways to cut out and eliminate the cancers in our world; those evil monsters that threaten us constantly. Those monsters that terrorise and kill people almost every day!"

"Are you understanding what I am saying, Csenge?" As Junior spoke, Csenge reached behind her chair for her jacket. "I think I do, and I am leaving. You are feeding me a load of bullshit; I'm beginning to feel I am in some sort of Cinema Movie!" Junior stood to block her exit. "Csenge, please let me continue, to show you I am telling the truth!"

Csenge sunk slowly back into her chair. "Ok Junior, so what can you say to convince me you are not some lunatic." Junior exhaled then whispered, "Csenge, please drink with me for a moment; we both need to relax." The waiter arrived again. "Are you ready to order, Sir?" "No, please give us another 20 minutes," replied Junior. "But we would appreciate another gin and tonic and a large scotch, Dalmore or an expensive one, please."

His red wine bottle held one more glass. He poured it and gulped a mouthful. A tender expression adorned his handsome face. "Csenge, this is not exactly easy for me, so please give me a chance. I can't tell you much about my work, but I can tell you a lot about your life, that may convince you I am an honest, sincere person." Csenge's attitude softened. She reached across the table to clasp Junior's hand. "Ok, Junior, I will listen intently to your every word. I'm sorry if I have made this difficult for you."

Junior's mind, hearing those kind words, livened once more. "Csenge, I am going to tell you things that may make you fearful. But please trust me. I have only had a few hours today to work on this, but with what I tell you, I am hoping you will see I am authentic. I have a massive organisation supporting me and can arrange, or do, anything I need to do!" Csenge and Junior quietened as the drinks arrived.

Junior, now they were alone, said, "I will try again." "Csenge, my gorgeous, beautiful Csenge; your full name is Csenge Schneider. You are Jewish, although not orthodox. Your father's name is Janos. Your mother's name is Lena. You have a brother that lives with your parents. He is disabled, suffering from cerebral palsy, since he was born. You have two sisters that live in New York. Your parents live on a farm in a town named Gyor, relatively close to Budapest. Your father also owns a tailors shop in Budapest."

Csenge, exclaimed "Junior, stop." She took a large gulp of her gin and tonic, and eased back in her chair, breathing heavily.

Junior offered a tender smile, then continued, "You visit your parents as often as possible, about every two months. You help with work on the farm and all domestic duties. When you are there in Gyor, on a Sunday, you always have two things you do. First, you drive to Budapest to have lunch with two married friends Reka and her husband Ferenc. After lunch;" Csenge clasped Junior's hand and with a tearful expression, asked him to stop for a minute. She inhaled and brushed her ebony hair away from her face. Another deep breath, then she softly smiled, saying, "Ok, Junior, I'll let you finish!" "After lunch, the three of you always stroll past the Parliament building on the Pest side of the River Danube, to the Danube Bank Memorial, known as the Danube Promenade. You all stand and stare at the 60 vintage style shoes, put there as a memorial to Jews massacred by the Arrow Cross fascists at the end of WW2."

Junior stopped, noticing tears streaming down Csenge's cheeks. "I'm so sorry, Csenge." As she wiped her eyes with a napkin, she croaked, "Take no notice; please continue." "The shoes are there, men, women and children, as a reminder of that cruel day. The Jewish victims were forced to remove their shoes before being shot and then thrown into the River Danube."

"I'm sorry Csenge to walk through that in detail. But that horrendous cruelty is magnified 100 times in the world we live in today. My life is on the line, every day, as I try to prevent it!"

Csenge, now feeling hot and bothered said she wanted to go outside and have a cigarette. They went together, passing the waiter who was still intent on taking their order.

They stood together on the pavement, Csenge frantically puffing on a cigarette. Junior moved very close, putting his arm around her shoulders. But silence retained its place in the quiet of Mayfair. Finishing her cigarette, Csenge swivelled and clasped Junior's waist. Her lips slowly moved forward to his. A tender kiss, then they strolled back into the warm restaurant.

Just seated, the waiter appeared. Hunger had started to overtake emotion. They both livened and enthused over the steak offerings on the menu. The waiter appeared relieved with their steak choices, and more drinks!

When he'd gone, Csenge asked "So what do you want from me? I have worked out that you are in a secret world that is usually invisible to the rest of us. But what do you want from me? What has caused you to tell me all this tonight?"

Junior realised he was now a third of the way into the driving seat, and had to be careful not to mess it up. He took a napkin and dabbed the corners of his mouth, in order to give himself some thinking time.

Staring into Csenge's eyes, he spoke quietly, but with feeling. "As well as the research I have told you, I am also informed that you have a degree in mathematics and all your school and university reports depict you as an honest, truthful and caring person. A person that cares about, and is knowledgeable about, what goes on in the world. So the bottom line is, I want to offer you a job. But right now, being totally honest, I'm not yet in a position to offer the job. I have to first get my bosses approval. However, in the meantime, I would like you to think about it. Because I am sure I can get their agreement. You have already been given clearance, both in Europe and the USA." His nose wrinkled as he smiled and said, "You are obviously a very good girl!"

Csenge wanted to know more. "So what is the job? What is the pay?" Junior held his hand up to halt the questions. The food was arriving, and as the waiter carefully placed it in front of them, they remained totally silent.

A few minutes later, they both began to tuck into their late-night steaks. Csenge, having worked a long, busy shift appeared famished. For several minutes, she devoured the delicious fare; rump steak. Half way through it, she placed her utensils to rest on the edge of her wooden platter. Junior watched her as she enjoyed chewing the morsels remaining within her gorgeous lips. She noticed his intimidating gaze and placed her hand over her mouth as she daintily finished. "Junior, you were staring?" "I'm not going to apologise," he replied. "Your lips are inviting!" "You, Junior are incorrigible!" Her expression became attractively sensuous; she leaned across and gave him a slow tender kiss. Then stretching back in her chair, Junior tried to ignore her voluptuous breasts. Csenge knew she now had his complete attention. "So Junior, please tell me more. Give me more detail, be more descriptive." she whispered.

Junior thought for a couple of seconds. Placing his cutlery down, he quietly began to provide more definition. "My colleagues are in Washington at present. It's not a certainty, but I am 90% sure their assignment will involve the ongoing conflict between Russia and Ukraine. They are both young women, in their late twenties. They are experienced agents, but have never been out of the Asian continent before. They have recently worked with me in Afghanistan."

Csenge recoiled in her seat. "My God, I didn't think anyone would be brave enough to work there!"

"They would definitely survive on their own in Eastern Europe. They are equipped to handle this assignment. However, it would be a massive help for them to have a knowledgeable, common sense person like you, working with them. You know the countries, logistics, the laws, the bureaucracy, they will face. And if you enjoy the work and learn from them, you may wish one day, to become a field operative like them. I would suggest you all live together in Hungary. But their main interest, especially in terms of intelligence gathering, will involve Ukraine and Russia. However, there is a strong suspicion that the Russians are looking beyond Ukraine, to countries such as Hungary and Poland. They are probably intent on re-establishing the USSR!"

Junior gripped his scotch and downed it; Csenge watched silently, with a mesmerised expression. Junior went on, "You would have phenomenal support. We have agents and military throughout Europe to ensure your protection. And initially, your salary would be in the region of £12,000 per month, exclusive of property and living costs and all other expenses. So please think about it, we would be offering you a lucrative career, and with all I have learned about you in this short space of time, you deserve the opportunity!"

Csenge now planted her elbows on the table and her pure, ivory cheeks dropped into the palms of her hands. Junior beckoned to the waiter. The dinner remains were relegated to the waste bin, and were substituted by more drinks.

Gradually recovering, Csenge leaned back. An excited smile emerged. "I am totally speechless! If everything you have explained becomes possible, I have no hesitation in agreeing to do the job. I will try to be the best assistant those girls will ever have!"

The drinks arrived. Junior, now relieved that he was close to success, clasped both Csenge's hands. "I will be in the hotel again tomorrow night, then on Saturday, the following day, I have to head to Washington DC. I would like you to come with me. I have my own work to do, but I also plan." He stopped in mid-sentence! "Csenge, this is a very serious request. Please do not speak a word of anything I have told you tonight, to anyone! Also, nothing I am going to say now! If you do, it is probable that all bets will be off!"

"Where was I? Ok I was saying, I also plan to meet with the CIA to get your appointment approved. I'm going to get my Mum to speak to them before we leave." Csenge, as she sipped her gin and tonic, began coughing violently. Junior slapped her back and, breathing deeply, she recovered. Her expression appeared strained. "Your Mum? What has she got to do with all this?"

Junior chuckled as he rubbed Csenge's back. "I'm so sorry! My Mum is the Director General of CECD. She will talk to the CIA before we arrive." "No Junior! I can't go with you. I've got several shifts and a month's notice to give!" Junior tugged Csenge close. "That should not stand in your way. Because it's the person you are! You don't want to let anyone down. But all costs will be covered, and more. We will settle with your employer. So please say you will come with me! It's important that they see you, and you meet Kainaat and Asha. In between times, fix anything you need to fix, and if you don't I will arrange for those things to get done!"

Chapter 10

Csenge Grasps the Nettle

Now outside the restaurant, Csenge clasped Junior, resting her head on his chest. She peered up into his eyes, saying, "So what now?" "Well, we both go to our beds; we both need sleep! It's been an exciting but stressful night!" Their taxis arrived. Junior was first to depart, shouting to Csenge as his taxi pulled away! "I will see you tomorrow to finalise arrangements!" She coyly waved goodbye, disappointed to be leaving Junior, but excited by the prospects before her. The taxi taking her home was right behind. In the solitary, quiet, darkness of the rear seat, her mind rapidly reviewed everything Junior had said. A gleeful smile emerged, as she realised this would probably be the most exciting and rewarding adventure of her life!

Saturday morning, Frank Junior's CECD driver pulled up outside Csenge's Romford rented apartment. She was ready and waiting. A single suitcase, loaded into the boot by their driver, a German named Wolfgang. The journey to Gatwick airport was stop/start until they crossed the Dartford Bridge. Wolfgang now accelerated and drove as if on a no speed limit autobahn. Very soon, they were through check-in, security and passports.

Now seated in American Airlines exclusive lounge, both sipping bloody Mary's, Csenge silently stared around. Junior, with a slight frown asked, "Is everything ok, Csenge?" With a startled expression, she replied, "Oh yes, oh yes, of course! I just still can't believe this is all happening. I keep pinching myself thinking it's all a dream, and I will wake up at any minute!"

Sitting next to Junior, in luxurious business class seats, her dream continued. The next milestone was their arrival at the FBI offices in Pennsylvania Avenue. They would be meeting Denton, a CIA Senior Officer, who had borrowed an FBI office to save them the trip to Langley. He respected the fact that Csenge would be tired after the over-night flight. And, in the back of his mind, he was unsure if this would work out with Csenge. He had already discussed the appointment with both Junior and Anneliese. Their recommendations were well accepted, but the final decision depended on this interview.

Denton's manner, throughout the interview, projected a grandfatherly, jovial attitude. He was acutely aware that Csenge was entering an unknown world, completely inexperienced, but academically highly qualified, and a quick learner. She had shown guts taking these first steps forward. She would only be required to provide support and assistance to his agents. She had a massive amount of local knowledge and, of course, had the backing of two of the most respected Secret Service personnel, Anneliese and Frank Junior!

Throughout the interview, Junior remained silent. Probably because Csenge made an impressive start, which strengthened as they progressed. She was personable, confident, and above all, relaxed. Denton was particularly impressed with two features that would be a big plus for his agents. Csenge, obviously fluent in the language of her homeland, could also speak Ukrainian, Russian and English. But the outstanding bonus was that she had family living in

Ukraine, in Kyiv and Mykolaiv. She said she tried to visit them once a year, and had done so for the past several years.

The interview ended. Handshakes came next, and Csenge was asked if she would take a seat outside. Denton went back in the office to talk with Junior.

Denton smiled at Junior as he sat behind the desk. "She fits the bill! Absolutely fits the bill! She is more than I could have hoped for. She will be a great asset to Kainaat and Asha. Indeed, the whole CIA. Thank you so much, Junior. We owe you! Would you call Csenge back in?"

Junior peered around the door at Csenge, smiled, nodded and winked. "Come in Csenge" he said, gesturing with his fingers. Csenge returned the smile, as she entered.

Denton stood, approached Csenge and shook her hand. "I am pleased to be able to offer you the position, which I hope you accept." "Yes sir, Denton, thank you so much." "This means so much to me. It will be a great adventure." "Please sit," replied Denton with a wide smile. "We should go through some details. And you have some signing to do!"

Just then, came a knock on the door. Junior, who had been casually sitting cross-legged in the corner of the office, stood and answered the door. Laughing, chuckling and squeals of delight were heard. Junior returned, followed by two ladies. It was Kainaat and Asha, both very smartly dressed in business suits.

Denton introduced Csenge and then spent about 15 minutes explaining Csenge's role. Kainaat and Asha were delighted to have her help in a country strange to them. Denton went on to explain that some of his European agents would arrange a property for them. Csenge would be involved in selecting the area, initially, in or around Budapest. A travel itinerary would be prepared and they would depart in a weeks' time. Immigration documents, for all three of them, would be available in a few days. They would also receive details of local contacts and all necessary support, including phones, laptops and all relevant addresses and phone details.

Addressing Csenge, Denton explained that she would have special fast-track training, with ongoing support from European CIA operatives, as well as Kainaat and Asha.

Tomorrow, a driver would collect them from their hotel and deliver them to the CIA HQ in Langley, Virginia, where they would be required to attend briefing meetings, over the next few days. In most part, the meetings would focus on intelligence gathering, regarding the ongoing Russian/ Ukraine conflict and any information pertaining to Russian antics, particularly troop movements. Denton stretched, inhaled and slowly exhaled. "What I am going to tell you now is totally classified. Most of our intelligence is, so far, indicating Russia will, in the near future, attack Ukraine and then initiate a full scale invasion. They will announce they are at war with Ukraine and try to justify it with as many laughable reasons as they can conjure up. Your main objective will be to indicate, with your intelligence reports, when that is becoming imminent. You will, after establishing contacts, and networking with our European agents, need to get yourselves into Ukraine."

"Fortunately, Csenge has relatives living in Kyiv, and so I think that would be a good place to start. Once you reach that point, you will masquerade as Press representatives. You will be given necessary documents and Press passes, when you leave for Budapest."

"One final thing! When you Kainaat, and Asha, are executing intelligence activities in field operations, especially if there is any likelihood of danger, such as being close to military activity or installations, you must ensure Csenge remains in your residence or in a safe place such as a hotel or hospital. She is only your command support. She is not a field operative. She has not received military training. She has not received training in weapons and tactics. Is that completely understood?" They both nodded and responded with "Yes, Sir!"

Denton shook hands with the ladies. Turning to Frank Junior, he uttered, "I am very grateful, and I'm sure we will meet again in the near future. A car is waiting outside the main entrance, to transport you all to the Hilton Hotel. Have a good evening and the very best of luck."

In the hotel lobby they agreed to meet for dinner in the hotel restaurant. All four of them dressed for the occasion. Junior, wearing a grey Prince of Wales check three piece suit, complemented by a mauve tie and pocket handkerchief, was first at the restaurant. All three of the ladies arrived together, wearing fabulous evening dresses and looking even more gorgeous. Junior welcomed them, and as they sat, two bottles of Champagne were delivered to their table. Junior stood, and in a cool, steadfast manner, proposed a toast to the Three Musketeers'.

As the Champagne gained ground, chatter, banter and storytelling became constant. Kainaat asked what print Junior's suit was. She would love a suit made in the same material. Frank Junior proudly responded, saying it was "Prince of Wales." Kainaat gasped. "You are not going to issue another surprise... that you are related to the Royal Family!" Csenge chuckled, leading to laughter from them all. Asha, during the main course, slowly and quietly, described her abduction in Afghanistan, her rescue and Kainaat's wounding, during the episode. Csenge was getting an insight into the work she would be involved in! Although gasping throughout the tale, she appeared stoic and unmoved by those fearsome events. The banter and chatter continued!

The dinner was close to ending. Asha chose to ask a question. As they all enjoyed sipping marvellous goblets of Californian Shiraz, Asha, with a slightly mumbled slur began with a giggle. "Junior, at the very start of the evening you proposed a toast to the Three Musketeers. I probably should know, and I would like to." She glanced at Kainaat and Csenge who were both developing expectant grins. "So Junior," she inhaled loudly, "Who were they; who were the Three Musketeers?" Junior took it as a serious question, and began to answer, but needed to increase his voice above the inebriated giggles and laughter coming from Kainaat and Csenge.

He drew breath waiting for the hilarity to subside. "Asha, take no notice of these two flippants; it's an excellent question! They were three French military men, around the time of the French Revolution. They feature in a very famous novel by a writer named Alexander Dumas. These characters were special, and got into all sorts of scrapes. They were inventive, tactical, quick thinkers who always put their compatriots first. And the endearing quality all three of them exhibited, was comical humour and love for one another. Indeed, it is a swashbuckling adventure that follows the story of a young man, named D'Artagnon who dreams of becoming a musketeer. He works with experienced musketeers, during a difficult time; full of political intrigue. The reason I chose that toast is that I view you, Kainaat and Asha, as the experienced musketeers; Csenge here is D'Artagnon, taking her first steps towards her dream of becoming a musketeer. And looking at all three of you now, you are all comical, humorous and caring. You will become the new Three Musketeers!"

Standing waiting for their taxi, Junior gestured for the girls to huddle with him. With his arms around the necks of all three, he muttered they could all meet, at 7am, for breakfast. They would then need to get on the road to Jackson. He would leave for the White House. He was due to meet with the Director General of Homeland Security, the Director General of the CIA and the President. Kainaat and Asha immediately broke away from the huddle. Csenge was first to screech, then blustered, "Junior you are kidding us!" Kainaat, then Asha, advanced again, each kissing his cheeks. Csenge following, attempting a slow, more passionate kiss.

Junior pulled away saying, "You all have my mobile number. Call if you need any help, and go and enjoy your week up in Jackson. It will be intense, but you will enjoy the experience, and you will be a very capable team at the end of it. Give everyone my regards! They are all fabulous people! And don't forget to call or text me when you are returning, as I will probably be around in Washington all through the next week."

He entered his hotel room, and as he sat on the edge of the king-size bed, shuddered, as he felt the draught of loneliness. He switched the radio on, hoping music would take him to a better place. The song playing was "A nightingale sang in Berkeley Square." It was his mother's favourite. His mind took him to the story she would tell him about her visit to the US Embassy in Berkeley Square, when she was arranging her first US visit; an assignment that broke her heart! She talked about Anya to this day, and still missed her dreadfully. She was her best friend who had been killed while they were on assignment together.

Now Junior's mood went unchecked. He began thinking about his university friend. His mother, killed by a terrorist explosion on a Pan Am flight in 1988. His thoughts painfully moved on through the constant atrocities. The Oklahoma bombing in 1995, the suicide bombers attack on London transport in 2005, and the attack by gunmen in Paris in 2015. Governments seemed to have no way to prevent these interminable, unspeakable acts against humanity.

Desperately trying to bring the barrier down on the real world, he went to the fridge and poured himself a large scotch. A Bells whisky, not a single or double malt, just one to pour down your neck to ease the pain!

The first glass definitely helped. It transitioned him to thinking about the girls. Those three beauties he had experienced such an enjoyable evening with! But no, his mind was intent on surveying horrendous possibilities. The conflict in Ukraine was not going to improve. Any day now the Russians would invade Ukraine. How safe would his friends be? And now he had involved Csenge, a woman, which if he allowed himself, would be his romantic involvement.

Two more large whiskies and his negative thoughts were defeated by numbness. Tomorrow was another day, and as he rolled into the king-size, he spoke out loud. "Sweet dreams, Csenge, Kainaat and Asha. God bless you. My brave little darlings!"

The next evening, Frank Junior again sat in the loneliness of his hotel room, reflecting on the muddled mixture of misery, expounded by the President and his key advisors. The meeting had begun with the President describing his concerns for the world; a dystopian view of a future bereft of reason, swamped in great suffering, inhuman acts, and widespread injustice. The Director General of Homeland Security took the baton and touched on several subjects. His dominant concern was the growth of both left wing and right-wing extremist groups.

Referring to the attack on the Capital by an extremist mob supporting Donald J Trump; the Director General viewed the period up to the next American election" in 2024. It would be a very dangerous period for America. The President continued on this theme; the situation in the UK was very similar regarding extremism, and the next UK elections would also fall in 2024.

Throughout these meandering deviations, Frank Junior wondered where it was going. Why had he been summoned to this meeting?

The Director General of the CIA had been waiting for his chance to square this circle. He had become very appreciative of Junior's ability, and, having worked with his mother on several occasions, had the utmost respect for Anneliese.

"Frank Junior, you know as well as any of us the serious threats that seem to seek us out every day." The Director inhaled sharply. "That is true for Europe as much as for America; I can list them, but you know them."

"We have, with a substantial amount of work, developed a strategy. The President, having talked and discussed this at length with the UK Prime Minister, believes we need a new approach to intelligence, security and defence."

"This new strategy requires a unified approach. Not, as we have now, two separate organisations, the CIA and CECD, working together when we see fit! We need and want a single organisation that combines these two units into one completely effective organisation. One that sees the same intelligence reports. Agrees and develops a single strategy! One that develops rapid response tactics that can be implemented anywhere in the world. Europe and America have the same values and objectives; therefore, they should work on defending democracy as one cohesive elite unit!"

"The proposal we want to put before you is this! Joint leadership of a single elite battalion made up of the best of European and American Intelligence Analysts and Field Operatives. Initially a team of around 120 people. They would have complete authority and responsibility, and sit at the pinnacle of the Intelligence pyramid. This would be the primary approach. If this proved its worth, we propose to amalgamate all Intelligence Organisations into this singular team, that for now, we are calling EuroAm Intel! EAI!"

Frank Junior had several questions buzzing around in his mind, but before he could speak, the CIA Director looked across at the President. He nodded! The Director, leaning forward in his chair said, "Frank Junior, we have, we believe, selected the best of the very best. We wish to offer you the job of dual leader. We will come up with a fancy title later. You would be required to work in complete unity, with a lady named Rashi. Her CV is absolutely fabulous, and her work, over several years, has achieved amazing results. Her systems and methodical analyses have thwarted more threats to this country than even Alan Turing did, in WW2, at Bletchley Park."

"Frank, please don't answer now! We have arranged for you to have dinner this evening with Rashi. We hope you will accept, as this will give you a chance to discuss our proposal, and start to think about how you would work together. And, by the way, forget the CECD assignment regarding China's involvement in the development of viruses. We will assign that to another operative!"

As they all stood, and strode towards the door, the President, with a mischievous smile, grasped Frank Junior's arm. "Your mother is a great friend of mine! Please send her my congratulations on her appointment as CECD Director.

Incidentally, she was the chief protagonist in this clever strategy." The President's mischievous smile widened!

Frank Junior's Hilton hotel room, once again, provided the solace that nurtured clarity of thought. Junior sat quietly, in the armchair in the corner of his room, analysing every syllable and thought-provoking word spoken during the White House meeting. In essence, he concluded his Mother's idea of a unified Secret Service was essential to counter the increasing challenges, and match their increasing complexity.

He breathed deeply as his thoughts began to applaud Anneliese's early, and probably first, strategic improvement. Suddenly his thoughts switched to Rashi. Looking at his wrist, his 18th birthday Omega watch stressed the need for urgency. He had about 30 minutes to get down to the restaurant. Tardiness would never be accepted in his vocabulary.

At 8pm precisely, he arrived at the entrance to the hotel restaurant. Confirmed the table booking with the Maître De, then stood upright, as if a sentry guarding the doorway!

Rashi appeared three or four minutes later, first asking the Maître De if Mr Frank Teer had arrived. Junior, hearing her words, stepped forward and introduced himself. They were shown to their table, and Junior's smile, as they walked, confirmed he appreciated what he saw!

They sat opposite each other and their eyes timidly glanced at each other. Rashi's feelings quickly appreciated the effort Junior had made. His attire was extremely smart but casual. A dark blue open-neck shirt under a light blue casual lightweight jacket. She had noticed, when they sauntered to their table, that his dark blue mohair trousers, fitted tight to his muscular bottom.

Junior, as some small talk began, was entranced by her cute, warm, dark brown eyes. Her eyebrows, neatly contoured, exaggerated her smiling eyes. Soft silky skin enhanced a lovable teenage look and her petite frame, with curves like a winding road, appeared exquisitely dainty!

A couple of glasses later, they both began to speak their minds. The whole truth and nothing but the truth trundled out with abandon. Rashi, a very strong forceful woman, explained she was Indian by birth. She had emigrated to the USA with her family at a young age. Mathematics had been her strong point, which as the world moved on, dragged her into systems analysis, and then, systems construction.

Although, compared to Junior, her height and tiny body structure appeared miniscule, her character and personality equalised their proportions.

Now, with dinner in front of them, they eventually began to discuss the potential to work together on this new assignment. And not just a new assignment, but also a significant promotion, and a massive future opportunity to wield substantial power to defeat the growing threat of evil.

As their conversation advanced into an exploration of their ideology, soon both realised they held mutual hopes and fears for humanity. The under-current in their thoughts, as they surfaced, confirmed a genuine and consistent belief in their ability to make a difference. Both recognised they shared the same destiny, and working together would double their power over evil!

Those intense shared thoughts took them to a joint vision of their utopia. A Utopian world, they were convinced, they could both work towards.

Both, now completely relaxed and euphoric, had only one course of action left to them. With the clinking of their wine glasses, as their arms entwined, they agreed that tomorrow they would jointly accept the leadership of EAI.

Over the next six months, they worked on their primary tasks of assembling a team, and getting it up to speed! Finding premises, interviewing and offering appointments, attending to constant questions from the hierarchy, regarding progress! In addition, a trip to Europe and the UK to talk progress, and deal with developing issues.

By September 2023, Frank Junior, Rashi and 120 Intelligence Officers were settled in the Old Executive Office Building at the junction of 17th Street and Pennsylvania Avenue, within a stone's throw of the White House!

Initially, they were all kept busy, following and understanding events as they occurred, almost every day. This was the continuing conflict in Ukraine. But was quickly superseded by the terrorist attack at the Nova Music Festival. Hamas gunmen had crossed the border from Gaza, attacking sites and indiscriminately, killing about 120 people.

Israel's retaliation was swift and ferocious. Torrents of missiles flooded the Gaza strip, almost every day and night. Hamas, the Palestinian terrorist organisation, had taken 250 Israeli's hostage. Later, Lebanon joined the conflict, firing missiles into the suburbs of Israeli cities. Israel responded with missile attacks on Beirut, striking the Lebanese capital's suburbs. Next came the killing of Hezbollah's potential next leader, with an airborne strike. Israel continued the deadly siege of Northern Gaza, demolishing residential buildings and shelling homes.

The US made several attempts to arrange ceasefires and peace talks. By November 2024, around 64,000 people had been killed in Gaza, and civilians, reportedly, accounted for most of those deaths.

Frank Junior and Rashi had been directed to collect, analyse and refer intelligence information to the US President and his White House team. The EAI team, working in shifts, provided such data throughout 24 hours of every day.

By the end of January 2025, their collective work had supported meetings, very hopeful peace talks, between the various factions, facilitated by a US envoy.

These efforts were protracted. The demands on Junior's and Rashi's EAI team became extremely fluid. The next security checkpoint was the inauguration of the new US President, Donald J Trump. The pressure was intense in view of threats from extremist factions, and the level of unrest in the country, since President Trump's supporters stormed the White House in January 2021.

Throughout these times, Junior, Rashi and their staff had made significant inroads in the invisible game of Secret Service. They constantly identified and pre-empted dangerous individuals and terrorist cells, identified and constructed strategies to pursue peace, and alerted the President to potentially explosive situations before they became uncontrollable.

Frank Junior and Rashi were now working together as if they were conjoined twins. However, the world was moving into uncharted water. Rashi had rationalised that, in her part of the business, the only possible way forward was to embrace AI... Artificial Intelligence. This quickly became more than an interest. More than a hobby. She would spend every free waking minute, exploring, understanding, and developing her ideas on this virgin subject.

Over time, Junior's interest in this subject gradually developed. The intensity of Rashi's enthusiasm began to engulf Junior. They would sit together, late into the night, discussing programmes that Rashi was attempting to develop. He was convinced that she would, eventually, invent a computer programme that would obsolete all previous Government security programmes used by Intelligence Analysts.

But right here and now, it wasn't Junior's big thing! Its value was only about 10% of his thinking. His mind was taken up by his concern for the UK. Since the Labour Party had come to power in 2024, profound hope had abounded in all sectors of the nation. The media, based on the manifesto, had painted an optimistic future. All generations had experienced an extremely difficult period in the run-up to the election. The pandemic, Covid 19, had taken over 120,000 lives. Neighbours, friends and family had been lost. Rules imposed by the Government had increased tension.

No Socialising, limited numbers at marriages, and funerals. But what followed alienated everybody. The media exposed the Conservative Government for not living up to their own laws and rules. Disgust and disillusionment spread throughout the country. An amenable population, that since the 1970's had been willing to rollover and capitulate, had become vociferously vocal!

However, the new Parliament lifted their hopes. Fears were not in people's thinking. Until the first Budget!

The new Labour Government tried, in the days leading to the budget, to alert people to the black hole they would need to address. A £22 billion black hole. This, they claimed, was their legacy from the previous Government. The Budget, never pulled any punches. Instead of good news expected by the country, everybody would experience a worsening world. A massive tax increase for employers, in terms of National Insurance was the demon's bullseye. The man-in-the-street knew this, ultimately, would mean higher costs, a reduction in people employed, and consequently, lower rates of pay and more part-time working. And these costs would pass to consumers.

But it didn't stop there! Inheritance tax on farmers' property, tax on pension pots, almost everything, including benefits for the less fortunate and disabled were to be scrutinized. And pensioners definitely felt the cold of winter; possibly telling them of their future fortunes!

In conjunction with all the budget effects, inflation remained almost stagnant. And, every day, all people were being exposed to everything concerning the Russian/ Ukraine conflict. The war between Israel and Arab countries. Immigrants continuing to pour in across the Channel. Climate change causing the worst-ever wildfires in Los Angeles, and the new American President constantly threatening protectionism. Just to make matters worse, billionaire industrialists, who seemed to be bored with making money, were interfering in politics and criticising the UK Government. How much longer would the populace stand for all this?

After hundreds of years, not even considering it an offence against historic religious teaching, the new Government floated a bill to introduce Assisted Dying. But stranger things have happened. And over the next few years they would!

Junior's mind watched, considered and reviewed every human mistake, over the next couple of years. But sadly, he found very few decisions that in his judgement were correct. Where were these supposed Government intellectuals taking the lives of ordinary people?

As time went by, the Ukraine/Russia conflict ebbed and flowed. Attempt after attempt to call a halt failed. It is said time heals, and in this case it did. Money and effort ran out. The sickening death toll weakened both countries. So, eventually it was reduced to sporadic clashes. Putin came under pressure at home and the UK and Americans no longer saw the need to provide support to Ukraine, Essentially, the same occurred in Israel. A ceasefire in early 2025 achieved release of some hostages. But like some cancers, the war kept coming back. Israel suffered constant dribbles of conflict with the Arab world, and just resigned itself to waiting for the next horrific attack that would light the media touch paper.

During the period up to 2027, there were, almost weekly terror attacks. Some in Western Europe, but by far the most, in the USA. Junior and Rashi had made tremendous strides with their Intelligence team. Particularly in the sphere of counter-intelligence. They had prevented or disrupted over 70% of likely or actual terrorist attack attempts. Their AI work had prevented many cyber terrorism attacks which had the potential to disable financial and health care systems.

In consequence, both the President of the USA and the Prime Minister of the United Kingdom were pressing to finalise a complete devolvement of CIA and CECD Intelligence responsibilities to the global force.... EAI. They would work together as one unit, one organisation, essentially with responsibility for the whole of the Western World; Western Europe and North America.

Day by day, since the US and UK elections, unrest had been growing. The electorates in both countries were losing faith. Both economies were in desperate situations, although the US was faring better than the UK. Investors were pulling out, unemployment continued to grow, with AI now a serious element. Industry, particularly manufacturing, was close to imploding as a result of higher taxes and low demand, as people's living standards suffered. Integrity of people governing was constantly attacked by the media, and usually with good cause. The remaining bastions of the economies, hospitality and service industries, especially retail, were on their knees. High Streets and Shopping centres were like ghost towns.

Europe was economically almost on its knees, with its car industry dying. Worst of all, immigration in both the US and UK, motored on, plundering the treasures of both countries. And to add insult to injury, the US Government had embarked on a policy of protectionism, applying harsh fiscal measures, in terms of import duties, to many countries exports.

2024 seemed to have lowered the chequered flag to initiate a downhill race. However, for the militants, the extremists, this had signalled the era of opportunity! Both left- and right-wing extremist factions began to gain ground. Their popularity, since the new governments were installed in 2024/25, became a growth industry.

In the UK, a far-right group had formed a party; its objective to compete in the 2029 elections. It named itself The Peoples Republican Party.

It appeared to be a mixture of far-right activists, football troublemakers who had been banned from football grounds, known assisted dying sympathisers, and several neo-Nazi militia groups.

This party, along with two left wing parties were slogging it out in the polls. The Labour Party had been in power since 2024, but after just six months, their ratings had nose-dived across the board. But the PRP were beginning to secure a commanding lead, according to various polls. The performance of the Conservative Party, during and after the Pandemic, along with the shell-shocked economy they left behind, had sealed their fate.... At least for the time being.

Frank Junior and his Intelligence Team had been closely following these developments. Intelligence reports regarding individuals in the PRP emanated constantly, as surveillance monitored their every movement, and recorded every written and spoken word. Their lobbying of major corporations, and supportive outspoken comments by Industrialists, were scrutinised to determine impacts on their power base and social media responses; from which an assessment could be made regarding the level of positive support in the country.

As Frank Junior sat in his office, his agile mind turning over all these political nuances, the phone rang. His secretary announced that Mrs Teer was on the phone. Anneliese spoke first. "Frank, I've got a heavy schedule, so I will get straight to the point. I need your help with a couple of issues. Would you be able to get over here for a meeting in the next couple of days, say Monday!" Frank Junior looked on his screen. His brow wrinkled for a few seconds as he thought." Yes, Mum" he replied. "Would you make us reservations in the Berkeley hotel for Monday night? It would be fantastic to have dinner and a long chat." Anneliese replied, "Yes, of course, but try to get to my office in the Foreign Office for the afternoon. Let's get the work out of the way first!"

Monday afternoon at the Foreign Office, Junior's first lengthy embrace was with Penny. As their cheeks met, Junior whispered, "How is it going with Mum?" Penny's lips brushed across his as she muttered, "Superb, she is lovely, just like you!"

Anneliese exited her office door; so came the next embrace! Anneliese then stood a pace back, her hands gripping his forearms. "Frank, you have not changed one bit!" Penny said. "Anneliese, I was just about to say the same thing."

Frank glanced and smiled at Penny as he and Anneliese entered her office. As they sat, Frank asked "So what's up, Mum?"

"Well, Frank, the song our Intelligence operatives are singing goes like this. Those strangers on the Right." Anneliese blended those words, very tunefully, with the melody of Frank Sinatra's classic! She inhaled, smiling at Frank, as she ambled around her office. She turned to look at Frank with a sombre expression.

"A new right wing political party has surfaced in the UK. Our Intelligence Analysts have been digging and delving into every member's background and philosophy. What they have found in there does not appear to be much philosophy. More an insidious belief that carefully executed inhumane, extreme violence will satisfy their personal fanatical extremism."

"These fanatics are now leading in the polls, and with the UK elections only 18 months away, we seem to be flying into very dark, ominous clouds. Cleverly, they are constantly getting their message across to the electorate on social media platforms. They camouflage their intentions with fake reports and fake news. It's almost at the level of brainwashing."

Frank interjected, saying, "Mum, I agree, they are a dangerous outfit. I've been following this from the sidelines. And, for the same reasons, extremism is also coming to the fore in America. Immigration and the economy have become the main talking points across the country. And that undercurrent of the North/South divide, the Johnny Rebs, remains with us."

"In summary Frank, I need the help of EAI. Your new organisation has been doing a superb job, so I want to ask you to put some of your staff on intelligence gathering, working with my CECD team. Incidentally Frank, I don't think it will be long before we are all in one organisation. A global EAI. That's the word on the street! But just to explain a bit further, my staff have been exploring and investigating the world's banking system. They have found that serious levels of funding are flowing into the UK's new PRP extreme right-wing fundamentalists. They are convinced it is originating from several Corporate Billionaires aspiring to become oligarch celebrities. Also, the Eastern and Middle Eastern world seem to be colluding in this venture against western democracy. Being truthful, Frank, our evidence is weak and circumstantial. That is why I need your help!"

"Mum, you've got it. My guys will work with your people! And the blessing is, it means we will be working together. The "Tears for Fears" group was one of my favourites. So, this should be this Operations title. And orchestrated by the Teers family!"

Anneliese and Frank Junior met again for dinner in the Berkeley Hotel restaurant. Their drinks arrived and their conversation drifted into nostalgic recollections and stories about family and friends. Junior moved into asking about his Dad, and then Frank. As the name Jerome started to pass his lips, two hands clasped his face, covering his eyes. His first reaction was to swiftly reach behind and forcefully grab the unknown's neck. His left hand formed a tight fist, as he began to swivel in his seat. "No Junior, no!" screamed Anneliese. The hands over his eyes released as three guys moved into his view. Half-standing, Frank spluttered, "You shits, I thought we were in for some real trouble." With adrenalin still pumping, and Anneliese giggling, Junior embraced each of them. "Dad, Frank and Jerome! What the Hell are you doing here?"

With that, the Maître De appeared saying he had reserved a large table for them in the middle of the restaurant, nearer the bar. They all got comfortable, as drinks arrived.

"Junior, I invited these three reprobates to join us for dinner." Anneliese leaned to Junior and kissed his cheek. "I knew you would love to see them. It's been a while since we were all able to get together!" Junior's expression was ecstatic.

The wine, food and especially banter and conversation, continued for over an hour. Then Anneliese slowly and quietly requested their attention. She wanted to explain a few things. Peering at Junior, she whispered, "Dad is going to spend more time with me, helping with my work. And I have persuaded Frank to come out of retirement and help with the issue we discussed today. And, of course, Jerome is here in the UK permanently, and manages all the intelligence work I rely on every day! But how fantastic is this!" Anneliese's eyes glistened with emotion. "I have managed to get the four men in my life, the four I adore, all here for dinner with me!"

Just a short while later, Anneliese asked Junior if he had thought about the people he possibly would select for this assignment. "Junior, I need people that can infiltrate this organisation, and gain their trust. Whoever we select will report to Frank, hope you are ok with that!"

Junior, with a pensive expression, thought for what seemed an age, as Frank, Jerome and Anneliese studied him. Anneliese broke the silence. "Junior, one thing to tell you, and it may lead you to a personnel thought that will help you back in the US."

"The three operatives we assigned to the Ukraine/ Russia conflict have done a fabulous job. But now, as the conflict has diminished, I have decided to bring one of them back to help me here with the issues at home. The one I am withdrawing quickly was promoted from a support role into a fully-fledged Secret Service Agent. Junior, you had found her and recommended her. She wants to return to the UK and I have a position for her. Your protégé, Junior, named Csenge!

Are you ok with that proposal, Junior? Denton is agreeable, if you are."

"Yes, that all sounds very sensible!" Anneliese decided some more explanation was necessary. "The things in her favour, Junior, are that she is an adopted Brit. Her English is perfect, and she is white. The people she will be tackling are racists, or at least, that is my belief. And the icing on the cake is that she is extremely attractive. Those bigots won't be able to resist." Junior worked hard to contain his agreeable expression!

Junior responded. "Those three out in Ukraine were a team. So maybe that indicates it's time for me to bring Kainaat and Asha back to the U.S. to work on our troubles." Anneliese, with a knowing smile, said "Exactly Junior." They all raised their glasses to toast a better future.

Chapter 11

Return of the Three Musketeers

Three days later, the Three Musketeers were dragging small suitcases through Budapest's Ferenc Liszt airport. Asha, Kainaat and Csenge all appeared tired and dishevelled. Their small back packs were dirty and torn. They had received instructions to return to London whilst on a tour of duty in Kyiv, Ukraine. Ostensibly, they had been visiting Csenge's family. However, the trick was they had stealthily travelled into Romania; close to the Russian border, their intention being to gain intelligence on Russian troop and armament locations and movements. They had accessed partisan Romanian groups who had supported and secreted them. The signs were that Russia may now attempt to invade Romania, as the next stage in Russia's strategy aimed at re-inventing the USSR.

The final element of their incursion had provided more adrenalin flooded exhaustion than expected. Near the Russian border, they were intercepted by Romanian troops that displayed allegiance to Russia. They began to rough the girls up, then attempted to abuse them. They were in a service area when Csenge and Asha decided enough was enough. As these soldiers clustered around Kainaat, Csenge and Asha, responded. With lightening execution, they drew their secreted revolvers and dropped three of them.

Continuing to fire, they dragged Kainaat to a car that was being fuelled in the service station. They bundled in; keys were in the lock; they took off with tyres screaming. The chase continued into Bucharest. Now recognising they were in sympathetic territory, the chase ended. They had lost their pursuers! Later, they gathered their belongings and drove, through the night, to Budapest.

In their small apartment, having read the message from Anneliese, they only had an hour to get out of there, to the airport.

The three slept through most of the flight, but as they awoke, circling Heathrow, they began to laugh and chatter. This team were tough. They appeared to have enjoyed every minute of that episode, and the hundreds of episodes that had gone before.

A single night in the Berkeley Hotel in Chelsea; the glorious rooms, fabulous bed linen, ablutions that provided every possible healing and cleansing, were the catalysts for a magnificent transformation. After fine dining, the girls enjoyed heavenly slumber.

Next morning, following a full English breakfast, all three of them proudly ambled into Anneliese's office.

Anneliese stood to greet them. Her expression was one of bewilderment. She took one pace forward to view the glamourous creatures before her. "You look like you have been enjoying a holiday in Barbados, but I know you have excelled yourselves in Ukraine!" They all moved forward to embrace, then shake hands. Anneliese turned, to move to her desk. "Ladies, just give me a minute to make a call." Deeply inhaling, she said, "Frank, it's me! I have the Ukraine team with me." Silence for just a couple of seconds. "That was Frank," she said peering at the girls! "He will be here in 10 minutes." She glanced around them saying, "You all know my son, Frank? I need him here with us to explain where we go from here." Kainaat, smiling said "Oh, you mean, Junior." "Yes, however my dear, I am the only person in this depraved world that's allowed to call him Frank. He was named after Csenge's new Senior, an older Frank. He is our best ever field operative. I have known him almost all my life and he also will be with us in a few minutes. He's always on time, never late, like an Omega watch!"

As she finished speaking, Penny held the door open and Frank strolled in, but not alone; following behind him were two other men. The three of them approached Anneliese. Frank offered Anneliese a gentle handshake, then a simple, single cheek kiss. He moved back as his colleagues stretched to shake hands with each of the girls.

A pregnant pause consumed the atmosphere in the room, as everyone's eyes studied all facets of the human Rubik's cube surrounding them. A loud double-knock broke the silence. In came a flamboyant Frank Junior, dressed as if he was going to be attending a wedding in the Chelsea Registry Office.

The girls poise lost its proportion. All three together rushed forward, embracing, clutching and kissing him. Stepping back, and ending with handshakes, Kainaat had to speak. "Sorry for all that fuss and emotion Anneliese, but this guy was our flat mate, mentor, teacher and protector in Pakistan and Afghanistan. He was the best person to be with us on that assignment, and me and Asha thank God, every day, for placing him in this world with us!"

Coffees arrived. The trolley rolled in. Penny stood at the door asking if anything else was required. As she closed it, Anneliese sat behind her desk. First speaking slowly, but then as she began, stood and strolled around them. "You all want to know what comes next. But before we tackle that, let's get some introductions done!"

"Ladies first," she uttered. "Kainaat is the lady in red. Next is Asha, in the blue dress and Csenge is wearing the black blazer." The girls stepped forward and hand shaking prevailed. Anneliese, smiling, shuffled into the midst of the girls. With an arm around Csenge's shoulder, she pointed to Frank first. "This gentleman is Frank. A long-serving, highly decorated, CECD Senior." Glancing to Csenge, and then the two yet-to-be- introduced gentlemen, she, with an assertive tone, explained that Frank would be their senior, their boss!

Anneliese grinned as she said, "And of course, you guys know Frank Junior, my son. But these days, I'm never too sure if I should be speaking in those terms, or introducing him as the Acting Director General and Commander of EAI. Incidentally, Kainaat and Asha, Frank Junior will be your boss and you will travel back with him to Washington DC. He will give you your briefing there!" Both girls' expressions showed appreciation.

"You have all heard the circulating rumours concerning the amalgamation of European and American Agencies. I am in no doubt that one day soon, we will all become part of a western-world secret service. Frank Junior has led the pilot scheme, which has proved fabulously successful. You, Kainaat and Asha, will join his organisation, to help fix the problems impacting politics and society in the USA."

Anneliese arched her back then strode to her executive chair behind her desk. She leaned forward, glancing around their faces. "So, why am I saying all this? Well, essentially, it's because, soon, we will be working as one unit. It's a big job, but we are bigger than the task it presents. And cohesive support from all areas, is what we need! So now I'll move on to our two colleagues that have not yet been introduced." Frank began to chuckle. Anneliese continued, "I know these two like the lines on the palm of my hands. So I will say it as I see it. They will not be offended by anything I say. I have worked with them for what seems an eternity. And the reason I am approaching it this way is that in a singular Secret Service, we may all be working together, out in the field, on assignment in the US, the UK or anywhere else throughout the world."

Staring at the unknowns, Anneliese's smile widened. "The tall guy on the left is Norman. We don't use surnames, but he's usually known as Norm. His long-term sidekick, is known as Sly. They are particularly competent Secret Service operatives, specialising in infiltrating subversive and terrorist groups. Essentially, I would say that, together with fear, their hearts are non-existent. They are known in the service as the Symbiotic Misfits." Both gentlemen smiled and nodded!

"Norman presents as a classical, but effeminate upper-class character with slow deliberate speech, which has a distinctly aristocratic tinge. When he speaks, he exaggerates this quirk by drooping the corner of his lips, intentionally imitating a royal personage. His attire, as you can see, is always impeccable. A three-piece Saville Row suit, adorned with all the embellishments; silk pocket handkerchief, striped silk tie and diamond cuff-links. A pair of Church handmade black leather shoes complete the ensemble." As Anneliese moved next to Norm's 6 foot two inch frame, they both began to chuckle.

Drawing a breath, Anneliese continued. "I will tell you".... She stopped to address the whole of Norm's being. Using both arms to depict presentation, she grinned as she continued.

"You should be aware that what you see is not what you get! Norm is a Chameleon. He is the perfect person for our type of work. Beneath that soft, aristocratic persona is a highly circumspect Agent, with the heart of a lion. He is the absolute best at locating infiltration opportunities and manipulating his targets. To the uninitiated, he appears faint-hearted. But beneath that ingratiating exterior is an ingenious, ferocious and resilient protector of our democracies. In short, he is the thinking man's bumper sticker!"

Norm stepped forward to shake Anneliese's hand. As he released his grip, and thanked Anneliese, his steel grey eyes scanned the faces. "Anneliese," he said, "Would you mind if I did the introduction for my soul mate, Sly."

Anneliese gesticulated and nodded a yes. Norm returned a smile as he stepped next to Sly. "We are sorry to take up so much of your time, but we talked this through with Frank and Anneliese. We think it's important because it's an absolute certainly that we will be working with you all, in the very near future. Initially our work will be with Csenge, but that could change overnight. Sly and I are willing to go anywhere in this job, a job we adore! But right here and now I want to tell you something about my buddy, Sly."

"Our names, Norman and Sly are pseudonyms. We don't use our real names because our recognised talents mean we are usually given fucking assignments that require us to infiltrate massive pieces of shit." Those words were spoken with an aristocratic edge!

Norm pulled Sly close. "Sly always epitomises the working class Scouser, but one with eccentric tendencies. Especially nefarious, eccentricities. He will do anything for someone that offers him a chance with a beautiful woman. In essence, he portrays a sex addict. I would stress, that is not Sly! He uses that persona with any organisation, to infiltrate them, by making them believe he will do anything for female payback. However, I would add that, in combat circumstances, Sly is an intelligent, ferocious, malevolent assassin."

Hearing those words, Sly, with a flamboyant regal bow, peered at each and every one. As he bent forward, his Baker Boy cap fell off, revealing short cropped blond, greying hair.

Norm grinned at Sly, looking down on his leathery face, some six inches below. Now Norm, releasing his grip on Sly, said, "We have been working on this assignment over the last year or so, since Anneliese took up her post. We have made inroads. Sly and I never appear to work as a double-act. Our characterisations are too dissimilar! But we do work together behind the scenes."

"We have determined that this new Political Party, leading the polls, the PRP, are receiving massive funding from a billionaire industrialist. An Oligarch who is attempting to stay hidden in the undergrowth. His protégé, and leader of the party, presents as a very wholesome, intelligent individual from a working-class background. He is an attractive proposition to the general population that have experienced several years of public schoolboys overseeing economic decline. Apparently he has had in-depth training in performing in front of cameras. He has received significant help with speeches that people can't wait to hear, from a working-class lad. A lad that understands the lives they are living! This dedicated but, seemingly unassuming, upright 27 year old's name is Adam Tibbs."

Norm eased away from Sly; as he turned to place his hand over his mouth, he coughed. Just as he pivoted back, a knock on the door preceded a confident entrance. It was Jerome! Norm strode over to him, and clasped him around his shoulders. All that knew him, Frank, Anneliese, Junior, Norm and Sly rushed at him; handshakes and a couple of cheek kisses followed. Everyone moved back to their original places, but Norm would not release Jerome. Seconds later, Norm edged Jerome to face the ladies; Csenge, Asha and Kainaat.

Norm uttered, "This guy has worked marvels. He has dug up enormous amounts of dirt on this guy that presently seems to be destined for Premiership in the UK. We won't be using any of it yet. It will remain in our back pockets until the time is right. Until then, we all should constantly work, and rely, on Jerome, to feed us the best, the very best, intelligence needed for our assignments." The ladies, suitably impressed, all moved forward to embrace Jerome!

Now came another knock on the door. A loud knock! Frank stepped forward to take a turn. It was Penny, Anneliese's secretary. She handed Frank a paper, whispered in his ear, then followed him into the room.

Chapter 12

Anneliese – Head of EAI

Inquisitive expressions appeared on every face in the room as Frank proudly stepped into the middle of the forum. With a knowing smile, Frank first peered at Penny, then his eyes glanced around every face in the room. Taking a deep breath, he began to speak. "I have been asked to make a very important announcement. Breaking news on TV around the world has confirmed that NATO met today. Their announcement was followed by interviews with the American President and the UK Prime Minister. They have sanctioned, following a pilot scheme, a singular Western World Security Organisation. It's title is E.A.I. No more information was given. But we have received an e-mail." Frank looked toward Penny, who stepped forward. With a wide smile, she said, "Yes Anneliese, you have been chosen to keep this world safe. You are now the Director General of E.A.I." Penny stopped, tried to breathe, but still spluttered her next words as she stared at Frank Junior. "I can't believe this is happening, but Junior, you have been selected to be Anneliese's Assistant Director General."

The show was over, nothing could better those announcements. Frank Junior stood quietly pondering. All assembled watched, waited and wondered what he was thinking. Instinctively, Anneliese knew that look!

Moving into the middle, Anneliese scoffed, then giggled. "You are all wondering, but I know exactly what he's thinking." Junior's brow furrowed as he stared at his mother. "The fact of the matter is that Frank Junior is feeling some guilt. He and I were informed yesterday that this announcement was a distinct possibility. But the fact is, there was nothing to tell until NATO had agreed!"

Little Sly was the first to move to shake Junior's hand. Norm, behind, with hands on Sly's shoulders followed. They both side-stepped to Anneliese, and everyone followed them.

The meeting was close to ending. Anneliese thrust to the front. With an assertive expression she said, "This is how we wish to organise the start of this new venture. Junior, along with Kainaat and Asha will head back to Washington to develop a plan with Denton and the US staff, to bring the US back to democratic normality. Norm, Sly, Frank and Jerome will tackle the more imminent threat to the UK from the new political party. I will be based here in London and also Amsterdam. We need to keep close to the European Parliament. Csenge will be based in Amsterdam, due to her extensive knowledge of Eastern Europe. And to demonstrate your value to this world, you will all be receiving a deserved promotion... a significant upgrade to Seniors of EAI!"

As Anneliese wrapped up the meeting, she took Csenge to one side. "Csenge, I am flying to Amsterdam this evening. I would like you to join me as soon as possible." Csenge asked, "Would tomorrow be ok, Anneliese?" Anneliese grasped Csenge's hand. "Of course, my dear. I will be staying at the Breitner House Hotel by the Oosterpark. I will book you in if you want, but talk with Penny first, then if you are happy with that hotel, I will book you both in, I would like you two to, initially, stay in the same hotel. Just call me later, you have my mobile number!"

Csenge smiled saying, "Thank you, and see you tomorrow." Next, Anneliese strode across the room and explained to Penny. She glanced across at Csenge and nodded.

Late afternoon around 4pm, Anneliese and Frank Junior met in the Berkeley Hotel restaurant. Closeted in their booth, Anneliese's expression became questioning. "Are you ok, Frank, with how all this is panning out?" "Mum, I'm over the moon. This is spectacular. Who would ever have imagined we would be working together, in charge of security and intelligence. By the way, where is Dad? I thought he would be here." Anneliese giggled. "No, I've given him a free pass to have a boy's night out with Frank and Jerome. And I suspect they have taken Norm and Sly with them. I dread to think what they will get up to! I have to go now. My flight is at 8pm, and my driver is picking me up in an hour. Dad is joining me in Amsterdam tomorrow, so you may bump into him later. We will be back in a couple of days, so hope to see you before you leave for Washington. But right now, my priority is tomorrow's meeting with the European Agency Chiefs!"

Junior, with a pensive expression said, "Mum, one last thing! I think you are going to have a massive amount of computer and technology intelligence work ahead of you. I am willing to loan you my IT partner, in about a month's time. Rashi is exceptional and has an AI programme she is about to launch. I think it would be a big advantage for the work you will need to do."

By now, Anneliese had gathered her things and was starting to edge away. Junior gave a finger wave as he shouted, "Think about it!"

Now alone and relaxing, Junior decided to award himself an alcohol rush. With a single finger in the air, he got the waiter's attention. As he moved closer, Junior, feeling jubilant and knowing the waiter was Spanish, expressively requested, "Camarero, whiskey por favor, grande!"

Smiling as the waiter turned back towards the bar, a beautifully serene voice from behind, softly uttered, "I love your Spanish, I love your everything!"

Junior, with spiritual rapport, turned in his seat and gazed up into her face; it was Csenge. She bent forward, and gently kissed his lips. Grasping his hand, she moved around to sit opposite him in the booth. The waiter, seeing Csenge, hot footed to them, and now stood asking what the lady would like to drink. As he left to collect a bottle of Malbec, Csenge, with a soft poignant expression said, "Junior, I have missed you more than anything!"

The subsequent ten minutes or so was mostly about their work, all quietly spoken. This whole period was interspersed with compliments, and a little romantic language. They were now enjoying the effects of the Malbec.

Csenge became slightly animated and more insistent. "And now as I eventually get back in the same country as you, I am being sent away again! You are at the top of our profession. So the least I would have expected was that you would keep me close." Junior, after a lingering pause, reached for Csenge's hand. That thinking time allowed him to choose his next words carefully. "Csenge, I treasure every moment I am with you. We will have a glut of chances to be together. You will be back and forth between London and Amsterdam. I will have the same opportunity for regular visits to London and Amsterdam. So all we have to do is stay in constant contact. But the priority thread, running through this time, is to work for a victorious ending. My fervent hope is that you won't lose interest."

"You have worked your socks off to become a highly respected and accomplished field operative. I need you to work at keeping my Mum, Anneliese, safe. She is always a target for those evil fuckers that we deal with every day. Then, when we are through this difficult assignment, I swear we will be together! I want that more than anything."

The sparks in Junior's words ignited Csenge's passion. She was compelled to slide round the booth next to Junior. His youthful face, with slightly sad eyes, turned to stare into hers. His hand drifted to the nape of her neck. Inch by inch he slowly brought her lips to his. He had wanted this explosion of emotion since they first met. Now the time had come. He could not resist any longer. The passion in that kiss would excite their beings, their souls, their hearts, forever more.

Csenge, eyes wide-open, breathed deeply as she leaned back in her seat. Junior's love for Csenge almost overcame sensible thinking. All his mind and body wanted was to share ecstasy with her. But instead, his responsibilities, his destiny, wrestled him to the evil yawning chasm that he must fill, and fill completely.

"Shall we have a last drink, then I need, and you need, to get to bed. Tomorrow will be an intense beginning!" Csenge, with a pleading expression, could only reply "Ok Junior."

Once again, he had rescued his destiny from the clutches of love. He wanted both, but knew that this was not the right time!

They all met at breakfast. Matthew and the rest of the guys were hanging, by their fingertips. Junior was planning to head to the Foreign Office to use their secure phone system, to phone Rashi. Frank and Norm were going, in the afternoon, to a PRP rally, hoping to find some chinks of light that would shine as they attempted to enamour themselves to the PRP hierarchy.

Csenge spent a few minutes, unobtrusively, sharing time with Junior. He asked her to attempt to find an apartment in Amsterdam, where they could meet whenever he was in Europe. As she departed for the airport, the smile on her beautiful face seared into Junior.

Early morning in Washington, Rashi took Junior's call. "I guess you have heard all the news regarding the new organisation," was his opening remark. "Those programmes you have worked on in anticipation. How are they going?"

Rashi, proud of her accomplishments, ran her hand over her shiny dark hair, as she exclaimed with excitement in her voice, "Junior, fantastic. The EAI programme, linking us all together, has had two dry runs. It was perfect on both occasions. I am going for a complete launch in two days.... The end of the week. I am even more excited by the AI Intelligence programme. It is fabulous! It can do things I have never even dreamed of. I won't explain everything now; I need to show you. We are close to launching in the next few weeks. So Junior, when will you be back so I can take you through it?" Junior sighed loudly. "Rashi, Mum is coming back Friday, and I would like to hear how her visit to the European Agencies went. Then I will be back at the weekend. And I will be bringing Asha and Kainaat with me. We need to determine their next assignment. They have been superb out in Ukraine and they worked to save thousands of lives out in Afghanistan. They rank at the top of our field operatives!"

The following week, Junior was having a meeting with Rashi and her Seniors in his office in the Old Executive Office Building in Pennsylvania Avenue. She had explained that the Western World Intelligence Programme had gone live and seemed perfect. All Agencies were now receiving intelligence and alerts in real time. All Agencies were training their staff, and so far it appeared flawless.

Her staff, attending, sat proudly smiling. Rashi leaned forward, to Junior's desk top computer. Tapped a few keys and Anneliese appeared on-screen.

"What's up, Junior?" Anneliese's expression was somewhat strained. "Nothing" responded Junior. "Rashi was just showing me how fast we can now reach anybody in our Security Services." "Oh, Frank, while you are online, could I talk with Rashi?" "Anneliese, I will call you later to discuss that subject. I need a bit of time. Not had any time since I arrived back from the US." Rashi stared at junior with a wondering expression.

Rashi decided it was best to move on in ignorance. "Junior, I would like to give you an insight into my AI system." Junior nodded. "Please follow us up to the laboratory cell!" They stood and followed Rashi. Before the stairs, Rashi stopped and turned to face her staff. "I think I need to do this alone. So would you please all get back to your work, and I will be with you in a short while." Glancing first at Junior, then back to the group, Rashi said, "These guys have been fantastic. They have worked day and night on both systems."

Junior's eyes moved around each and every face. "Thank you; heart-felt thanks! This, I am sure, will move us ahead of the game."

In the laboratory, with banks of computers surrounding them, Rashi, with a fierce expression, eyeballed Junior. "So what the fuck is all this with your Mum that I am not aware of?" Junior blinked, stared into space and scratched his chin, before he spoke. "Rashi, we are not hiding anything from you. It's only that I haven't had time. This is my first day, indeed, my first couple of hours when I have had the chance for a face-to-face with you. In fact, the whole thing is about how appreciative and excited we are with your new systems. And not just those. Your work overall is a fabulous asset."

"So down to brass tacks. Mum has a very dangerous political situation building in the UK. In less than six months, they will be into an election. The party, with a substantial lead in the polls is, a relatively unknown right-wing party. Her intelligence people have, in a very short while, determined that this party is made up of criminals, communists, neo-Nazis and extremists. They are funded by industrialists that appear to want to re-arrange the economy in their favour. You know how important the UK has always been to world peace; it is a pivotal force throughout the democratic Western World. So I will drop straight to the bottom line. Rashi, I know similar issues are developing here in the US, but I think the UK is in need of Emergency care. So, on the spur of the moment, I put you on a platter and offered you up. I am being completely honest with you, Rashi. I'd had a couple of glasses of wine and wanted to help my Mum. I just blurted it out! She has got a big job, that's so important to us all. And I know you would make such a difference. So I said I would talk to you about going to London, to work your systems magic, for a couple of months."

Rashi stood upright and inhaled a slow deepening breath. Her burning stare gradually softened. "Junior, I know you don't give a toss about how computers work. You only care about how they can work for us. And I respect that, both you, and Anneliese, see my work as valuable."

Rashi sidled across the laboratory, and stood before him as she reached to caress his face then neck. Slowly, she lowered onto his knee. The palms of her hands caressed his cheeks. As his emotions overcame him, he stared up into her glistening eyes. Rashi, kissing his forehead, assured Junior she was OK with the idea. "Now we are one magnificent Secret Service, I suppose I can't refuse my new boss. And I will find it thrilling to see new scenery, especially in Europe!"

A relieved Junior replied, "And I will be over to work with you every few weeks. Because, I will have to check in regularly with our new boss, Anneliese!" Chuckling, he kissed Rashi's nose!

Over the next few months, their work in London began to get some results. During this period, the UK's economic situation had significantly worsened. The PRP political party were making the most of this, with weekly rallies, extensive media coverage, and social media which PRP swamped daily with their propaganda. But on the other side of the coin, Norm, unexpectedly had managed to convince the PRP hierarchy to appoint him to the second tier senior team. He had presented himself as a staunch supporter of their ideology, as well as being a qualified solicitor. The PRP leaders saw Norm's persona enhancing the depiction of PRP as a party with beliefs sacrosanct to the working people of the UK. A party that was upright and committed to integrity as its key value.

The strategists in EAI Intelligence had originally thought that Sly would be considered more acceptable to the PRP leaders. An intelligent working man that presented as such. An enthusiastic Scouser that would criticise the establishment with convincing rhetoric and humour. But no; they preferred Norm, because they were taking on both the Private School Conservatives and Labour. Sly had gained acceptance, but needed to wait his chance to move into the arena where he could make friends and influence people.

Over in Washington DC, Rashi was preparing to depart to London. Junior had prepared a list of everything he thought she needed to know, as it was her first time in London. He had summarised everything in an email and ended by saying he would be in London in two weeks' time.

Despite jet-lag, Rashi met with Anneliese at lunchtime, the next day. They sat and discussed the intelligence that would be most useful in the present circumstances. Rashi detailed the possibilities that she knew AI systems could deliver. As background information, Anneliese explained the political situation. The party in power, the Labour party, had recorded constant failures throughout their term of office. The opposition, the Conservative party, had not recovered from several years of inept attempts to tackle major issues; both whilst in power and also in this last period as the opposition. But a new political party had emerged; the PRP, which had become dominant due to the electorates disappointment with, and apathy towards, the usual ruling parties. Now, only several weeks away from the UK election, the PRP were ahead in the polls and continuing to gain ground.

Anneliese stood and walked round beside Rashi. "I have been through our intelligence, time and time again." Peering into Rashi's eyes, she inhaled and then took a quiet moment. Sighing, she continued. "Rashi, this PRP party will probably gain power. Under the surface they are a toxic mob. I have looked at them from every which way, and it's the only conclusion I can reach. So, I need you to track their every movement and if I am correct, help me disable them, before they become too powerful."

Over the next few weeks, Rashi, with the help of local IT specialists, had set out her stall. Norm had provided her with strong, detailed intelligence which had made two spectacular advances possible. The first AI programme, based on Rashi's original concept programme, had the ability to track all funds and fiscal arrangements, in real time. It was impossible to detect, and could follow funds throughout the world banking and black market systems; however, the development had needed to overcome many difficult operations, iterations and complications! Rashi's new staff were spellbound.

The second AI programme allowed access to all PRP incoming and outgoing electronic mail, again, in real time. Rashi's development was based, initially, on sending a scam-type email to the PRP mainframe computer and computers belonging to every known member of the PRP community. As they attempted to delete this email, the AI system automatically set-up a surveillance system which showed and recorded every movement. And if they used a video link or face-time, they were recorded!

Norm had done a wondrous piece of work, providing Rashi with accurate primary data. Rashi's new staff were amazed at how easy she made it look. Anneliese was astounded by these technology achievements! She now had the tools to evidence every piece of their lives.... their funding paths, their communications,... and most importantly, their intentions.

Now, with just two weeks to go until the UK 2029 election, nothing incriminating had shown up. PRP were playing an astute game; still gaining ground in the polls, they were receiving the lion's share of media coverage, especially with the tabloids. Their leaders were being depicted as salt-of-the-earth people, with distinct advantages.... Real wholesome people with real working experience. Indeed, they constantly paraded their senior people, with personal histories that ranged from owners of private companies, to lawyers, accountants, to bus drivers and factory workers. Every one of these party members had come from poor backgrounds and always had a great story to tell about why they had joined PRP and how they believed this party would deliver a better life for all!

Tomorrow looked like a big day. The PRP were publishing their manifesto. Just in time for the arrival of Frank Junior!

At mid-day Junior turned up in Anneliese's office. She had just begun to read through the PRP manifesto. Two seconds after Junior entered, there came another knock on the door. It was Norm.

Anneliese and Junior both scrutinised Norm's expression. Anneliese beckoned to Norm to come closer. "What is it, Norm? I guess it's something important."

Norm, with respect, replied, "Yes Ma'am. You know I've now attended several PRP meetings and rallies. They are widespread, extremely widespread; fanatical activists. I think I've done a pretty good job collecting objects with their fingerprints and DNA. But their core numbers worry me! So I would like to ask a question. How many Agents do we have assigned to this operation?"

Anneliese's response was assured. "Norm, at present I have fingered about eighty. All you have to do is say what you need, where and when." Norm winced and, as his lips tightened, retreated a step. "Anneliese, Ma'am, that's great, but I have to alert you to the fact that this well-organised, fanatical crew can call on people up and down the whole country. If the worst comes to the worst, we will need at least 130 Agents, possibly with military support! They are training strong-arms, and forming militia groups that are ready and willing to use force whenever they need it."

Anneliese's expression soured. Looking sideways out of the window, she grasped 30 seconds of thinking time. Turning to Junior, her expression transitioned into a wry smile. "Norm, if that's what we need, that's what we will have." Glancing to Junior she then stood and uttered expletives she hardly ever used. "These fuckers may gain power. I am not sure we can prevent that! But these atrocious evil, racist bigots are not going to be allowed to put the people of Britain through hell. The Nazis did that all across Europe, but the Brits stood up to those rancid, evil demons and won! And I will categorically assure you Norm, I will not let such a thing happen again! We will win again !"

With a quarter turn to face Junior, she continued. "Norm, I don't have to ask Junior for his opinion. I know what he's thinking from his expression. It's this! If we need help from America, we will get it. Whether it's more Agents, military or weapons. Because the USA know we are two countries that live together, with the same doctrine." Junior chuckled, and replied, "Correct Mam."

Norm, with an expression that exuded belief and confidence, stepped towards the door. With it half-open, Norm paused and looked back, with relief in his face. Nodding to Anneliese and Junior, he quietly uttered, "Thank you! This, with you two in charge, will be the beginning. Not the beginning of the end! Forget that manifesto; it's all bollocks! I have heard their plans, which are the work of demented, callous treacherous bastards. The work of Satan."

Chapter 13

The PRP are Elected

The UK election run-up saw the polls reflecting continuous gains for the PRP. And on Election Day, the polls were proved to be completely accurate. The Peoples Republican Party would be forming a government. Prime Minister Tibbs was installed as leader of the Government in August 2029. From that day, British values of social care, truth and integrity would be threatened, as never before! An evil contagion would be spread by PRP from day one. The only weather pattern that Anneliese and Junior could visualise was calamitous clouds gathering on the horizon.

Junior, sitting in his office in Pennsylvania Avenue, exhibited a numb, nothingness stare out his window. He was feeling concern for his mother, Anneliese, and almost as much concern for the people of the world.

President Trump had retired from politics at the end of 2027. The 2028 US election resulted once again, in a win for the Republican Party. But, different to President Trump's volatile eccentricity surrounding moderate governance, the subsequent ruling Republicans were beginning to demonstrate far-right tendencies. However, reflecting on this, Junior perceived the US situation as a drop in the ocean compared to the recent adverse intelligence he was getting concerning the UK situation.

Norm, Sly, Csenge and, of course, Frank, had been leading the work of the undercover UK field operatives. Everything, landing on Anneliese's and Jerome's desks reflected a deteriorating situation. Now the government's first budget was staring them in the face!

In the Houses of Parliament, the PRP Chancellor opened the Budget speech and debate. James Maddern, attempting metaphoric splattered humour, chuckled as he explained that when he had studied the books, he had suffered a severe spasm of shivers. "We are new to this business of keeping the country afloat, but compared to the previous incumbents, the Labour Party, we are real people who have worked, and have real experience. So, we can quickly spot the scandalous truth." Boos and cat calls erupted from the opposition benches!

Maddern's smile transitioned into a menacing stare. The Chamber gradually suffered a deafening eerie silence. That stare, a threatening stare, penetrated every one of the Opposition front benchers. They all, everyone in the Chamber, now knew this would be an abnormal and aggressive Parliament.

The silence continued as Maddern, with sarcasm in his voice, loudly exclaimed, "The previous Government has put all of us, in the near term, close to the breadline. But be assured, we, the PRP, will ensure that life carries on! We will suffer for a while, until we gain some traction. Then we will keep the pedals turning until we cycle into the garden and smell the roses!"

Now, everyone was about to be treated to the new Parliamentary language, the PRP language! Even TV commentators became silent and showed surprised, fearful expressions.

The leader of the Opposition, Aubrey Holderness, rose to his feet, and as he crashed his rolled-up papers on the ballot box, screamed "We don't want to see your showboating and hear your far-right attacks on Labour. We left you in a good financial position; something you could build upon!"

James Maddern, head bowed for around 20 seconds, slowly looked up and then stared into Holderness's eyes. His grinning expression became hostile. "Sit down you useless little fucking piss-head. The country wants us real people to take charge and deliver. You had your time, and spent it on booze and mental masturbation; you achieved nothing!"

As a shocked Holderness flopped back into his seat, surrounded by lingering silence, the speaker shouted "Order, Order!" Just as he was about to reprimand Maddern for his language and aggressive tone, the new Premier stood and screamed, "Shut the fuck up! Give this guy a chance. Remember this is his first time, but unlike you lot, he has worked, run a business and been successful." His expression was fearsome, as he, with threatening, squinting eyes, stared at the Opposition front-benches.

The Chancellor began to rattle off the elements of his Budget, occasionally embracing the TV cameras focused on him.

First, and as expected, all except the poorest would pay more tax. Businesses and the rich would be expected to pay more!

Migrants were next on the agenda. Prisons would have inmates seconded into defence, army, navy and air-force. Migrants crossing the Channel would be immediately taken to prison. Those with skills could apply for factory work or work on farms. Any attempts to abscond would attract a long prison sentence.

Now came the warning sign of things to come. Things that would not be popular. The Chancellor, straight faced, stated that Defence would be bolstered. National Service would be re-introduced, after almost 80 years. Maddern used all the soft soap he could find in his twisted bathroom. Apprenticeships, skills for life, comradeship and pay, would as a result, all be enhanced.

That previous part of his statement was designed to somewhat soften the blow and appease the nation. The Chancellor took a deep breath as he puffed out his chest. Then came the sucker punch. National Service will be served for a three-year period, and will apply to all people over the age of 16 and under 21 years of age. The gasps around the house shook the rafters.

Youngsters aged 16 to 18 years would be required to serve in a Cadet Force, subsequently transferring to the Senior Services at 18.

The Chancellor asserted that this National Service Programme would have substantial benefits. A massive skills increase to take young people into civilian work. A substantial reduction in criminality, especially Knife Crime, and a significant boost for intelligent citizenship!

Saving the best until last, Chancellor Maddern referred back to the increase in tax rates. All tax rates would be increased by 5% except for those with incomes above £125,000 per annum, and exclusions would continue for those people on low incomes.

Gasps from the opposition parties expressed disbelief. However, the Commons quietened as the Chancellor quickly continued his statement. "Those lucky people with incomes above £125,000 will, obviously, be only too pleased to assist their country. The tax rate for those citizens will increase to

65% which will go a long way to getting the NHS and other services back on track!"

There was enough meat in this sandwich to keep the media bloated for days, if not weeks. The electorate would see, hear and read their analyses over the next few days. Debates in pubs, cafes, restaurants and clubs would go on for quite some time. Mostly, full of fear and apprehension regarding where the PRP would eventually drive their wagons. Would it be into a desert lacking empathy, a deep chasm requiring sympathy, or over the precipice of hatred, racism and conflict! If the last of these, there would be no rescue. Truth and values of right over wrong, and conscience, would be irreparably broken, as the wagon bit the bottom!

Anneliese, having read, and heard the Chancellor's Budget speech several times, had already analysed every word, and possible hidden meaning. Her first action was to request her Intelligence Analysts to review the speech and provide their interpretation. Her second action was to call a secret meeting of her European Senior staff, and also the American side of the equation. They would meet in Amsterdam two days hence. Anneliese opened the session by introducing the American contingent, then the European country directors. Lastly, she stood to introduce her Senior European staff. She completed this mammoth task then introduced Penny, saying Penny would take minutes and therefore, probably have to concentrate and work harder than the rest of the assembled company! Everyone smiled and giggled at these words!

Anneliese paced around the conference room for a few minutes, shaking hands and welcoming everybody, mostly in their own language. Ambling back to the head of the conference table, she sat in silence for a minute, gathering her thoughts.

Looking around the faces, in a quiet voice, she began. "As you know, I have been appointed as head of a superstructure organisation responsible for counter espionage, surveillance and security in the Western World. But I would be ineffective, indeed useless, without your efforts and support. We seem to be entering a period where our ideology is under attack. The UK has, during and since WWII, carried a torch to remind the world of the constant need for vigilance, to nip evil wickedness in the bud. But, from every direction, that torch flame is beginning to flicker, due to strong evil winds blowing from every corner of the compass."

"I asked you here today because I sense, indeed my intuition tells me, the UK will experience an extraordinary deterioration in its ability to keep the peace in its own country, let alone continue its diplomatic role and efforts to keep peace throughout the world. The UK electorate, probably unknowingly, has placed a right-wing Government in power. Our intelligence indicates they will quickly transition to a far-right Government. Possibly one with ambitions dedicated to oppressive, tyrannical rule. Our people's intelligence identified funding flowing in from a subversive country. The evidence so far, indicates Russia!"

She stopped for a few seconds and glanced around the room, at the faces that had expressions demanding to hear more. Anneliese stood, then smoothing her dress, sat down again. Seeing the concerned faces around the room, Anneliese began to chuckle. "Please, please don't get worried by this. I have been fighting evil all my life, and now my son, Frank Junior is working with me. We will win! We will surprise these monsters with our hearts and souls dedicated to defence of peace, and our people."

"I have only talked about the UK so far, but let's expose how widespread our enemies are." Looking across the table at Frank Junior, Anneliese continued. "Frank will tell you that the legacy left by President Trump has continued. Trump's protectionist convoluted business thinking and interference policies, with continued non-sensical statements, remains an issue. The American people are now sceptical about every word spoken by the new right-wing President. Then if we look around Europe, Germany is now dominated by fascists. In France, left-wing extremists are in control and they are sliding, day by day, down the economic ladder. Italy has resurrected its far-right stance from the days when Mussolini led them to join with the Nazis. Spain is a mess, not knowing where its heading, because it believes their problems are caused by the countries surrounding them!"

Peering at the faces around the conference table, Anneliese only saw knowing acceptance in the expression of the assembled emissaries. Frank Junior now decided the time had come to assert the position of America.... The most powerful nation in the Western World.

Junior stood, adjusting his striped tie as he did so. One by one, he slowly addressed and welcomed each Director General. Each and every one were treated to a respectful welcome in their own language. Although these emissaries had translation earphones lying on the table in front of them, their smiles confirmed their appreciation!

Now, with microphone in place, Junior, with an appealing smile began. "Well, like me, you probably perceived the opening remarks from Anneliese, Western World's Director General, as pretty pointed and hard-hitting. Maybe, that's because she is not a politician. She works on facts, figures and intelligence. And she has told it to you, in truth, the way she sees it panning out before her. We should all remember that she was appointed to this job because there is no one better. I won't take you through her career history. You can do that for yourselves. But I have done my homework, and I know she is right! This is the time we all must be concerned, and get prepared to resist attempts by fundamentalists, extremists and insurrectionists to destroy democracy. Today, we are asking for your total commitment to the defence of security in every country and region that has joined EAI. As you know, we now have an Intelligence Secret Service system that links us together. Totally together, in real time!"

Junior smiled. "I must take this opportunity to introduce you all to EAI's most valuable, Director of Technology. Rashi developed our programme, and has more on the way!" Junior held his hand out towards Rashi, who stood with embarrassed reluctance. Clapping and some cheers overwhelmed Rashi. She, enjoying the moment, slowly sat as her eyes sparkled.

Junior now waltzed into the middle of the horseshoe conference table. Looking around, his voice began meekly. "You all have people like Rashi. People that want democracy for their countries. People that work hard to feed their families and have Governments that keep democracy sacrosanct. Governments that work to make lives better for people. Put very simply, our job is to keep them safe and secure!"

Standing behind his chair, he further explained. "All we want from you today, ladies and gentlemen, is this. Presently, we are all exposed to advancing evil and wickedness. All Anneliese and I want is agreement that if any country, any region, needs our help, we will provide it. As we see it, with all the intelligence we have, the first will be the United Kingdom. So please, ladies and gentlemen, before you leave, sign the acceptance and obligation papers before you."

That evening, in the Amsterdam Breitner House Hotel, the EAI team met for dinner. The relief from the stress of the day gradually took them all to a much better place. Anneliese and Frank Junior thanked their staff, saying they thought the day had been successful. No dissenters, no anguished expressions! As the wine continued to flow, dignified humour enveloped the whole table, Anneliese inched her chair back and stood. She slowly meandered around the table to Csenge and leaned to whisper in her ear. Csenge smiled, stood and asked her compatriots to excuse her. Anneliese and Csenge sauntered outside. Standing together in the hotel entrance, Csenge asked Anneliese, "Do you mind if I smoke?" Anneliese grinned saying, "No, of course not. But could I have one too?" They lit their cigarettes, both enjoying the first gasp, as they watched their first exhale float plumes into the dark night air.

Anneliese grasped Csenge's vacant left hand, and with a tender smile, led her ten yards or so away from the hotel entrance. Standing under a street lamp, Anneliese leaned slowly forward and kissed Csenge's cheek. "You, my young lady, have been extraordinary. Indeed, magnificent! But now I am needing more from you. And I am convinced you will deliver. I know I originally asked you to be based in Amsterdam. But I have changed my mind. This is not all bad, because you will need both bases, London and Amsterdam. However, right now I need you, with me, in London. Many things in the UK need our attention. My strategy involves you working with Norm and Sly. I would like you to come to my office in London tomorrow. I will have Norm and Sly with me and then will explain all."

Csenge, with a somewhat disappointed smile said, "Anneliese, I have just signed to rent my apartment in Amsterdam." Anneliese chuckled." That's ok, keep it! You will need it. I am learning to rely on you, and so you may be coming and going from London to Amsterdam for some time to come! So when we arrive in London, take the opportunity to select an apartment there also!"

Csenge, now elated, settled gently back into her seat at the dining table. As her mind backtracked through the conversation with Anneliese, she reached for her wine glass. She needed to calm her excitement. It seemed her value to the organisation had been recognised and in consequence, she now would be expected to fulfil a senior role. Indeed, her assumption was she would become Anneliese's right hand!

Her wine glass slowly approached her lips as her excitement eased. Before taking a sip, her eyes met Frank Junior's. His gaze seemed to be searching for Csenge's heart. Her glass remained at her lips as his eyes, then expression, were enchanted by a delirious passion!

Frank Junior, with an enigmatic smile, looked away as his hand searched around the table for the wine menu. "Would you all agree we deserve another bottle? We have had a successful day, and probably only have this last chance to celebrate together, before we enter a very difficult period!"

Everyone uttered, "Great idea, we would love another glass!" That was, all except Anneliese." Junior, I'm getting past late-night alcohol and need my bed. Please, everyone, enjoy yourselves. However, I would request you to attend a meeting with me tomorrow evening. That is Frank, Csenge, Norm and Sly. And of course, you Jerome. Tomorrow evening at 7pm in my office."

Junior stood and kissed Anneliese on the cheek. Now standing, he reached out to Csenge. "Please come with me, Csenge, to the bar. You should select the wine to gird our loins ready for battle. Just as the Vikings did before they invaded!" He smiled with demanding eyes!

As they slowly ambled toward the bar, Junior whispered, "Csenge, there will be no raping and pillaging, but I am struggling to resist the temptation to ravish you tonight!" His grip on her hand tightened.

Standing at the bar, Junior passed Csenge his pen. "Write your room number and I will visit you later," Csenge stuttered a resistant response. "No, Junior, we mustn't!" His soul-searching smile spoke surrender! As they walked back to the table, he could feel her hand trembling!

Another hour of unimpeded conversation and humour took them all to the point of needing sleep. Both Csenge and Junior had resisted much more wine, knowing that their later meeting could not be sustained in a drunken state.

Chapter 14

Csenge's Night with Junior

Every step along the dimly lit corridor was placed quietly and softly. Junior, reaching Csenge's door, gave it a gentle, two knuckle tap. The slowly opening door revealed Csenge standing in the low light of the hallway. Her bright white towelling dressing gown gave some illumination. Her soft smile gave an innocent invitation to enter. As the door clicked shut, Csenge turned to lead Junior in. But with just a single movement, Junior's hand encircled Csenge's waist. His grasp tightened as he pulled her into him; her body brushed Junior's upper thighs. His pronounced thigh muscles aroused Csenge, but then, in a split second, he spun her, and she faced him. Her lips were first to seek his. Her hands clasped his neck, forcefully pulling his lips further and further, deep into hers. Kisses explored her throat, then tongues became entwined, raising their passion.

The pure white robe fell to the floor, and as it did so, Junior picked Csenge up and without pause, carried her to the bedroom. Almost dormant love, that had been resisted for so long, was now victorious!

Lying on the pure white bed linen, the morning sun streamed in and touched Junior's eyes. As he began to waken, the memories of that idyllic night in paradise returned. He was now in love! He had always loved Csenge, but this last night confirmed the feelings he had held for so long. His mind was constantly intimidated by his yearning for Csenge!

Mornings were never something that Junior or Csenge found easy. This one was stressful. Junior and Rashi's flight back to the USA was due to take-off at 2pm. But Junior wanted to spend more time, much more time, with Csenge. They eventually met the rest of the team for breakfast, about 10am. Although that gave them a few hours after waking, that time had been eroded by romance and love-making. In all the affection, Junior admitted to Csenge that he loved her from the very first moment he saw her. He topped that by admitting he had only been in any sort of relationship, once or twice before, and one of those had been a girl in his hometown, during his youth! Csenge listened but did not speak of her previous relationships. She now realised she was an experienced woman that had met a relatively young, handsome man; a man that was honest, truthful and loved her. The dawning came. She was obsessed with him. She loved him! She had thought she did, but now there was no doubt. He had to be hers! For life!

Their flight was two hours away, half-an-hour before Junior and Rashi. Au revoirs on the hotel steps were exuberant. Junior and Csenge appeared rather reserved, however, once in the airport, Csenge received a text message. "Be back in a week or two! I love you!"

Mid-afternoon, Penny, Csenge and Anneliese were in the Foreign Office building. They would all meet with Norm, Sly, Frank and Jerome at 7pm. In the meantime, Csenge was frantically ploughing, page by page, through estate agents websites, searching for a flat to rent. Penny eventually joined her saying that Anneliese had drifted off to meet with Jerome.

At the point Csenge was becoming despondent, Penny raised her arms above her head to stretch. Her pretty, slightly upturned nose slowly and quietly inhaled. Holding breath for a few seconds, she exhaled as she leant forward, forcing her words to blast out!

"Csenge, the budget for this is non-existent, open-ended. You have three months as an ex-pat, to live in a hotel whilst you find a suitable place. Now to the point. There is a fabulous hotel that was recently built. It's a stone's throw from the Foreign Office, with views of St James Park, Pall Mall and Buckingham Palace."

"But, Csenge, really, this new hotel has only been available for a couple of years, and is unbelievable. It's named the "Victory", after Admiral Nelson's flagship. And such a worthy name for the job we do."

Penny eased her chair back and stood. "Csenge, would you like me to cancel the booking in Trafalgar after I see if I can register you into the Victory. It's a shame you relinquished your apartment in Romford, but I suppose it's a bit of a way out, now that you are one of the Seniors' here." Csenge's eyes traversed across to Penny. "Am I really in the Senior group?" Penny, surprised by Csenge's question, replied, "Yes, of course, you have earned it! So, remember, I am your first port of call with anything you need help with."

Csenge now feeling exhausted, stood and stepped away from the computer. "Penny, you are an angel. Yes, please see if you can get me in. If they will accept a week's booking, and I like the place, I will reserve a further three months with them. If you could do it now, I would be very appreciative, as I am tired and need to get myself organised for our 7pm meeting!"

One by one, they arrived in the Palmerston Conference Room. A luxurious historic room with a ceiling some 20 feet high. As their chatter reverberated around the room, it mystically returned to them as it echoed off the ceiling, and central carved medallion.

Csenge had never been in such a splendid room. Overawed, she sat quietly admiring the exquisite architecture and furniture. Seeing the intensity of emotion in her eyes, Jerome leaned towards her and placed an arm around her shoulder. "Csenge, enjoy every moment. You are now in the upper echelons, and should be very proud. You will get used to it, but I suspect you, like me, will always be mesmerised by this new chapter in your life!" Csenge turned slightly to reply with an innocent wide-eyed smile. "Thank you, Jerome, it's like I'm in a world that, in my wildest dreams, I never imagined!"

A loud creaking sound, as the oak doors opened, signalled Anneliese's arrival. She elegantly breezed in, loudly exclaiming "Hello again everyone, it is always very special to meet with you!" Penny ambled in, almost pacing in exact time behind Anneliese's silent steps.

Csenge leaned toward Jerome and whispered. "Anneliese is so beautiful. In Hungary we would comment szep noi" Jerome whispered from the corner of his mouth. "Yes and I have known her since she was 23! And she continues to be a goddess with brains!"

The silky Dutch accent that was Anneliese's, filtered through the room. With a glowing smile, she requested their attention. "I am going to explain the difficult situation we find ourselves in." The room developed an eerie silence. "We are obligated to protect and work with the ruling party, the PRP. The party this country elected in the 2029 General Election. But as we all here know, we also have a responsibility to, and are accountable to, the organisation for Western World security! We work for EAI and, following agreement by all NATO countries, must not forget we are accountable to the EAI Intelligence Service. In the case of the United Kingdom you are, my team Seniors. I, as Commander, Director General, will not be affronted if you simply refer to me as Anneliese. This is not about titles, climbing the ladder, being awarded higher positions and salaries. It is about working to keep this world safe. And by that I mean, protecting and improving the lives of people in the Western World. Hopefully, we may begin to drag the rest of the world into a place that declines conflict, racism and a whole list of abhorrent things that surround us today. Has everything I've said so far been acceptable to you guys; right in the here and now!" The smiles from around the table confirmed their agreement and commitment!

Anneliese now moved from her chair and began to stride into the middle of the room. "So now I would like to move to the nitty gritty that is the next step we should deal with."

"It comes down to this, we must, on the one hand, ensure our operatives out in the field, and our Intelligence Analysts, in GCHQ, are dedicated to performing and providing outstanding Secret Service advice, support, and security to the UK Government, the PRP!"

"On the other hand, you, my EAI Senior UK team will devote special efforts to monitoring and surveillance of every element of the PRP Government and its complete organisation. You, and only you, will be involved in this secret operation, which will be totally classified in EAI headquarter files. There are two exceptions. Frank Junior and Rashi will join us next week, and form part of this team's operation. But, make no mistake, our commitment to the rest of the NATO countries will continue as normal. I, along with Frank Junior, will direct any necessary global assignments, alongside our work with you!"

"In general, I visualise individual responsibilities in this way! Jerome will manage GCHQ Intelligence. Jerome, you should work in conjunction with Rashi when she arrives." Anneliese glanced around everyone, and as she enjoyed her own thoughts, smiled saying "Rashi has pulled some more rabbits out of the hat, and has a few new spectacular intelligence systems to show us!"

"Norm, Sly and Csenge will be our field operatives, and in a moment Norm will give us a report that will engage these three in their next assignment." Anneliese stepped forward and shook Norm's hand!

"Penny will stick close to me, for obvious reasons. Now I get to our elusive pimpernel! Frank!" Anneliese pivoted and smiled as she walked toward him. "You all know Frank and the exploits that are documented in his career history. He will be our floating consultant. He knows every aspect of our business inside out. If any of you need assistance, he is your man. He will be around me most of the time, and I and Penny will ensure he is contactable, if you need him."

Norm glanced at Frank then Anneliese. Frank gestured to Norm to take the floor. Norm's towering frame moved out of his seat. He was immaculately dressed and his smile seemed to capture everyone's attention. He stroked his shaven, baby soft chin as he prepared to speak. The intensity of his expression gained complete attention.

"I am now accepted in the PRP organisation. Rashi has been recording in her system every important person in the PRP Government. I am a back bencher, but because I am legally trained and professionally qualified, I am, on occasions, invited to sit in on Cabinet meetings. Indeed, sometimes top level secret government meetings."

"I recently attended one of those secret meetings. Several things were discussed. In my opinion, outrageous things. Top of the agenda was a mandatory assisted dying programme. Previous governments never got past discussions and years of work on getting this through Parliament. The PRP are planning to force it through, with commitments to funding all the necessary support and medical forces within specialised clinics. They also have an intention to widen the scope to people with severe disabilities that cannot contribute to the world of work and commerce."

Norm stopped. He stood and turned towards the window. The deafening silence in the room seemed to last forever. Slowly, he turned back to face them. "I am so sorry! I apologise to you all for losing it. I have a younger brother who was born with a severe disability and will never be able to work. But to him just being alive is wonderful. When our family meet with him, the look of ecstatic joy is heavenly. Then there is my Mum. She has been suffering from cancer for almost ten years. She has suffered almost every treatment that is available. But with the medical advances, she still has a chance. And she wants to be with us. So who, amongst us, is going to allow that to be taken away from her. Certainly not these PRP bastards that believe they can do whatever they want, because they have the power that decides whether we live or die."

Norm stopped and stood quietly for a few seconds, as he gathered himself. To begin with, his voice was timid and emotional. Once again, he applied the brakes as his eyes peered up to the ceiling. As he slowly looked down and stared deep into the sympathetic eyes watching him, his voice and tone strengthened!

"Over the last couple of weeks, that magnificent expert, Rashi, has communicated with me constantly. Her systems interceptions have evidenced PRP's thinking and longer-term planning. Indeed, I cannot wait for her to be here with us. Not just because I must thank her. But also, because we clearly need her expertise!"

Chapter 15

The Liverpool Protest March

" **I** am not going to take you too far forward in what we may be required to deal with, in terms of PRP's objectives. However, we must work on an imminent threat. PRP have discovered a serious level of unrest in the North-West of the country. Liverpool, in particular. Police informants have alerted them to suspected protest rallies in two weeks' time. The intelligence that Rashi intercepted, dovetailed with mine. The rallies will commence in an area of Speke, known as Little Beirut. The focal point, where they will assemble, is a working men's club alongside a pub known as George and the Dragon. My research tells us, the Scousers are very angry with the PRP. And Scousers are people that will always stand up against injustice!"

"Now, to put this into a context that everyone in this room understands. These people, and I don't say this with any strong past connection with this area of the country, will never allow anyone, any government, to harm their families. I have spent hours talking this through with Sly. I trust him as if he were my brother. Indeed he's more to me than a brother. He is comical, fearless and supremely clever. And he is a well-worn Scouser!"

"He tells me that the route the protest march will take is up through Speke, Garston, Toxteth and all the way up to Albert Dock, past the Merseyside Docks. These are deprived areas. They have improved, but finding employment is still a major problem. These were industrial areas that have now almost disappeared. But Scousers are resilient. Although most may be out of work, many on benefits, and disabled people suffering from benefit cuts along with the rest; they are always people ready to stand up and be counted."

Norm, as he finished, breathed a sigh of relief. He looked across to Anneliese, who immediately took charge. "Thank you, Norm! So, from what we have heard we need to deploy our resources. I would suggest that the first thing we should attempt is to get Csenge and Sly up to Liverpool. We will, hopefully, get Csenge work in the working men's club where this protest will start from. Sly will do his best to ingratiate himself with the locals in the pub. I know he will manage this! Norm will get up there with the PRP to try to evaluate, and alert us, to their intentions."

Frank, Csenge, Sly and Norm had arranged a breakfast meeting with Jerome. Early morning, they all met in a GCHQ room to discuss the Liverpool protest march. Jerome was unusually late. The expression on his face as he entered the room said he needed to speak. "I've just had a secure teleconference call from Frank Junior and Rashi. The new "Search and Find" system broke through the government's security system. The PRP hierarchy are organising an urgent COBR meeting next week. The key topic is the Liverpool march; how they want it managed, specifically instructions to Police and Military." As Jerome peered at the group, he remarked that the mention of the Military indicated that this affair may become excessive, indeed extreme! There would be a few other items on the agenda, but so far, unspecified.

The COBR invitees were limited to what appeared to be a minimum Cabinet, predominantly yes-men. " The good news is that Norm is on the attendees list! To me, that says they are concerned about the legal aspects of their plans."

"Just a couple more pieces of information. I have talked with Anneliese. She is thinking about approaching the Chief Constable in the North-West to get his agreement to Csenge joining his force as an undercover policewoman. But this will have to wait until his instructions have been issued."

"Next point is, Frank Junior and Rashi will join us on Monday. And to add another great weapon to our armoury, Denton will be coming with them!"

Jerome settled in a chair, his mind continuing to analyse the difficulties they would be facing. Norm was the first to speak. "I've got to see this communication for myself. I was away too early this morning, and don't know if I've received the information on this meeting" Csenge, Sly and then more from Norm, formed a tsunami wave of questions to Jerome. He listened intently to all, but admitted he had the same questions tormenting his mind. As he was about to attempt some answers, Frank stood! "Give Jerome a break! He doesn't know more than he has told us. So there are no more answers than we have already!"

Frank, with a strict teacher's expression, slowly wandered behind the group. "Listen you lot. I am no fucking genius or intellectual, but I know what this PRP will end up deciding to do. They will want to scare the shit out of the whole population!" Placing his hands on Norm's shoulders, he uttered, "Norm, you and Sly, just like me, have seen people like this before. Not so many, and not with such a power base. But they will be planning to agitate, then threaten the protestors. They will have arranged their supporters, mindless idiots, to do the work for them, so later they can go on TV saying they did their best to calm everything down. The Police will be drawn into combat. Also the military, and it will be similar to the riots in Northern Ireland. And the violence that took place between the police and the striking miners of 1984."

"There will be bloodshed, and for what? All to satisfy demented power egotists that simply want to dominate the country. I will tell you all something now. I will spend the next couple of days talking to Commanders in the military. I know most of them, and they know me. And I will assure you that, although I'm not a youngster any more, I am going to be there with you. No one, absolutely no one, is going to fuck up the lives of people in this country."

The meeting, for the moment, was at an end. They would be in constant contact over the next few days. As they left, all faces had strained serious expressions, thinking about where this was all heading. That was, all except one, Csenge; her mind was on Junior's visit!

That weekend, Frank Junior and Rashi arrived. Denton would be landing early Monday morning. He was flying in from Peoria, Illinois, where he had led secret meetings, with several of his senior EAI Agents, to review developments regarding the American North/South divide issue and Far Right politicians' involvement.

With the establishment of EAI, Western World Secret Service, Denton had been appointed Director of Intelligence in the USA, reporting to Frank Junior. Denton and Rashi worked in harness together, which was proving to be a very successful duo!

Anneliese had called a meeting with all her seniors, at 7pm, Monday evening. Her intention was to detail the structure and responsibilities of her EAI team during, and leading up to, the Liverpool protest rallies.

This meeting was to take place in the secret GCHQ London offices. Vacant offices within Blackwall's East India Docks. Secure high perimeter walls surround the site, and it was invisible from all aspects!

Anneliese and Jerome had discussed the need for secrecy, and had agreed this EAI property was the most secure. They could not afford this meeting being exposed to the PRP Government.

Spaced well apart, the delegates, Anneliese's team, were delivered through the manned security gates, in vehicles with rear blacked-out windows.

In this outwardly decrepit building, Anneliese and Frank were first to arrive. Anneliese, eager to get the show on the road, fidgeted, first with her close-fitting trouser suit, then her folder. Norm, Sly, Csenge and Penny were next, all arriving together. A couple of minutes later, the American contingent shuffled into the reasonable, but relatively sparse room. All appeared weary, but smiles soon appeared as Anneliese quickly welcomed them; however, obviously in a driven mood, said, "Ok team, let's get to it."

"We will start with target dates. Norm, Rashi, anyone, what is the latest intelligence?" Norm's eyes tracked to Rashi. "Norm, please go ahead, I am sure we have the same information." Norm began to speak in his Royal voice, his mouth withdrawing at the corners. "The Government COBR meeting is scheduled for Wednesday, at Chequers. Not the Cabinet Room." He stopped, realising his Royal imitation had invaded. "I'm sorry, I will try to speak," he chuckled, "with my normal voice and tone. My guess is it's not in the usual Cabinet Office, because, like us tonight, they want this meeting to be completely secret and secure!" Norm continued. "I am invited and will feed all important intelligence as soon as I can do so."

Rashi now peered across at Sly. Rashi took the bull by the horns. "I'm hoping that Sly will confirm what I am about to tell you. With Jerome's help, we have accessed all local community e-mails. The protest march will commence on Friday. They will assemble at 9am. The pub, The George and Dragon, will serve drinks. I'm guessing that heavy drinking will start well before the usual opening time of 11am. It is expected that hordes of local teenagers from the Little Beirut estate are planning mayhem. It's not surprising, as it's only a couple of years since buses came out of there without any windows intact."

Anneliese now asked "Does anybody wish to add anything, any new or salient points?" Nobody answered. "Well, in that case, we should move onto your jobs, your responsibility!" Anneliese gave a loving smile to Junior.

But her gaze had no chance. His eye line was elsewhere! Anneliese followed it to Csenge's wondrous, craving eyes. Anneliese's early, demanding work ethic, softened. She had seen, in his expression, in his eyes, this was something really special. She was good at secrets! For now, her intuitive knowledge had to be secret. And it would be! She would just watch and wait!

Anneliese stood. "So does anyone mind if I do this on the flip-chart?" Every element of this assignment was listed, explained and discussed. At around 10pm, Anneliese asked her Seniors if they fully understood their roles and the strategy and tactics to be employed. There were no questioners or dissenters. As well as directing the Seniors, Anneliese had explained that six undercover field operatives would support them. Most were Agents that worked directly for the Seniors or had worked alongside them, sometime in the past. They had been briefed to focus on gathering intelligence and, to remain passive unless circumstances became dire.

The unexpected boost to their launch plan had been delivered by Frank. He had, with Anneliese, secretly met with an old comrade, Major General Alan Fisher, Director of Special Forces. He had fully understood the need for secrecy and had agreed to deploy an undercover SAS unit to work alongside the EAI Agents. They would only intervene if any serious conflict occurred. During the meeting with Frank and Anneliese, he had eluded to serious concerns within the armed forces, regarding the Governments' intentions and behaviour.

A surprise package was floated by Anneliese, at the very last minute. Sly would behave as a protester, but would pretend allegiance to the PRP hierarchy if the situation demanded! He had already spent time in the area, and his comical Scouse personality was well-accepted. He would stay close to Csenge, in her undercover role as a Police Officer. The ultimate surprise package was Frank Junior! He had insisted on working alongside her as an undercover Police Officer. With a raised voice, he asserted he hadn't come all this way to sit in an office staring at his computer screen. He was very capable of handling such an assignment. His words that clinched it were "for fuck sake, I've been out in Afghanistan, fighting the Taliban and ISIS. So it's not beyond me!" Csenge's heart rejoiced!

The next crucial point was reached on Wednesday. The meeting at Chequers was scheduled for 3pm. Early morning, Norm's encrypted messages, shooting back and forth with Anneliese, Frank and the rest of the Seniors, kept them all busy. After 1pm all was quiet. Norm was on his way to Chequers, in Buckinghamshire! In a Government vehicle, the chance to communicate came to an end!

Intuition is a fabulous thing, and in some instances, can be spot on. Anneliese's mind, as she sat in her hotel room, was in a concerned spiral. There were things that were bothersome. She was certain she had pinpointed Junior's relationship with Csenge. That was not the real worry. She knew everything there was to know about the relentless need to be with someone; that magnetism which dominates your every thought! This may distract Junior!

As she brought her wine glass to her lips, the torment eased. She convinced herself that Junior would always recognise danger signals and only continue if he believed that, whatever the disturbance, they would, indeed, their love would, overcome it!

It had been the same for her. She had experienced intimacy with many men. Indeed, for almost a year, she had, in her early years, worked as an "on demand" female in the Red Light district of Amsterdam. However, the truth was that this had been her first assignment as a Secret Service Agent for CECD, requiring her to obtain intelligence from members of the European Parliament.

But then she met Matthew. A young man on a work trip to Amsterdam. That was a long while ago. But they fell in love and that overpowering feeling was still something they both lived for every day.

Matthew, Anneliese's husband, was due to arrive soon. He was an ex-secret service agent, and would help Anneliese in these difficult times! Her thoughts moved on to Norm. She hoped she would hear soon concerning the discussions at the Government's Chequers meeting. Then, there was her concern for Junior and Csenge at the Liverpool protest march on Friday.

Anneliese had informed and discussed with the Chief Constable their involvement. He had issued warrant cards for them both. Prior to the protest, they would be introduced to the undercover detectives, and work with them on this assignment. A similar approach had been adopted with the SAS unit. All Junior and Csenge would have to do was phone a dedicated number if they required assistance. These arrangements would provide protection for Junior and Csenge if an emergency arose!

Close to midnight, Anneliese phoned, on her secure line, and spoke with Rashi. "Have you heard anything from Norm?" Rashi said she had been on the secure system all evening but nothing had materialised from Norm! Anneliese gave a heavy sigh and was about to speak, but Rashi interrupted. "Norm probably feels his position is insecure! Knowing that Government mob, they are all together, partying before what they believe will be their big day, tomorrow." Rashi continued to explain she had also been working on the financial tracking system. "Anneliese, I am seeing serious levels of funds being transferred into private off-shore accounts from the Government coffers. I know you are very busy, but there is another thing I must report. Enormous levels of funding is flowing into the PRP accounts. It is travelling sometimes through as many as ten accounts. Some even being exchanged for gold bullion. It is set up this way to make it impossible to track. However this new AI programme is meticulously thinking for itself. It is giving me the same answer over and over again. The funds are originating from …. Predominately Russia, but also Iran."

"Rashi, your ability with this technical stuff is amazing! Thank you so much for putting in so many hours work on this. What you have told me, and have evidenced, may soon become of primary importance. I have to go now, but one last question. Do you know where Junior is, he's not answering his phone?" "No Anneliese, he went out earlier saying he had to prepare for tomorrow. I'm sorry I can't help." The phone line dropped. Anneliese's intuition came back into play. She half smiled as her feelings for him were generously loving. The voice in her head screamed, he is with Csenge!

Chapter 16

Norm's Intelligence

The rising early morning sun broke through Anneliese's dreams. Curled up on her settee, her mind launched full tilt into her concern for Norm. Gathering herself, she began by organising her coffee percolator, then strode to her secure laptop computer. It bleeped and flashed as it recovered the information and data waiting for Anneliese's retrieval. After striding back to the coffee, she poured an early insipid cup and rushed back to sit with her laptop. Around 30 messages started to appear, one by one. Her eyes scanned the growing list, searching for one from Norm.

And there it was, encrypted within Norm's codename, Wonky Wheels! A play on Norm's all-time favourite food; jellied eels!

Anneliese immediately sent the message on to Jerome in the secure system, for him to decipher it for her. She relaxed for a few moments then returned to the coffee pot. Just as she was filling her cup, the laptop began to bleep once more. This was a message from Rashi. Her system had automatically and within seconds, intercepted Anneliese's forwarding message, translated the whole thing, and it was now available for Anneliese to view. Rashi concluded by saying she would call Anneliese in an hour's time, at 7am.

Now with a decent cup of black coffee, Anneliese retrieved the whole message from Norm. Yes, he had been partying with the PRP government into the early hours. Always with people around. He didn't want to take any risks. There was a massive amount of intelligence he needed to pass on, but would try to keep it to the minimum, for now anyway. It continued:

1. They were planning to import youths from the South, mainly Neo Nazi groups and football hooligans. They have been paid to stir up trouble and attack the protesters and police.

2. They have a mercenary group that will blend in as the troubles escalate. Some will be armed. They will also have snipers on roof tops.

3. Most of the youths will be knife-carrying. Apparently, their choice. That is their usual modus operandi!

4. Some of these kids see this as fun. The PRP have given them the impression that this country needs them to wake people up. So, a few will be in cars and be willing to drive into the marching crowds!

5. PRP have assured the Chief Constable that if there is any violence, especially use of firearms, they will support the use of firearms by the police.

6. At the end of a late night of alcohol drinking, the Cabinet Ministers, talking in the bar, came up with some explosive new ideas. They will find a way to ruin the reputation of the Monarchy. And the next late night drunken suggestion, was that all people over the age of 70 should register with their doctor or local hospice for assisted dying. The regulations were being withdrawn. But action was needed now because the programme was being overwhelmed. A downright lie! The discussion had moved on to

include mental health and disabled people that were not contributing to the economy.

7. Although these were late night inebriated words, the Chancellor saw it as very positive. "We will save bucket loads of money, not having to pay pensions and benefits to those people."

"We should have more meetings on this subject." Prime Minister Tibbs put his arm around the shoulders of the Chancellor. "You can be assured we will! These are great ideas. We need new measures that are explosive but explainable. The need for something new has been months coming and our performance has been irritating Europe and America. This may be the answer I've been looking for!"

Norm's message rounded off with" We need more than good luck! See you soon."

At 7am, Rashi called on the secure line, "Anneliese, are you ok? Norm's message is terrifying. Absolutely disgusting degenerates are in power in the UK! I can imagine that you are as sickened as I am!" Anneliese's dismal tone characterised her feelings. However, her response was strong and courageous. "Rashi, we will defeat these evil bastards. Right now, one thing you can do to help us is to use your AI systems to leak evidence that will damage the PRP. Include anything in their background. The media will lap it up. Comb through their history and that of their close families. Nothing you put out must be traceable back to us. As well as the media, issue it to the Labour Party and the Military hierarchy. If you can get it out before tomorrow, we may put them on the back foot." "Great idea boss, I'll tackle it immediately."

As Rashi clicked off, the phone rang again. It was Matthew! Before he could say more than "hello darling" Anneliese took control. "I know you had to visit friends and family in the East End, but I am drowning in developments that require attention. Please get back here with me and I will bring you up to date, and you can tell me all about Joan, Jess and all your old buddies!"

With Anneliese's appointment to the pinnacle of the EAI Security organisation came a totally secure and secret office. As far as the Government, media and outsiders were concerned, her base was in Amsterdam.

Penny stuck to her like superglue. They shuttled back and forth between London and Amsterdam, every week or two. As did Csenge, whose residence was only twenty yards away in the Victory Hotel.

Their new office property was in Admiralty Arch. A prestigious, historic building, at the entrance to Pall Mall with a direct unimpeded view of Buckingham Palace. Although Anneliese hardly ever seemed to leave work, her residence for rest and recuperation was on the other side of Pall Mall, opposite Canada House. She had decided to stay, when in London, in a hotel close to her heart. The Trafalgar Boutique Hotel! Essentially, she had decided this was the hotel for her in order to avoid crowding Frank Junior if and when he decided to visit Csenge.

As Anneliese stared up Pall Mall, enjoying the view of Buckingham Palace, the amazing architecture of the buildings on the right, and the God given greenery of St James's Park, Penny tapped her usual 3 knocks on the door. She opened and peered around the edge of the door. "Anneliese, your husband is here." "Penny, please show him in!" Penny could see from her expression how pleased she was to be seeing him.

Matthew struggled in, around the leather-topped desk and almost pulled Anneliese out of her chair. The embrace was more than passionate. Matthew stepped back and slumped into the easy chair. Although immaculately dressed, his weary face told the story. "So, Matthew, how did it go with your old mates and Joan and Jess?" "All getting old, but fine!" And I suppose seeing your old stomping ground again must have been nostalgic!" "Anneliese, I can't start to explain the feelings that erupted in me as I drove over Canning Town Bridge into West Ham. The place, the buildings, the enormity of the developments, the progress, took my breath away." His voice faltered, as his eyes began to glisten. Anneliese rushed out of her chair and clasped him to her breast. His eyes looked up into hers. "Darling, I'm feeling my age! But I'm so grateful that we've done so well together. And that son of ours, Frank Junior, leaves me speechless!" His hand reached behind her neck and pulled her lips to his. His eyes began to sparkle again. "You make me feel so young! In just a half an hour, being with you has brought me back to life."

With supreme elegance, Anneliese slowly and gracefully edged around to confront Matthew. She leant forward, grasped his cheeks, and then slid gently onto his lap. With a tender smile, she whispered, "Matthew, it's been longer than I can remember, since I lost my heart to you. But I am always excited to be with you, every day and in every way!"

"I have to get back to work in a moment. Tomorrow may be a disastrous day, but tonight I will organise a romantic dinner for us in the hotel. I can assure you, it will be delightful, delicious and at the end of it, I will make sure you are delirious. I have missed you more than I can explain, so tonight I will make you feel 40 years younger!"

Now it was Csenge's turn to be fulfilled. As she stepped out of the shower, she was sure she heard a gentle knock on her door. She grasped her bright red Indian silk chemise as she, uncertain if there had been a knock, stepped toward the door. As she peered through the security peephole, she struggled to slide her wet body into the chemise. Attempting to cover her saturated curves, the chemise clinging to her body, began to saturate her feelings, as she realised it was Junior! Love and lust now compelled her mind and overcame her body. The chemise, completely forgotten, hung loosely as she opened the door to ecstasy. Before Junior could move, Csenge clasped him around the neck as her legs, like a ballerina, slid elegantly up his thighs, grasping his waist.

The raging intensity of this sensory encounter laid waste to every muscle, sinew and nerve. They lay together on the sweat soaked bed linen, staring up at the dimly lit chandelier.

Csenge had powerfully dominated, teased and tormented throughout what seemed an eternity of rapturous passion. Junior, staring at the light above him, found his mind wandering beyond the feelings he had for Csenge. Other than her beauty, he had been immediately attracted to her personality. He was aware of her history that was above the surface, but he knew nothing of anything that may be hidden below that surface! Her prowess and stamina this night had alerted him to how little he knew of the real Csenge!

Csenge's thoughts also swirled around Paradise Island, but soon her mind stepped onto an unsteady path, paved with guilt. She glanced at Junior there next to her, his eyes now tightly closed. That irritating confused feeling strengthened. Until recently, she had not seen Junior for several years. She had never had a deep conversation with him, or got into details about her years in Eastern Europe. He may have seen the CECD reports but there was much more to her time there. She made a deal with herself. She would make a concerted effort to tell him everything, every angle and episode. She wanted this man, her man, to know everything there was to know!

Anneliese had begun to experience that stomach fluttering feeling that relationships sometimes cause. She glanced down at her watch. It was 7.20pm. She stepped out from behind her desk and shouted to Penny. "I am leaving to have my first date in several years with Matthew. I know I never go this early but if you need to contact me, I will only be in the Trafalgar." Penny helped Anneliese on with her coat. "Anneliese, have a wonderful night and give my regards to Matthew."

Anneliese and Matthew worked their socks off, and everything else, to make this the most splendid night of romance they had managed in the past several years!

Lying in those tangled crisp sheets in the Trafalgar king-size, exhilaration had taken them into the top sails of the ship. The gentle breeze of the air-conditioning gradually eased them both into consciousness.

Matthew's agile mind was first to grasp the tiller! He quietly moved to sit on the edge of the bed. Thinking Anneliese was sleeping, he slowly turned to adore her face, the face of this beautiful soul he had loved and become part of, over so many years.

Anneliese's eyes flickered. She could feel his stare, his heart-beat; even his adoration penetrated every morsel of her waking mind.

Matthew's expression, as he stared at Anneliese, appeared to become guilt-laden. After so many years, and so many grievous situations, her intuition announced an issue!

She sat up and reached out to Matthew. "What's going on? Why do you look like you should have told me something?" Matthew, still sitting naked on the side of the bed, stood and pulled on a pair of lounge trousers. "I need a nightcap. Would you like one?" Sitting back on the bed, he handed a large vodka and lime to Anneliese. He began to sip his Glenmorange, but Anneliese would not relent. As he swallowed, Anneliese persisted. "Matthew, I know you need to tell me something; you may not want to but I know you need to!" "It's nothing serious darling, the first thing on my mind is that I have to be up very early. And you have exhausted me." Anneliese's retort was short and sharp. "Oh, I'm so sorry, you've never complained before!" Matthew's head dropped into his hands. His slow sideways glance allowed him time to inhale deeply. "Anneliese, I'm so sorry, it's not about our love-making. It was fabulous and has been for over...." His face developed a huge grin. "As Americans would say, it's been amazing ever since God was a boy!" His grin transitioned into laughter. Anneliese began to chuckle also.

Anneliese then asked, "So why do you have to be up so early?" Matthew developed a sheepish expression. "I know, Anneliese, that you are not going to like this, but I must do it!" "Do what? What are you ranting about?" "Early tomorrow, I am going with Frank up to Liverpool! I had a lovely conversation with Frank. And yes, we had had a few drinks. But we both agreed, and even now being here, sober as a judge, with you, I feel the same." Anneliese raised her hand and with a semi-glare retorted, "Matthew what the hell are you going on about? What did you agree? You are starting to worry me, so please tell me what you two are planning!"

Matthew's expression, after a minute's thinking time, gradually became serious. "Anneliese, I am here in the same country as my son. He is heading into something that may become a dangerous confrontation. I can't let him do that without me. Frank feels the same. We will join the protest march and protect his every move. I know we are oldies, but we are experienced professionals. So the bottom line is, being here with him, neither I nor Frank, can let him do it alone!"

Matthew rolled back on the bed. Pulling Anneliese close, almost nose to nose, Anneliese, in absolute silence, peered into his eyes. As the seconds rolled by, Matthew realised he had touched a nerve. Her eyes signalled an emotional tsunami. Suddenly the wave struck. A massive wave of tears that terrified Matthew!

"Darling, what is it? You never cry so you are scaring me!" Clasping her close, the sobbing slowly eased. Anneliese, being Anneliese, switched, almost instantly, to a personality that existed on fortitude. Shuffling across the bed, she stood. Pulling her silk nightdress around her, she straightened until she towered over Matthew.

Anneliese bent forward, clenching Matthew's chin. Her lips attacked his with intense passion. Slowly, very slowly, she eased away. Anneliese gradually leaned back to stare at the ceiling. Her wrist swabbed her tearful eyes, as she inhaled a deep shuddering breath!

"Matthew, sometimes my love for you and Junior is overwhelming. Tonight has been one of those occasions. You thought I would be annoyed with you going to Liverpool. I am not! But I am drowning in a mixture of emotion and fear."

Penny, knowing this day could be extremely testing, arrived in the office at 7am. She hustled and bustled around her domain with a determined, urgent expression. With all necessary switches flicked on, her next task was the coffee maker. Just as she attacked the sealed bag of coffee granules, the door slammed open. Anneliese purposefully strode through the office door.

"Morning Penny", she uttered, "I'd love a coffee to get me going!" Her tone was exuberant. Penny recognised and appreciated that Anneliese was in a victorious combat mode. "Penny, get the television on please. BBC Breakfast are bound to cover the events in Liverpool. And at 8.00am, would you open the secure lines to the Chief of Defence Staff and Connaugh Brien?" Penny stopped, turned to Anneliese, asking "Who is Connaugh Brien?" Anneliese turned to Penny. "I'm sorry Penny, I met with him one late night when you had already gone." Stroking Penny's blonde locks, their eyes met and both experienced that bonding feeling strengthening. Anneliese, now preparing to leave for the GCHQ satellite at Blackwall said, "Penny, he is the Chief Constable of the North West Constabulary. I came away from that meeting with him convinced that he had all the same concerns as me. He distrusts the PRP as much as we do! And so he is valuable to us, probably extremely valuable!" Anneliese's face broke into a smile then a grin. Penny had seen that look before. This would not be a day to tangle with Anneliese. Today would be the moment, however it turned out, when she would begin her work to get this nation to rise against tyrannical adversity!

The BBC breakfast programme was already giving the protest march coverage. Intermittent interviews with PRP MPs' all saying these protesters were rabble rousers. It was now 8am. Frank and Matthew would arrive in Runcorn, close to Speke, at 8.50am. They planned to meet Frank Junior and Csenge at The George and Dragon pub. They would have driven most of the night to be up there on time. Norm was travelling with just a few PRP government people and would reside in the Liverpool Council offices, to watch on television and answer questions from the TV researchers. Sly would be at The George and Dragon pub, ready to march with the protestors.

Frank and Matthew, with about 30 minutes to go, were sitting in their compartment chatting. "We'll be there soon Frank!" With a pensive expression, Matthew continued.

"Anneliese will be watching all the screens in the GCHQ satellite centre in Blackwall. So Frank, what is your thinking, your intuition, telling you about today, and where this all may be heading?"

Frank lent forward, his eyes stared authentic belief in what he was about to say. "Matthew, you and I have been around the block several times over many years. I am not going to beat about the bush or express platitudes that you have to decipher and analyse."

"This government will prove to be rancid. Today will not be pleasant. I have talked with most of the military commanders. They are as bewildered as the rest of us. There is a feeling amongst them that this government is ruthless. Possibly trying to take this country into a world where they can flourish as tyrannical despots. I've never felt or heard anything in Britain like this before. And to go on from another angle. I have been on the phone for several hours with Rashi. One of her new AI systems is intercepting every email communication that they send. Even encrypted messages are deciphered immediately. Rashi's take on what she has seen is that they have initiated a destructive, toxic set of offensives that will seriously test the Police and even the military. But what they don't know is that we have been working with the Police, the military and our ace card, the SAS."

Matthew shuffled forward in his seat and reached to grasp Frank's arm. "Thanks, my old mate. You and I will make sure that they don't win today. And more than that, we will work with Anneliese and Junior to topple this PRP Government. It may take a while, but Frank, you know, Anneliese will come out the winner!"

Frank, Matthew, Csenge and Frank Junior joined the growing numbers in the pub. Friendly chatting with everyone, but they kept well apart, attempting to appear completely independent supporters of the march. The exception was Csenge and Junior who behaved and pretended to be a couple that supported the views of the marching people.

Outside the pub and inside the working man's club, banners were unfolding. Flags, and banners which were hard hitting.

The protest marchers, runners and riders, were now at the starting post. Meanwhile, Anneliese was watching every screen in the Blackwall satellite control room. Although glancing around every screen, her mind constantly brought her back to the screen showing the marchers, as they set off along the East Lancs Road, with Junior and Csenge amongst the leading group. Two or three rows behind was Sly, and behind him, Frank and Matthew.

A computer programme, surveying the screens, registered the number of marchers. As they reached Garston, including onlookers, it registered over 400.

Anneliese's secure mobile vibrated. It was a message from Rashi. She would call in five minutes! The phone silently trembled, and as Anneliese answered, she turned to Jerome. "Keep watching the screens. I need to take this call from Rashi."

"Ok, Rashi, what is it?" "Anneliese, I have several new AI programmes; two of them are a first, and I have been testing them." A ruffled Anneliese responded. "Sorry, Rashi, there is a lot going on here that needs my full attention. I don't mean to sound abrupt but can you get straight to the point."

Rashi was heard to gasp. "I'm so sorry but it's important! I have amalgamated a generative programme with a neural network. It's fabulous!" Anneliese frowned and as she looked at Jerome, raised her eyes to the heavens and twirled her right hand, indicating a need for urgency. Rashi's voice strengthened with confidence. She knew what she was about to tell Anneliese could, possibly, be a game-changer. "Anneliese, this programme is indicating that the PRP will select from three options. The first option is they will initiate vicious conflict. Their second option is they will take hostages, intending to blame this on the protesters. There is a third option which is they will activate both!"

Anneliese took a deep breath, but before she could comment, Rashi interjected. "I'm sorry Anneliese, but please let me finish. My programme, that has the ability to infiltrate all PRP communications, has confirmed these predictions! They have identified Junior and Csenge as undercover Police. They are now the target hostages. I'm only guessing, but the PRP probably have a Police informant!"

Anneliese stood and began to wander the room as her mind, full of concern, tried to think through the situation. Her deep breathing was heard by Rashi who loudly spoke again. "Anneliese there is more! I may have overstepped the mark, and if so, I am sorry. I have securely contacted Sly. The PRP have a Neo-Nazi group working for them and they will attempt the hostage taking. If you watch your screens, several of them are around Junior and Csenge. I have messaged Sly and said he should befriend them. Work hard to convince them that he is a PRP member. And when the abduction is attempted, he should try to appear on the side of the Neo-Nazis'. But he should get in between them, Junior and Csenge, so that the kidnapping is done without violence. Sly understands that he should convince the Neo –Nazis' that extreme violence was not on the PRP agenda. All the PRP want is to be able to claim that they rescued Police officers from the protesters!" "I am now in the process of sending all this information to Junior. But I know, whatever I tell him will not necessarily have enough impact to control him!"

Anneliese closed her eyes for a few seconds. Her thoughts were never jumbled, but always controlled and orderly. "Rashi, please send that same message to Frank and Matthew! We will talk again soon!"

As the protesters marched through Toxteth, the numbers exploded. The TV cameras now were focusing on the myriad of banners. Short sharp messages were clear for the whole country to see. "I can't survive without benefits," "my disabled kids should be welcome," "I need my Nan and Grandad," "When can we get work?" "Why do I need to beg for an operation 'cos I'm over 70?"

The Breakfast TV Programme was in the middle of presenters discussing the banner meanings when the computer number count flashed up on the screen. The protest had grown to over 15,000 people. Before the presenters could comment on the extent of the protest, breaking news flashed on the screen. The PRP Government had been accused, on social media, of planning and orchestrating tyranny within the UK. Indeed, the publications went further. Insurrection by a foreign power was one of the accusations listed against the PRP.

It ventured to explain this by saying that evidence had been ascertained that money was flowing into PRP off-shore personal bank accounts from Russia and Iran. This accusation was magnified by the accusers. Apparently, they also had evidence that funds were being electronically transmitted out of the Government's coffers through a multitude of transactions that eventually bedded the funds into Russian and Iranian coffers. Rashi had done a faultless exposure job.

⸺⬗⬖⬗⬖⸺

Chapter 17

All Hell Breaks Loose

The protest march reached Albert Dock. The procession of protesters reached back 3 miles. As the march leaders began to assemble on the edge of the dock, all hell was about to break loose!

Denton, sitting with Anneliese, had been quiet until now. He had been listening to Anneliese's softly spoken commentary on Denton's first views of Liverpool; landmarks, buildings, the John Lennon Liverpool Airport and anything she thought would be of interest to him. All the time, Anneliese's eyes searched the screens, but predominantly, the screen showing Junior and Csenge.

As the marchers' entered the Albert Dock area, Denton's phone started to vibrate. Opening an email from Rashi caused an immediate reaction. Denton interrupted Anneliese's commentary. His arm reached across Anneliese's shoulder as he pulled her close. Passing his phone, he, with a concerned expression turned to Jerome. "Got a message for Frank. I am about to send him face photos of the mercenary PRP activists that are all around Junior and Csenge. And tell him to expect some acute violence, within minutes; I advise he alerts our operatives and his SAS chums!" Denton retrieved the phone from Anneliese and pressed the send key.

They watched Frank opening the email. He began to search the faces surrounding Junior and Csenge. A large group that was now encircling them. The command centre room fell quiet. Anneliese stood, her eyes transfixed on Frank as he called the SAS emergency number on his secure mobile.

A second or two after his call, the screens shuddered and flashed. Some blacked out, but just for a few seconds. As the visuals were restored, the cause became obvious. Bricks thrown by the teenage sideliners were raining down on the marchers. Some had been aimed at cameras and reduced transmission!

Chapter 18

Hostages Taken

The second wave attack followed. A Transit van scorched into the dock area, driving straight through the stream of marchers. Several innocent bystanders were tossed aside, as the vehicle ploughed into the marchers. Four people were ploughed into the dock water as the Transit came to a halt.

The PRP mercenaries surrounding Junior and Csenge attacked! These hyenas attacked in numbers. Several grabbed hold of Csenge, attempting to drag her into the van. She kicked, punched and even managed to bite an ear off one that was trying to toss her into the van. They found it just as difficult with Junior. Seven blokes beat and kicked him. He feigned injury, then fought back at them, destroying three that now were lying prostrate on the ground. However, the rest overwhelmed him. Like Csenge, he was thrown into the van. Five vicious bastards clambered in behind them. Before the doors closed, Sly managed to wrestle his way in and dropped bodily onto Csenge. Now gunfire shattered the silence. Shots from the rooftops all around the dock were drowned out by shrieking, screaming, squeals and pitiful bellowing as protesters were seen to drop to their knees to comfort the wounded, the dying and.... the dead!

Gunshots began again, blotting out the screaming emotion. The marchers were now dropping face down on the floor, covering their ears and eyes. This gunfire was return fire from the SAS. The gunfire increased as the police joined the assault on the assailants.

Just as two SAS troopers were running to the van, its tyres screeched and it sped off out of the Dock Area. Its departure through the hordes of marchers caused a stampede. All around, innocents dived for cover, some throwing themselves into the dock. The march was halted at the Albert Dock entrance. The noise and commotion had stopped the procession in its tracks. But some, concerned for their loved ones, continued to run on into danger!

Anneliese, now standing, was anything but emotional. Denton and Jerome, watching her face, her expression, her eyes, was a demonstration of their intense respect and regard for Anneliese's stoic courage.

Denton, about to speak, now saw emotion slowly beginning to swamp Anneliese's eyes. Her control was beyond belief. "So you guys, what shall we do now? Two of our own have been taken hostage. How do we find them and get moving ahead on a rescue?" Denton noticed small tear droplets easing from her stunning blue/green eyes!

Denton stood and stretched a hand out to hold Anneliese's. "This team will get it all back under control!" Anneliese stared back into Denton's eyes. Denton continued to reach out to Anneliese. "I watched the screen showing the van. Last to get in was Sly, so we have someone with them!"

Anneliese's concern softened. Denton smiled. "And more than that, both Junior and Csenge will give us their location. We can track them!" Anneliese's jaw dropped. "How? How is that possible?" "Because," and at this point Denton uttered a subtle chuckle. He gained a breath and started again. "Because, Anneliese, yesterday I recognised how much they meant to one another. I'm only guessing, but I think you also know. And I certainly know how much Junior means to you and Matthew!"

"So, yesterday I used a trick we are using in the US constantly. They have both had implants. By that, I mean a small chip in the back of their neck that attracts satellite transmissions to tell us where they are. But it does more, much more. We can see if they are being mistreated. It registers their health condition. The best of it is that it will record everything, and can be used as evidence."

Anneliese's smile widened! She grasped Denton, then Jerome. "Thank you, guys. You are and have always been fabulous. So now, we have to work on the next steps."

The SAS had shot three of the snipers dead. Two more had been wounded, and the Police had overcome and arrested two more. These terrifying events at Albert Dock were all over the mid-day news. The TV editing presented a totally horrific scenario!

As Anneliese and Jerome were calling Rashi, she sat sadly watching the aftermath at Albert Dock. Police, military and paramedics attending to the wounded and injured. Dazed protestors, no longer even knowing where they were, or why they were there!

In that short period of anguish, Anneliese's mind was imagining the horrendous things that may be happening to Junior and Csenge. The reality, at that exact point in time, was that the Transit was speeding through Liverpool City, into the suburbs. As the van twisted and turned, rattled, shook, with tyres squealing as it cornered, the mercenaries pulled Sly off Csenge and were now applying cable ties to the hands and feet of both Csenge and Junior.

The brute with the missing ear lobe, and probably, missing conscience, had revenge top of his list. As he pulled the cable tie tight on Csenge's wrists, and then yanked it even tighter, his grimace turned into a look of sheer evil. He slowly lowered his lips to Csenge's. Holding her chin, he began to slobber around her mouth. Sly tapped the guy on the back. "Let's have a go mate! I'd do anything for time with this beauty!

The brute froze. He eyeballed Sly. "Ok mate, you can have her all night, for a thousand pounds. But I want it transferred now!"

Sly, with a look of greed, said, "You are on, mate." Pulled out his phone, got into his internet banking account and pressed various keys. Passing the phone to Brute, Sly said, "Mate, what's your name?" "I'm Boris," as he smiled and held out a hand. "Well Boris, I am Sly and if you tap your details in, the money will be transferred immediately." All the time they were talking, Sly had been stroking Csenge's thighs. Just to give an impression of his lust! "I've got it" shouted Boris. "I've heard about you. You're the sex addict. The PRP pervert. They have lots of work waiting for you."

As they cornered, Boris fell across onto Sly. Settling down again, he said, "Thanks Sly, good deal." They now had reached their destination!

Denton jumped out of his seat just as the Blackwall door opened. "Hey you guys, they have stopped travelling, and our satellite has homed in on them." Denton peered up from his screen. His face lit up. Rashi was strolling toward them. "Rashi, you are just in time. I need your help to access the info from those implants we did for Csenge and Junior."

Rashi chose to walk around behind Anneliese and Denton. She stood behind Anneliese, and as she massaged her shoulders, bent to whisper in her ear. "Anneliese, we will get them to safety. I promise!" With that she reached to kiss

Denton's forehead. Jerome stood and gestured for Rashi to take his seat next to Denton. With Jerome looking over Rashi's shoulder she, without hesitation, began to tap keys on her laptop. "They are in a place called Cronton, not far from the city centre." Jerome, working on his phone, interjected. "It's a suburb. Rashi, can you access a postcode?" Within seconds, Rashi was slowly and clearly detailing it. Jerome, now working in unison with Rashi, was tapping it into his mobile phone. "Anneliese, I've found the place." Jerome before continuing, stared deep into her eyes. "It's a large property with several acres of open ground surrounding it. Once, it was owned by a major company, it was their sports ground, but has been vacant for a few years."

Jerome stopped talking and began thinking! Immersed in his silent thinking space, Jerome's mind returned to his roots! He stood straight and then screamed at maximum pitch. "c'mon you Irons, you can score." Anneliese peered at Jerome. With a puzzled expression, she asked, "Jerome, what was all that about?"

Jerome apologised. "It's a trigger I use when I'm under pressure and need to get to a decision. And I think I've found it. Anneliese, it's a massive property. There are three exits. But, in our favour is that they only have five or six baddies in that place. We have three of our own. Sly, Csenge and Junior. My thoughts say we need to get Frank and his SAS comrades there!"

Anneliese interrupted. "Frank is injured, in hospital, so that's not possible." Jerome replied; "We could really do with Frank now, but ok, I understand! So, should we get the SAS to secure the exits and drop in on them. But now I've said that, I know that will put Junior and Csenge at risk."

It was now mid-afternoon. "Let's take half-an-hour break to put some petrol back in our tanks." As Anneliese spoke, she forced a smile at everyone, despite feeling despondent. "Then we will all get together to determine a way through this!"

Coffee was the first stop. Then the tarmac driveway at the front of the building, bathed in warm sunshine. Jerome and Anneliese slowly meandered in separate directions. Denton and Rashi walked and talked together. All the four exhibited thinking intensity in their expressions!

At the end of the 30 minutes respite, they were all seated back around the shiny walnut conference table.

In opening this session, Anneliese commented that the evening TV news would probably cover the Liverpool events. They should all watch!

Denton now, with his weighty Boston accent, secured everyone's attention. "That 30 minutes break gave Rashi and me time to explore the art of the possible. And I think we may have the answer. In a moment I will ask Rashi to explain, but before I do, I will cover the preparatory work."

"Our thinking goes like this. The bedrock to this rescue will be the SAS, the Police and possibly the Military. Discussions on their roles will come later. Next thought is our key operative, Sly. We could get an encrypted message to him to tell him when the rescue will commence."

"Rashi and I agree that's too risky. If one of their mob heard his phone bleeping and found encrypted messages, well....he would be in a canoe without a paddle!"

"We think; that's Rashi and I, that Sly will do everything possible to stay in the room with Csenge and Junior. And if Sly has managed to get a level of trust, he may be left alone with them at some time. Rashi tells me that her satellite tracking shows Junior and Csenge in the same room in that sports complex building. We don't know about Sly, but we need to trust he has managed to stay close to them."

Denton, looking at his watch, passed to Rashi. Before she spoke, Denton reminded her that TV news would begin at 6pm.

Rashi explained that whilst talking in the break with Denton, an opportunity began to stare her in the face. "I have not attempted this before. Indeed, this advance with the satellite human tracking is new to me. I will try to explain the possibilities simply. If I can access the programme, it has the capability to do almost anything that is wanted. In terms of the implants, they have been programmed to record. Indeed, after recording, AI takes over. It will give us not only commentary, but also observations, and options for action. But there is also a programme to send messages from the implant to a person's hearing....a verbal message, clearly spoken!"

"That would take me a day or two to input, and I know we don't have that much time. However, there is a simpler task. It will take me two or three hours. If I can do this on this new equipment, it will have the ability to send a Morse-code message to Csenge and Junior. It will repeatedly cause the implant to pulse, shudder or vibrate."

Rashi, taking a breath, pondered the faces before her. All, including Anneliese, had expressive wonderment immersing them in expectation.

Rashi, in her head, was fighting those negative feelings that were attempting to engulf her. After a few minutes composing herself, Rashi spoke again.

"I'm so sorry, but I don't want to let any of you, my colleagues, down. And, especially not Junior and Csenge. I am going to use one of your expressions.... Although, to be honest, I'm not certain what it means. I am sheeting myself! But I will do it." "A few hours from now you will be able to tell Junior and Csenge when the rescue will occur. In my homeland, there is a saying; you either try to survive in the jungle or live in the zoo. The jungle is freedom. The zoo is living under the dominance of PRP. I will make this work; we will live in freedom."

Chapter 19

AI and Morse Code

"Just to sum up, I will use this new technology, the most advanced technology of our time, in combination with an age old, historic messaging system.... Morse-code. I am a firm believer in utilising tried and tested methods if they fit the circumstances!"

The team breathed a sigh of relief. Anneliese was about to speak as Rashi decided she needed to ask a question. "I know Morse-code and I am certain that both Junior and Csenge do. It was used out in the field by operatives when the occasion required it. What I want to ask you guys is the type of transmission I should programme into the communication. As you all are aware, it must clearly represent dots and dashes, and be recognisable as such. My preference is a strong pulse for a dot, and a shudder for a dash." After looking around at one another, all the team nodded agreement.

Rashi smiled then moved on to her next question. "We need to give them a time. To spell it out in Morse code may take too long. So, I suggest the following. And this is just an example. I will transmit the word ATTACK, using Morse code. Then the word AT, also in Morse code. Then the time of the attack. If, for example, it is 6:00pm I can use either six pulses or the word six in Morse code. My decision will be based on the time selected!"

Anneliese responded. "Rashi, that sounds perfect. But now the news is only a few minutes away. But before we switch to the news, I think our next step is to meet with the SAS Commander and Police Chief Constable." Anneliese glanced across to Penny. "Please, Penny, contact them and ask them to join us for a meeting at 10:00pm"

As Prime Minister Tibbs began to speak, everyone around the table in Blackwall was incensed and angry at every insincere word he uttered.

He had the utmost sympathy for the wounded and injured. He was still traumatised that a Liverpool Protest March could lead to so many deaths. 18 in total, was the latest count.

The Protest March, according to Tibbs, had been orchestrated by Liverpool fundamentalists and terrorist groups that were unwilling to accept the result of the 2029 election. A national election that had, clearly, demonstrated that the people of the country knew that the PRP would take them into a caring world!

He finalised his 30 minutes of downright lies with his version of the hostage taking of two police officers. The protesters had planned this atrocity from the outset. But the Government would do everything in their power to bring these brave police officers' home safely.

Anneliese, now incensed by Premier Tibbs bare-faced lies, glanced at Penny. "Think we can turn that garbage off now Penny, and get back to business."

With that last word, a loud knock on the door distracted everyone. The door then smashed open. There was Frank, bathed in sunlight, leaning on a crutch. With a large protective boot on his left foot, he began to hobble in.

Anneliese questioned, "Frank, what have you done to your foot?" She could not wait for the answer. "And where the hell is Matthew? I've been worried sick. I was told you had both just gone for a swim in the Dock!" Another character stepped into the doorway's sunlight. It was Matthew. He ambled in behind Frank, and as the beam surrounding him cleared, his wide smile came into view. He scuttled around Frank to Anneliese, leant across the conference table, grasped her cheeks and softly kissed her lips.

Her face, as he eased away, became anguished. "Matthew, I've been out of my mind. Why didn't you call me?" Matthew peered into her eyes. "I suppose there were many reasons. But the main reason was we thought you had enough on your plate, and would guess we weren't seriously hurt." Matthew chuckled, "Frank and I just went for a swim together in the warm water of the Mersey!"

Anneliese, softly slapped his face, just as Frank began recounting the event. Apparently, as the Transit screeched into the Dock area, its bumper clipped Frank's legs. Frank fell backwards into the Dock, but his numb left leg scraped down the edge of the brickwork. So more cuts and bruises!

Matthew, just about to jump in, was kicked by one of the assailants. That kick toppled him in to join Frank. They had to swim about 40 yards to a ladder up the dock wall. Paramedics insisted they needed hospital treatment. Frank had an Achilles injury and Matthew, a haematoma swelling on his thigh. Frank's SAS chums helicopter flew them back!

The room settled, knowing that two of their key strategists were safe, and almost well. "Frank, Matthew, we need your thoughts, advice, expertise." Anneliese, her eyes beginning to exhibit emotion, stuttered, "Our boy, Matthew, is in the clutches of this mob. Frank, he's your Godson! We have to get him back to us, safe and sound!"

"We are meeting with the SAS and Police at 10:00pm tonight. I know you have had a tough day, but we need you here." Her eyes were pleading, although she knew they would never let her or Junior down.

As Frank prepared to respond, he glanced around the room at his comrades. In his usual cool, calm, collected, and always charismatic way, he slowly built a grin. His eyebrows lifted as his expression confirmed his confidence. "Anneliese, my darling Anneliese, with all the help we can muster, we will get Junior and Csenge back safely with us."

Frank, sometimes a comic, reached inside his grubby white polo shirt. Pulling out a glistening, sliver cross and chain, he glanced around them all. With a broad smile, instigated by belief and excitement he asked, "Is the Pope a Catholic? Your eyes confirm the answer is, yes. And you are all correct. We will be with you tonight and throughout this assignment!"

A break now was essential. Energy levels needed to be replenished. As they advanced toward the coffee trolley, Anneliese stopped Frank. "I have known you for years but never knew you were Catholic." Frank's smile was consuming and intriguing. "No, I've never advertised it, but I was born in Ireland, and my family were, and are, Catholic. Everyday my Catholic faith soothes my soul. It is my mainstay every day. We all need faith and my religion has helped me through many difficult, indeed horrendous times, especially when I was in Northern Ireland during the troubles."

Chapter 20

The Rescue

In the Cronton Sports Club, the mid-evening late summer sunshine was streaming into the front entrance. The vast reception area led to an expanse of staircase which gradually tapered to the upper floor.

Boris had left Sly alone with Junior and Csenge. He'd gone to find the rest of his mob. Sly, in a ground floor room at the back of the building, knelt in front of Csenge. Both Junior and Csenge had been hog tied to their chairs with cable ties.

Sly, glancing at both of them, whispered, "Sorry but I must make this look realistic. They need to think I have been having some fun with Csenge." Junior's expression became tormented, as Sly ripped the front of Csenge's blouse. Closing his eyes, he then reached under her skirt and ripped her panties off. Deliberately leaving them laying on the floor, he approached the door. "I'm going to find my way around this place. I'll have to lock you in, but I'll only be a few minutes." Standing in front of them he whispered, "When the time comes, I will cut you out of those cable ties. Then we will all need to be ready to fight our way out of here. We could make a run for it, but that could be dangerous." Junior whispered, "no Sly, we should stay and help capture these bastards!"

Sly added, "you can be assured that Frank and Anneliese are already deep into a plan for our rescue!" Junior nodded!

"I bloody hope so. We had those implants so they could track us, and that was more than painful!"

Sly slipped out of the door and moved stealthily along a corridor. At the end, he began to enter the reception area. Closing in on the carpeted staircase, he could hear loud voices, laughter and a voice he recognised, Boris!

As he slowly, inch by inch, step by step, climbed the stairs, he could see the crowns of four of the kidnappers. His eyes searched around them. They had found the bar and were draining the left behind booze.

He had seen enough. He had a good picture in his head of the layout, so quickly headed back to Junior and Csenge. Locking the door behind him, he quickly and quietly explained the layout, and then said, "Best of all, they are in the bar getting drunk!"

The Blackwall team had been advised that the Chief Constable for the North West and the SAS Major for Three Squadron, the team that had defended in Albert Dock, were only five minutes away. Their helicopter blades were heard as they landed in the flat concrete area in front of the building.

Rashi entered the room. Glancing around them, she announced, "The satellite implant system has a green light." As she took her seat, Major Tony Fite of the SAS and Chief Constable Connaugh Brien were shown in by Penny.

Following rapid, but polite, introductions, Penny got them both coffee. The SAS Major was first to speak. "If we are going to have the best chance of success, the rescue should be tonight! I don't think it's a good idea to leave it until tomorrow! With this type of assault, we stand the best chance around 3.00am. That gives us slightly less than five hours. The better news is that my men and Chief Constable Brien's police have been prepared and are ready. They are only a few miles away from the target area and we can be back with them in two hours." The major gulped some coffee as his eyes looked for Frank and Anneliese's' acceptance!

Denton politely thanked the Major, who was slightly shaken by the strong American accent. "My God! I am impressed. You EAI guys really are tuned into the whole Western World!"

Denton, then Anneliese, chuckled loudly. Denton's face moved back to business mode. "Rashi, are you certain, completely certain, you can get the satellite implant system to work. We need your messaging to be flawless and be repeated several times. If Junior, Csenge and Sly are aware of the timing, with them working from the inside and the SAS and police from the outside, this mob will stand zero chance!" Rashi replied, "Denton, I am as certain as I can be!"

Connaugh Brien broke into the arena. "We have studied the plans. The second floor of the building has a large bar and then a dance hall out to the front of the building. It has a flat roof. We plan to drop special service troopers on the top of that roof. Some will be winched down to smash through the large plate glass windows. The police will break through the main entrance door and find the hostages."

Frank smiled then laughed furiously. "Don't think your policemen will have to look too far. If I know Junior, Csenge and Sly, they will be in the thick of the assault on this mob!"

The Major stood. Taking one last swig of coffee he reiterated, "So, it's 3.00am precisely!" Everyone nodded as Anneliese thanked them. Frank escorted the Major and Chief Constable out to their helicopter. Timing now gave them four and a half hours to complete the operation.

For the mob in Cronton, the scene was becoming drunkenly hazy and distorted. Not for Sly, who was wandering their room looking for anything that could be used as a weapon.

A loud knock on the door pressed him straight back into action. "Csenge, scream, rant, make it sound as if you are being abused. Junior, shout loudly, you bastard, leave her alone, that sort of thing!" The wailing, screaming and swearing deserved an Oscar.

The knocks got louder. Sly went to the door. "Who is it?" "It's me, Boris." Sly took a deep breath, counted to ten, then shouted, "Boris, fuck off. You've had your money so don't come here destroying my pleasure."

Boris screamed, "Sly, we are in the bar having a great drink." Sly butted in. "Boris, I am having the best time ever, so please fuck off and leave me to enjoy the night I have paid for. It's even better because I've got her boyfriend watching, and I can give him a smack whenever I want to!"

Now Boris became pushy. "Look Sly, we are going to sleep in the rooms upstairs and there are some things I need. My rucksack is in there, so let me in!"

Sly stood back for a second as he glanced at Csenge. Yes, she looked the part. Sly let Boris in. He stood in front of Csenge, giggled as he struggled to keep his balance. Junior began to scream, "You fucking bastards will pay for this." Boris returned a smile. "We won't, you know. We have asked half- a-million for you two and it's been agreed!"

Rucksack on his back, he wafted past Csenge, picking up her panties as he left.

Just after 2.00am, Tony Fite was briefing his squadron. He stood facing his men in a dimly lit building that backed onto a wild part of Eaton Hall, the Duke of Westminster's Estate, on the outskirts of Chester.

The Major was spoilt for choice. His Three Squadron totalled 65 troopers. He reckoned that 13 would be more than sufficient. Having handpicked them, he called out the names of the 13 one by one. He expected the rest of his Squadron to work with the Police, blocking all exits and remaining battle-ready around the property in Cronton.

The assault group of 13 would travel to the property in a Blue Thunder helicopter. This chopper would also transport four stretchers in case of medical emergencies. Two medics were in the team!

The briefing ended. The 13, with all their gear and weapons headed out, about 100 yards, to the Dauphin, better known to the SAS as Blue Thunder. The other 52 troopers would leave immediately in a nondescript coach. They would silently meet the police on the perimeter of the property.

Blue Thunder took 10 minutes to get the troopers and equipment seated and stored away. Another 15 minutes, seated on the helicopter, was used to work again through the whole plan. Also to check every element of the weaponry and equipment.

At 2.35am, the engines were engaged and throttled up. The rotors gradually accelerated and began to shudder and shake the trees around the helicopter pad. The troopers were totally silent as the chopper scorched, upwards.

Their intention was high flying to get the locals accustomed to helicopter noise. They flew over Liverpool several times, gradually descending as they traversed the area of Cronton. The pilots and the Major were searching every part of Cronton to establish if the increasing decibel level was causing any disturbance.

The time now was 2.56am; the chopper was hovering directly over the Sports Club property, but at a height of approximately 900 feet. At 2.57am Major Fite gave the order. They dropped like a stone, towards the flat roof of the dance hall.

The Blue Thunder was renowned for its ability to hover low and close to buildings. They were only about 20 feet above the roof when several troopers winched down and began to smash through the door. The chopper eased southward 15 feet, and then hovered over the lower section of flat roof. Here were the large glass patio doors on the barbeque platform area.

The remaining troopers dropped down to this lower area, three at a time. As they landed on their feet, the patio doors opened. Some of the troopers that had landed on the main roof were now clambering down using drain pipes, using ropes and ingenuity!

Now the sound of pile-drivers being used on the front door could be heard. Glass smashing, splintering wood, then shouting as the police entered.

The rumpus inside grew louder. Glasses smashing, bottles flying through the air....then a gunshot! As the SAS approached the open patio doors, a body came hurtling out. Then a man; Junior with two men, one on his back and one grasping his leg as Junior kicked out to get loose. Next a woman appeared, Csenge, fighting to release the grip of the bloke on Junior's back.

Csenge leaned back and with all the force she could muster, delivered an accurate karate chop to the attacker's throat. A direct hit on his Adam's apple dropped him to his knees; his tongue drooping out of the corner of his mouth. Her karate training in Eastern Europe was paying dividends!

The police arrived. They had arrested and cuffed two of the mob, and now were just standing, watching the antics of

Junior and Csenge. The finale was Sly. He strolled out onto the rooftop patio looking very pleased with how it was turning out. As he edged towards the SAS troopers, Boris scrambled to his feet and grabbed Sly around the throat. "You fucking arsehole, I'm gonna throttle you." Sly mumbled something that nobody understood. Boris dropped to his knees. Sly coughed to recover his voice. Boris toppled over holding his groin. Sly could now speak. "Sorry Boris, what I was trying to say was, I don't think so! I've stabbed you in the dick and hopefully, you will never have kids that have your mentality!"

The Blackwall team erupted. Rashi had excelled herself. She had initiated the Morse code pulses at 2.45am and continued through to 2.55am. Junior and Csenge, early on, accurately interpreted it. Having told Sly, he cut their ties, using his Swiss army knife. Indeed, the knife he had used on Boris, and that had saved his life so many times before!

Rashi had delivered an extra bonus. She had activated a Generative AI programme that had made a satellite recording of the whole rescue event. Well not exactly! This programme had artificially replicated the actual content it was recording. Although it had a few seconds lag time, the animation was realistic.

The team in Blackwall had been on the edge of their seats, watching the whole episode. But they need not have been! Sly, Csenge and, especially Junior, had given a masterclass in escapology and self-preservation!

Following a swift debrief meeting with Police and the SAS Commander, the EAI team were driven back to London. With a Police escort, one car in front and one behind, the three Police cars whistled through the dark rain-soaked streets of Liverpool, occasionally with sirens blaring to alert any upcoming congestion.

⊷⊷⊷◈⊶⊶⊶

Chapter 21

Safe Return to Blackwall

They approached the Blackwall gate just after 8am, and were waved straight through. Anneliese, Denton, Rashi and Jerome were waiting on the steps of the GCHQ satellite building.

Stumbling into the conference room, tired, exhausted and somewhat battered, they sank into their chairs. The Blackwall team, also exhausted, looked toward Anneliese, knowing she would take the lead.

Slowly standing, her voice began as a murmur, but rapidly strengthened. "You are all probably too tired to listen to me, but my heart is screaming at me to say this. I commend all of you today! Every one of you were outstanding. Your work was beyond the call of duty. And that is an expression that is nowhere near sufficient. My English is good but I cannot find anything that is better, other than, hallelujah!"

"So, get off to your beds. I'm sure you all realise this pressure may continue for some weeks yet. And tomorrow is no different. I would like you all with me at midday as Tibbs; sorry. I should say Premier Tibbs, is on TV news at 12.30pm, giving his version of today's events."

At that point, Penny sauntered into the room. "Would anyone like a coffee or a sandwich?" Anneliese scuttled towards Penny. "This lady has worked and looked after us for more than 15 hours. Penny, you are amazing. I don't know how we would cope without you."

The whole room stood and applauded Penny. She attempted a curtsy. As she looked up, her eyes were welling up with tears of pleasure.

They all set off to get some sleep. Although exhausted, Junior, and probably Csenge, were now becoming exhilarated by their love for one another. As they closed in on the Victory Hotel, endorphins and adrenalin stealthily combined to raise enlivened passion.

Their footsteps to Csenge's room gradually quickened, and as the key turned in the lock, a gush, then a wave of testosterone captured their bodies and souls.

Love-making, throughout the day, was relentless. There were only two occasions when relaxation insisted their bodies took a sleepy interlude.

Next morning, as daylight seeped through the blinds, Junior's arm, already encircling Csenge's waist, tightened. His early morning libido was the first to raise its demanding head!

As Junior attempted to increase Csenge's pulse rate, she pushed him away and rolled to the side of the bed. In the dim morning half-light Csenge sat, head in hands.

Junior, with a puzzled expression rolled towards her. Leaning his head on an elbow, he asked, "Csenge have I upset you? If I've done something wrong, it was not intentional. I would never hurt you!"

Csenge's face raised out of her hands. A tiny stream of tears were trickling over her lower eye-lids. She gasped a breath, leaned back and brushed her hair from her face.

Csenge returned an intense, enigmatic stare. "No, Junior, you have done nothing, other than be the most wonderful man I have ever met." Her world was spinning as she fought to compose herself.

"Junior, you explained your loves and life before we met. But you know nothing about my life, since we first met. We've been apart for six years, and I've thought about you every day. But in between times, things happened. You've never questioned me." Junior stopped Csenge! "Darling, I don't care, I love you! We are human and we were separated for a long while. But from that first meeting, your first interview, I couldn't get you out of my head."

Csenge stood, leaned across the bed and kissed Junior. She straightened, turned and shuffled to the window blinds.

As she opened them bright sunlight flooded in. It helped; the mood lifted as Csenge returned to sit on the side of the bed. "Junior, I promised myself I would do this. I want you to know everything about me!"

With a nervous smile, Csenge outlined her early life. "Junior, I admit I had several boyfriends, but nothing was anywhere close to serious." Junior gave a throaty chuckle." I can understand that! You would attract attention from any and every man!" "Please, Junior, let me get this off my chest. This is difficult for me because I cannot lose you." Junior frowned, as if he was trying to understand how she could even think that!

Csenge turned away from Junior, staring out of the window at Buckingham Palace. A very deep breath, then she spoke with momentum. "After you sent me to Hungary with Kainaat and Asha, I thought any feelings you had for me had drifted away. I met a CIA agent, a Hungarian we worked with. He was a lovely caring man and we had an affair. But all the time I was with him, I couldn't stop thinking about you. It didn't last for long, because he sensed that he was not the one! So there it is, I've got it all out into the open!"

Csenge peered at Junior. Longing to see a tender, loving acceptance. Junior threw himself across the bed and pulled her backwards to lay next to him. He clutched her face and pulled her lips to his. "My darling Csenge; I can see that was difficult for you, but by now you must realise how much I love you. We will be together forever. There's a song that Mum would play constantly. It goes "fairy tales can come true; it can happen to you!" Darling, it has, and we have our own fairy tale."

That same morning, just after 6am, Norm was in Penny's office waiting for Anneliese and Penny to arrive. About half-an-hour later, Penny strode into Anneliese's office with coffees for her and Norm.

Chapter 22

Norm's Warning

Norm had arrived early because he guessed that some of his news would dictate Anneliese needing time to organise a response. He stood in front of Anneliese's desk to deliver his latest intelligence. "Anneliese boss, the first thing to tell you is that Tibbs and his Chancellor have arranged a TV slot next Monday at 12.15pm, ostensibly to deliver the PRP Autumn statement. This is several weeks early, so this urgency may indicate some crucial, and probably ruthless, new initiatives."

Anneliese's brow wrinkled as she waited for the rest of Norm's intelligence. Norm's brow also frowned. "He has had some of the Metropolitan Police working day and night to determine who caused the ruckus in the media, and who had orchestrated the rescue of Frank Junior and Csenge."

"Mam, there are not many in the Met that demonstrate allegiance to the PRP, but the ones that do are mostly senior experienced and accomplished detectives. Essentially, the bottom line is they didn't have to look far to discern that Sly was a key player for the opposition."

"So, they spent serious time and effort digging and delving into his history. Using every form of intelligence science, facial recognition, fingerprints, voice recognition and military and police informant networks, they have concluded he is part of our EAI organisation!"

"He is now their "most wanted" and the word is out in all their supporting forces to capture and detain him. Indeed, I believe they will identify him as a wanted terrorist in their upcoming TV broadcast."

Norm's expression had never looked so serious. "Mam, we need to get him out of the country, to safety. If they capture him, there's no telling what they will do."

Anneliese, with a thoughtful expression replied "Norm, of course, we will get him away today!" But Norm, leaning across her desk begged "please let me finish."

"Those PRP bastards didn't' stop there. Using their government contacts and every shadowy corner of their network, they have developed a patchy picture of our EAI organisation. As you know, we have always seemed pretty secure, but they have worked upwards through our organisation and, somehow, they have pinpointed some of our personnel."

"I have not been privy to this intelligence, but they are convinced it is accurate and valuable to them. I only have one suggestion I can possibly make. Mam, you and your Seniors should withdraw to Amsterdam. We can work from there, and maybe we can be just as effective!"

Anneliese's head rolled back onto her chair's headrest; she stared at the ceiling. A few seconds later, she prepared to respond. "Norm, I will".... But before she could continue, the office door sprang open. It was Frank Junior and Csenge.

Seeing the serious expressions, Junior chuckled and turned to Csenge. "I think we should go out and come in again!" "No, please stay, I will explain all in a few minutes, but I need to conclude with Norm!"

Norm's Royal flush returned. He grasped Csenge's hand and softly kissed it. Then a handshake and a bow for Junior!

"Anneliese, Mam, I have to leave now! I am expected at the House of Commons for 10am. And then some PRP meetings afterwards." Anneliese uttered, "No Norm, from what you have told me, I'm not letting you back into that viper's nest."

Norm moved back to Anneliese. "Mam, I'm probably one of the few not on their wanted list." Norm now took Anneliese's hand and planted a gentle kiss. "Mam, you need me there. I'm your only link-man, and at the moment I believe I am key to our success!" Norm, holding the door handle, grinned, then murmured, "As Sir Winston Churchill once said, we are at the point of uncertainty, poised on the edge of catastrophe!" This remark had Norm's usual Royal tone and wide smile.

The next 20 minutes involved Anneliese explaining all to Junior and Csenge. At the end they both had concerned, but thoughtful expressions.

The next key topic on the agenda was Sly. "Junior, the first thing we must tackle is getting him out of harm's way. So where is he now?"

Junior's face appeared, like a rabbit in the headlights. "That is the million-dollar question! Apparently, after the rescue, he just disappeared."

Junior continued, "I remember seeing Sly, outside the building. As we were leaving with the police, Sly was talking with the SAS troopers. Then I saw him, with his phone up to his ear, as he strode off with the SAS guys towards their chopper."

Anneliese immediately grasped her mobile. "Frank, we have a new issue. Do you know where Sly is?" She began to smile as she listened to Frank's reply. "Thank you, Frank, but would you please round up everyone and get to me in the next few hours. The key word is urgency!"

Junior's eyes met Anneliese's. "Did he have anything that may help us find him?" "Yes, oh yes! That clever Frank had worked out that Sly would become an immediate PRP target. He got assistance from his SAS mates and spirited Sly off to a safe house. Frank will give more details when he arrives. The Tibb's broadcast has been cancelled due to the Sly search!"

Everybody had arrived in Admiralty Arch by mid-day. Anneliese, in a quiet voice that demanded complete attention, spoke. "We are all now in danger. The PRP have unearthed our involvement in undermining their insurrection. The first and easy instruction I need to give is this. You, my senior team, must withdraw immediately to Amsterdam. The second urgent arrangement involves Sly. Frank, where the hell is he?"

Frank, as relaxed as always, smiled. "Anneliese, I have sent him on holiday." After several seconds, Frank chuckled. "He is with an old SAS friend in a Welsh castle. Once we have figured out how to get him safely to Amsterdam, he will be with you. He's in no danger, no one will ever find him in the depths of wild North Wales."

Anneliese relaxed in her chair! "Frank, thank you." Now looking around the rest of the Senior team, her voice strengthened. "Please, all of you, get out of this country until we can stabilise everything."

"I will meet you all in a couple of days in Amsterdam. Penny, please help everyone make their arrangements. In the meantime, I will work with Frank on how we get Sly safely out of the country."

Most of the assembled team departed. Frank, Junior and Matthew, moved close to Anneliese. Csenge stopped at the door. "Anneliese, please don't be long getting to Amsterdam with us." But, as she spoke, her eyes were peering into Junior's. "No Csenge, you, me and Penny will go together as soon as Tibbs finishes his TV slot."

Chapter 23

Sly's Escape

The next task was to plan Sly's exit to Amsterdam. "Has anyone any ideas?" asked Anneliese. Her unwavering stare searched the silent audience. Matthew, thoughts scurrying through his mind, appeared to be getting his mouth in gear, when Anneliese began coaxing. "Come on you guys. We need a trail that is really difficult to follow. Lots of changes and diversions. Don't forget, this Government will have alerted airports, seaports, immigration. They have law enforcement looking for Sly. They have his picture and probably his bona fide passport details. But he does have a false passport as part of his EAI kit!"

Matthew now edged forward on his seat. "I hope you guys don't mind. I'm going to think aloud. I need to get my ideas straight. Frank, where is Sly? Let's start at the beginning!"

Frank's answer was detailed, but necessarily so. "I had a good mate, Bunny, in the SAS. I suppose we almost became inseparable. He always said, if I ever needed help, he would be there for me. I haven't seen him for a few years, but we have managed to keep in contact."

"As Sly was leaving the Cronton Sports Club, I was rattling through how to keep Sly safe. I phoned through to Major Tony Fite, the SAS Commander. We had met before, and now I threw my mate's hat in the ring. I knew he lived not far from Liverpool, somewhere in the wilds of North Wales."

"The Major had known him. Indeed, Bunny, as sergeant in the training camp, had trained the Major. So, he was excited to meet my old buddy again. "

"Sitting in A&E with Matthew, Rashi was constantly emailing me with updates on the events at Cronton. I realised that Sly would become the PRP's most wanted, and needed a short-haul safe house."

"Talking on the secure emergency line to Major Fite, he agreed to get Sly to my buddy.... Bunny Evans. A proud Welshman who, after he retired from the SAS, bought a Welsh Castle. So Sly is living in luxury in a Welsh town, Ruthin."

Matthew drew a deep breath. "Frank, thanks for that diatribe. And I'm not being facetious. We needed to have the complete story, and now we have, we are all so grateful you got Sly to safety."

"But where do we go from here?" Anneliese asked. "It's critical we find a way to get him out of this country. Then we all have to exit the UK. Well for now, anyway."

"Ok, now I have the start point, I will fill you in on my idea. Anneliese, you want a convoluted passage and I think you are correct. But first let me ask Frank another question." Matthew smiled at Frank. "Would it be possible, Frank, to get your buddies in the SAS to fly Sly to Manston airport in Kent?" Frank's eyebrows raised. "How does that help?" Anneliese also appeared confused!

"Well, Frank, it goes like this. My brother has a helicopter company at Manston, it's at the farthest point south in the UK. Only 26 miles from France! If your SAS mates can get Sly there, I'm sure my brother, Alfie, could get him across the Channel. The trick would be to fly Sly, as a tourist, to Toulouse.

Thousands visit the town for leisure, vacations, and Sly will like this…. gourmet experiences."

The evacuation of Sly was agreed. The plan would be the responsibility of Frank. He would initiate the first phase with Major Fite and his SAS troopers. Matthew was going to take charge of Phase two…. the flight from Manston to Toulouse. Alfie agreed to the plan. Indeed, he was quite excited to be involved. The SAS Blue Thunder chopper would arrive close to Ruthin Castle at 4am Sunday morning. They were scheduled to land on Alfie's heliport at 6.30am. Then to Toulouse, where Sly would take a train into Amsterdam, arriving around 9.30pm.

Everything went to plan. Not a single issue! Anneliese received constant progress reports as she sat with Frank and Matthew in her Admiralty Arch office.

Junior had stepped into an adjacent office to make contact with his EAI staff in Washington. Denton and Rashi had accompanied him as he was updated on issues in the US.

The cauldron in America was continuing to bubble away, but it had not worsened. Junior's subordinates convinced him that they had everything under control, and had managed to calm the senators in the worst affected areas. As the American people watched the events in the UK and were beginning to draw their own conclusions, the heat under the cauldron was diminishing. The far right's support was dwindling!

Junior, relieved at how things were going in America, returned to his concerns for the UK and his mother, Anneliese. Junior's tempo increased. His eyes were now sparkling and his pulse racing. "Denton, we need to get Anneliese out of this country before the PRP can find her. I know she will want to stay. Want to brave it out. Want to listen to the Autumn statement!"

Their EAI forum, led by Junior, began to formulate a plan. Junior, Denton and Rashi would leave for the USA just after midday. They would all meet in Anneliese's office to listen to Premier Tibbs. A complicated plan for the evacuation of Anneliese, Csenge and Penny was eventually agreed. They would travel by Eurostar train to Paris. Then onto Amsterdam. Jerome, Frank and Matthew would remain in London, with GCHQ intelligence operatives and their expert undercover Agents.

Immediately after Tibbs Autumn Statement, they all set off to their target locations. Junior and his team were aiming to work on the US Government and military to get commitments to support the UK with offensive action, if and when it was necessary. Frank, with a sombre expression, said he, Jerome and Matthew had a similar objective for the UK. "It may come to the point where a coup is our only option."

Anneliese, Csenge and Penny were probably more at risk, since the PRP had managed to access some EAI European personnel files. The travel plan for them was therefore, deliberately complex! They would be driven to St Pancras station to catch the Eurostar train into Paris. Then, onward by road, with an EAI driver to Amsterdam.

All of them were equipped with false passports and documents, and this route would not be on a 'highly probable' list!

Once in Amsterdam, Anneliese's objective was to lobby for support from NATO. She was convinced that this would be forthcoming, particularly as NATO were key to the instigation of EAI. The more difficult objective was to gain acceptance and support from the United Nations Assembly. Anneliese's mind, moving at light-year speed, had figured that eventually the UK may require a UN Peacekeeping force.

During the next few hours, the American contingent and Anneliese's small Amsterdam group, had quietly discussed Prime Minister Tibbs statements. The Chancellor deliberately presented depressing economic news, and stressed that the National Debt was reaching danger level. All income from tax levies and investments were falling far short of that needed to sustain benefits. Unemployment was at record levels. Company failures were reaching a point that had never been experienced before. The stock market, in recent weeks, had fallen almost 2000 points. Personal pensions and now Government pension payments were seriously under threat!

Premier Tibbs, staring into the TV camera, smiled as he remarked, "The only good news we can offer you is that we have almost totally precluded the influx of immigrants. As they arrive, we arrest them, tag them, and immediately settle them in labour camps or Army training camps. Those that prefer the Navy are sent for training on prestigious Cruise liners. I will explain this element in more detail later!"

With a serene expression, the Prime Minister looked directly into the camera, attempting to appear sincere. His tone, initially was assertive. "We, your Government, the Peoples Republican Party, have today found it necessary to invoke Emergency Powers!"

"Our Counter Terrorism Policing organisation has unearthed a serious and widespread threat to the UK's national security. The CTP had suspicions and misgivings when viewing the events at the Liverpool protest march. Their investigations have conclusively proved that there is an ongoing attempt by a foreign power to infiltrate, damage, and distort our security, and our organisations that work to keep us safe."

"They have initiated cyber-attacks on several of our government's security and defence systems. Our intelligence people advise these foreign fundamentalists operate from within the dark web." "It is likely they have developed biological weapons and are about to execute severe bio-terrorist attacks."

"With this knowledge, we had no choice other than to introduce Emergency Powers. I cannot tell you yet what this will involve. But I can assure every person in our country that we will do whatever is necessary to defeat such insidious insurrection!"

Junior, Rashi and Denton were, by now, well on their way to Washington. But still huddling together, discussing Tibbs Autumn Statement. Apparently, he had completed his litany of lies by announcing he would talk again to the country in two days' time. He needed to work night and day to develop the necessary plans to protect UK security and prevent an economic implosion!

⋯⋖❮❰❱❯⋗⋯

Chapter 24

Eurostar to Paris

Anneliese and her two colleagues were now arriving at St Pancras. All three stood, passports in their hands, at the passport control desk. They had practised this part. Penny would do the talking. Csenge and Anneliese both had slight foreign accents. Whereas Penny exhibited a personable disposition and a classless English accent.

They were facing a young ambitious immigration official. He had watched the PM's speech and was attempting to be particularly diligent.

He casually asked Penny the reason for the trip to Paris. "Well," replied Penny, "We are hoping to have a glorious time to celebrate our friend's birthday." Turning to smile at Anneliese, she then peered back at the official. "Can you believe she is nearly 75?"

His attempt at diligence was negated, as all three beautiful ladies' pheromones, perfume and sensuous smiles overwhelmed him. Ten minutes later, they were sitting in comfort, around a table sufficient to cope with several drinks on the way!

They all relaxed, having no other immigration checks until they were out of the UK. Similarly relaxed, Sly was ambling alongside the Singel canal toward his hotel. The late afternoon sun was reflecting off his Ray-Bans as his mind continued to work through what may happen next. Little did he know that his face had just appeared on UK television. A newsflash purporting to show a terrorist, wanted in the UK, had just shown a serious, but flattering picture of Sly.

The Eurostar meandered slowly into Folkestone as it approached the Channel tunnel. The train came to a halt, just before the tunnel entrance. Vehicles were now being loaded into the wagons.

The ladies, trying to get into holiday mood, had organised a bottle of Champagne. Penny carefully poured this into the flute glasses. As they were warily enjoying the first sips. Two lady immigration officers walked in from the previous carriage. They came to a standstill at Anneliese's table, smiling as they searched the faces.

Anneliese, with a carefree demeanour, held her glass high. " It's my birthday tomorrow! Would you like a drink with us?" Under the table, Penny had gripped Csenge's hand, and clenched tighter as the immigration officers, peering at Anneliese, revelled in her joyful expression!

"We would love to" replied one of the immigration officials, "but we are working. Hope you enjoy your birthday in Paris." Anneliese, with a sweet smile, replied, "Oh, I will, officer. I am 75 tomorrow but the one thing I remember is how to party!"

Both immigration officials politely touched the peak of their caps, and eased away down the aisle.

Anneliese whispered to Csenge and Penny, "Enjoy your Champagne, we are home and dry!"

The Eurostar initially sauntered, then gathered speed though the Channel Tunnel. All three were now relaxing; work talk was replaced by girl talk.

The champagne bottle emptied at a speed approaching that of the train. Stories, chatter, giggling and wobbling walks as they accessed the toilet during the 3 hours to Paris.

Csenge, zig-zagging back from the toilet, giggled all the way as the train slowed, entering Gare-du-Nord. Her footsteps stuttered and stumbled as she reached their table. Penny, and then Anneliese, applauded as she, literally, fell into her seat!

They helped one another onto the platform. Weekend cases were placed on the ground as their giggling continued. They stood peering around the station, particularly Anneliese, who was assessing the likely danger areas. At the end of the platform was both French and UK Border Force checks. Also, a customs check which was selective....Anneliese counted about 20% having luggage investigated.

Anneliese concluded there was no need to be concerned about customs. They were only carrying minimal clothing, underwear and cosmetics. Therefore presenting as weekend visitors!

Walking toward them was a tall, dark haired handsome man. Wearing a long grey lightweight raincoat, with upturned collar. He drifted directly to Anneliese. "Bonjour boss, ca va?" Anneliese smiled as she replied "Oui, tres bien. Merci beaucoup Louis." "This is one of our French colleagues. He will be driving us to Amsterdam." As Anneliese began to introduce Csenge and Penny, two French immigration officials were approaching. Louis with an urgent tone said, "Ladies, please give me your passports." They were quickly passed across; Louis commented, "Tres bien, they are biometric." He turned away and strode toward the two French Border Force officials.

They stood talking for three or four minutes. Louis reached inside his jacket and showed them his identification. They perused the passports and then a few more words were exchanged.

Louis paced back to the three ladies. His English was excellent, with the added attractive tinge of a French accent. "Ladies, follow me closely and we will be in the car in a few minutes. It has been raining but our colleague, Michel, will bring the car to the station exit."

They, as a group, purposefully strode past the Border Force desks and Customs. As they passed the two officials that had spoken with Louis, both saluted. The UK Border Force personnel appeared confused and one ran to talk with the two French officials. With raised eyebrows and a quizzical expression, he returned to his desk.

As they walked through the exit archway, Michel arrived with the car. A brand new, gleaming, Mercedes 500 EV. Luggage and passengers loaded, they sped off. Next stop Amsterdam!

It wasn't long before Anneliese asked, "Louis, what did you say to the French Immigration officials?" Csenge and Penny were all ears. Louis, with his French accent causing rapid heartbeats, explained. "I showed my EAI identification. Did you know, the French love EAI due to our successes against terrorists. But I did not lie or exaggerate! I said you were here for important meetings with Gouvernement Francais and also NATO.I just added that the discussions were addressing the need to keep us all safe and secure!"

At about 10.30pm they arrived in Amsterdam. Louis explained they would all be staying in the Hyatt Regency. It was thought best not to return to the Breitner House Hotel, in case it had been identified as Anneliese's place to stay in Amsterdam.

At check-in, they all agreed to meet in the bar for a nightcap at 11.30pm. Anneliese managed to convince herself to give her people a chance to get to know one another. The day, a very long day, had been a complete success. No mishaps, and exemplary work by everyone. Although her astute, active mind would always search out more progressive moves, she could afford to relax a little.

The ladies had all been on the phone to one another. Penny, Csenge and Anneliese arrived together. The bar was busy, as most places in Amsterdam usually are. Csenge pushed the double doors open, and, dressed to impress, these gorgeous examples of femininity sauntered toward the bar.

The room quietened as Anneliese led them to the bar. Settling on the bar stools, they ordered their drinks.

Anneliese asked for a Californian Cabernet Sauvignon. As she took the first sip, Louis and Michel appeared. The chatter and banter gradually increased. After ten minutes or so, Anneliese grasped Csenge's wrist. "Could we have a word?" as she whisked her away apologising to Michel, Louis and Penny.

This hotel had fabulous, although man-made, garden areas. They, hand in hand, ambled past exotic plants, lit by solar lights. Anneliese found a table at the edge of the exotic area. A waiter arrived and they ordered more drinks.

Csenge pulled out a pack of cigarettes. "Do you mind?" "No, indeed; I am tempted to ask for one! But I won't" Csenge enjoyed the initial impact of nicotine, as the smoke billowed upwards. The waiter returned with their drinks. Two or three sips and Anneliese leaned toward Csenge. "My darling

Csenge, you have been through so much, but you keep coming back for more. You are so much like me when I was younger. I feel I have to warn you; it's not going to get any easier. Try to keep your mind focused on intelligence and surveillance. We are in a very dangerous phase!"

Anneliese, with an expression that left Csenge wondering what was coming next, toyed with the edge of her wine glass. It was obvious she was trying to find words that would not unsettle Csenge.

In the seconds that followed, Anneliese's eyes peered into Csenge's. With a soft, caring tone she asked "How are you getting on with Frank Junior?" Csenge, with surprised eyes and an uncontrollably drooping jaw, spluttered as she attempted an answer. As her beautiful lips were forming the answer, Anneliese began to say "I know".... But Csenge's mind forced out an answer. "I love him, I love him more than anything!" Csenge bent forward, rushing her wine glass to her lips. Anneliese's loving smile stared into Csenge's heart and soul. Csenge gasped a breath and leaned back in her chair.

Within a few seconds, they both settled and began to relax. Anneliese, continued searching Csenge's eyes.

As their eyes met, Anneliese said, "My darling I know you do, and I know he loves you! And I am totally convinced you are made for one another and will have a fabulous life together." They floated back through the gardens, and into the bar. As they approached, the attraction between Penny and Louis was unavoidable. The body language, as they leaned towards one another, spoke volumes. Anneliese and Csenge gave them room as they joined Michel. Their conversation, polite conversation, mostly between Anneliese and Michel, was almost totally in French. It was punctuated by continuous glances at Penny and Louis as romantic magnetism drew them closer.

They reached a point, just after midnight, where Louis' hand now rested on Penny's thigh. Louis' eyes were incessantly browsing the beautiful face before him. Penny's salacious eyes never moved from his.

Anneliese, an expert in human behaviour decided this was the time for her exit. She whispered to Csenge, "I need my bed, it's been a very long day. Oh, before I go, just one thing, Frank Junior and Rashi will fly in on Friday. By then we all will have heard Premier Tibbs broadcast on Thursday. Would you please arrange with Penny to get all our Seniors here for a meeting early Friday."

Anneliese knew, as she walked to the lift, Csenge's feelings would be at fever pitch. Csenge, after a few seconds rushed to catch Anneliese before she entered the lift. She clutched her arm! Anneliese turned with a knowing smile. "What is it Csenge?" "Would it be ok, Anneliese, if I moved into my apartment tomorrow?" "Of course, my dear, but I really need you at my meeting Friday morning." "Of course, boss, that's a given." "Csenge, you mean a lot to me, so please continue calling me Anneliese. Boss is not necessary."

The lift arrived as Anneliese stroked Csenge's cheek. "I'll see you all at breakfast, about 10am."

Chapter 25

Sly Surprise

Their group were assembled for breakfast, just after 10am. As they were beginning to stand to go and view the buffet, the double doors opened. The newcomer, dressed out of character, was not immediately recognised. Anneliese's eyes studied the man for a few seconds. Smartly dressed in a navy-blue blazer and grey flannel trousers, his face gradually developed a wide smile. In that blink of an eye interval, Anneliese's mind clicked into gear. It was Sly!

Although his stature was relatively slight, his personality was gigantic. His physicality grew with every comical word he uttered. As they slowly eased through breakfast, Sly recounted stories, quietly, about the hostage taking, the rescue and his travel with Alfie to Toulouse and then, his journey to Amsterdam. His gastronomic experience in Toulouse was a story that had the whole table engulfed in loud, wild laughter!

Breakfast over, Anneliese walked around behind Sly and whispered in his ear. As he stood, Anneliese asked for them to be excused for a moment as they needed to talk. As they, arm in arm, ambled into the garden, unending laughter and chuckles drifted away behind them.

They sat at a table in the farthest corner of the exotic rain-forest garden. Sly appeared slightly nervous as he faced

Anneliese. Her gracious smile relieved his nervousness. Sly spoke first.

"Mam, would you like a drink?" Anneliese, sensing his stress, leaned across the table to hold his hand. "Sly, yes, but don't worry. The waiter will appear in a few minutes."

Anneliese brushed her locks away from her face. Sly just stared. Anneliese returned an admiring smile. "Sly, I am finding it difficult to get the words to express my feelings. First, I am so happy you are safe, here with us. You looked after my son and Csenge and I will never forget that. I owe you so much and want to reward you. You are the salt of the earth and are very special in today's world."

Sly could see the emotion building in Anneliese. Leaning across the table, he grasped her hand. As he was about to speak, the waiter arrived. Anneliese asked Sly, "What would you like?" Sly immediately replied, "A large Napoleon Brandy and a black coffee." His eyes turned to Anneliese. "Sir, I will have the same, thank you!"

As the waiter retreated, Anneliese, once again, reached across the table for Sly's hand. "Sly, you have proved yourself, time and time again. I am wishing to upgrade you to the Seniors group. If you agree, you will be a lieutenant in EAI. But I do need one thing more from you. I need you to accompany me to Brussels. I believe we must persuade NATO to support us. You have experienced the sinister world that the PRP are dragging us into. You can talk about the depraved minds of the mercenaries they are employing. You can help me calibrate a clear understanding, and belief, in the need to depose this lethal government. They will not stop at insurrection in the UK. They will attempt to extend their coercive tyrannical control into European countries. They have a massive power, indeed possibly two, driving them on!

Russia and Iran. We have conclusive evidence, and two eye witnesses. You and Norm."

"So Sly, what I am asking from you is your dedicated unflinching support. I know this is not the sort of thing you usually do. But you are essential, and with Norm's evidence, I think we could present a cast iron case. Please, think about it. I will attempt to contact the NATO Secretary General, later today, to arrange a meeting. In the meantime, I was hoping you would give Norm a 'heads up' and tell him I will be in contact."

Sly began to grin. His eyes sparkled with excitement. He pondered for a few seconds then his lips tiptoed into Scouse mode. "Hey Wack, you will never walk alone! Not while I'm around! I am grateful and will work my boots off to help you, and our green and pleasant land! So, let's go and have another bevie and then scavvy a bifta to seal the deal."

Anneliese's expression developed a confused quizzical look. They stood, as she snatched hold of Sly's hand. Peering into Sly's dark brown eyes, she quietly commented, "Sly, I don't know what the fuck you said, but your tone made it sound attractive!"

They strolled back to the breakfast restaurant. As they entered, Anneliese clutched Sly's arm and tugged him to a small corner table. "There are a couple more things I should tell you before you speak with Norm. Tomorrow we will hear the details concerning Emergency Measures from the Premier. Friday, Frank Junior and Rashi will arrive. I will attempt to arrange the meeting with NATO's Secretary General for Sunday or Monday. We all need a break! I am hoping Junior will attend with us. The NATO supremo, Jasper Ankenbauer, is American and has had a good relationship with Frank Junior, going back several years. I have met him twice before and, apparently, he was a vocal lobbyist in the establishment of EAI; and me as Director General! But we are entering unknown territory in attempting to overthrow a maverick insidious Government. So we may need the strong persuasion of Junior to obtain solid, reliable support!"

Sly, nodded in agreement. "Mam, I'll feed all this to Norm. If he can escape those PRP fuuckers" … his scouse accent accentuated that word, and he repeated it! "those fuuckers' will wish they'd never started down this road!"

Anneliese smiled and slowly stood. Sly followed and, together, they moved across the restaurant to join their colleagues.

—◄❖►—

Chapter 26

Tibbs Broadcast

The Amsterdam group, with Penny as organiser, travelled, early morning to the Hague Binnenhof Parliament buildings. Louis and Michel escorted them on the 50-mile drive. At the Binnenhof, Louis produced his EAI Security pass and the guards waved them straight through into the courtyard. They were expected! Penny had arranged everything!

Following Louis and Michel, they quickly paced through a large oak door at the top of a set of Delft tiled steps. The door opened, before a foot was placed on the steps. Out bustled a stocky dark-bearded gentleman with a welcoming smile. "I am the Foreign Affairs Secretary and I will be looking after your needs today. My name is Josef Kalkwarf." At that point, Penny stepped forward to shake his hand. "Hello Josef, I am Penny. We have spoken about today on the telephone."

Josef's smile widened. "Please come in and we shall talk some more!" He led them a short way down a corridor and opened another large oak door. As they began to enter, Anneliese stopped dead in her tracks. The room was full of Dutch Government personnel. Seated in five rows, they all peered at Anneliese's group.

Anneliese turned to Josef. "Are we in the correct place, Josef?" "Madame, yes, these are my colleagues who also wished to watch the broadcast. We all love the United Kingdom and are sad to see what is happening there. We, and the whole of the Netherlands Government, will give you our total support. Madame Anneliese, the front row is reserved for you and your people. We have a large, drop down, TV screen. Please be seated and, in a moment, we will offer you refreshments."

Anneliese sauntered, with elegance, past the front row, then up and down each row, shaking everyone's hand. The rest of her team followed closely behind.

After about 5 minutes, listening to well-wishers and being provided with coffee and soft drinks, they took their seats. Anneliese, seated with Louis to her left, whispered, "I came here thinking it would be totally secure, and nothing could leak to the PRP." Louis gripped her hand. "This is the most secure place you will ever find. These people, the Dutch people, and generations before them, remember what the UK did for them in WWII. They can see the sedition endemic in this UK Government. It is constantly discussed in Parliament and throughout Holland. You have nothing to fear in the Netherlands. Indeed, they consider you, Anneliese, as one of them because you lived amongst them for many years and have many friends!"

The screen lowered and the lights dimmed. An eerie silence descended. The broadcast began. Prime Minister Tibbs launched into detailing a series of measures. He described them as Emergency Measures, but no emergency was apparent to anyone, other than the fact that the PRP were in power.

The broadcast ended. Everyone in the room remained silent in their seats. One gentleman in the third row stood. Waving his arms around the room to get the attention of his colleagues, his emotional speech blistered into the forum!

"They are depraved! This is the return of the Nazis'! We cannot, and will not, let this happen." Pointing at the front row, his voice tempered. "Anneliese, we are going to be with you, all the way. Whatever help you need, you will receive it. It was a God-send that we all supported the establishment of the EAI security organisation. And you at its helm, in particular. Thank you, Madame Anneliese, and your brave staff!"

As the room began to clear, Louis indicated they should leave. As they strolled out, Josef Kalkwarf caught up with Anneliese. "Madame, just one last thing. The Government have allocated you a complete floor in this building. Six large offices for your permanent use. I have been assigned to address any of your needs or requirements. I know its 50 miles away from your present Amsterdam base, and we can move you here, if you wish. But going back and forth, and its only 40 minutes, will increase your security. I have spoken with Louis and Michel. They say they are assigned to this operation for as long as it takes. So, just let us know how you would like to proceed."

Anneliese held Josef's hand and with a sublime stare said, "Josef, thank you so much! At the moment, I need all the help I can get. And today, you and your people, indeed the Dutch Government, have lifted my spirits to the point where we will not fail the UK." Josef grasped her arm. "Madame, I have put hours and days into this. It's not just the Netherlands that perceives the danger. You have world-wide support!"

For the first 20 minutes of the journey back to Amsterdam, a stunned silence soaked up the pain that Tibb's speech had inflicted. Penny, eventually began to sob as the sad atmosphere dragged her thoughts into fear for her family. Michel and Csenge comforted her, whilst Anneliese, with a numb expression, stared at the nothingness world flashing by.

A severe looking Sly was standing on the steps of the Hyatt Regency as they pulled in. He walked to the car, approaching the driver's window. Louis flicked the switch and the glass rolled down. As Sly leaned both elbows on the door window frame, Anneliese spoke first. "Good to see you Sly. As we are all here, I would like to ask you all to meet with me, first thing tomorrow."

"Penny, would you please book the Penthouse Suite for tomorrow. If not available, get us a conference area as far away as possible from other guests and staff."

They all clambered out of the Mercedes, with Penny dabbing her eyes, and now Louis, with an arm around her shoulders, offering sympathetic comfort.

⋯⊷⊷⧫⟨⟩⧫⊶⊶⋯

Chapter 27

Nostalgic Walk with Anneliese

Anneliese, as Csenge was passing, asked "Would you take my stuff in for me. I'm going for a walk to clear my head and get my thoughts together. Sly, would you care to accompany me?" Csenge smiled at Sly. "You make sure you look after the boss."

Sly and Anneliese ambled off together. "Where are we going, Anneliese?" "I want to take a slow stroll along by the canal." They smiled at one another and Anneliese took hold of Sly's arm. They strolled alongside the canal and were now entering the Red-Light district. Anneliese stopped, turned and sat on the wall opposite a shop window. The almost naked girl, sitting in the window waved, and to Sly's surprise Anneliese waved back, then blew her a kiss. Sly sat beside Anneliese, his expression somewhat unsettled.

Sly, with an angry tone, began to comment on Tibbs speech. "Thaat Fuucker today".... but he got no further. Anneliese ignored his words. "Sly, do you know my first job as an undercover agent was here. I lived in that same apartment, and day after day, sat in the same shop window." It was quiet for almost 30 seconds. Sly was lost for words. He'd never heard this story before.

Anneliese's voice, breaking with emotion, continued. "Sly, that demeaning job was a trial, and I survived it! And it thrust me into the most wonderful, rewarding career that I am now at the pinnacle of. But a career that I am also at the end of! I met my husband right here, at this shop window." As she pointed, she flexed her fingers into a wave to the young lady sitting, in what had been, Anneliese's shop window.

They both sat through a long quiet phase. With sun beaming on their faces and canal cruisers floating by; passengers waving and music leaking from the Red-Light apartments, Anneliese's mind was surfing back through her career.

Sly, in contrast, although enjoying the pleasure of the canal and its ambience, was ecstatic that he had been selected to hear Anneliese's story and sensed the immense impact her work had bestowed on her!

Anneliese snapped out of her mind's solitude. "Sly, that's it! I have it!" she grasped him and kissed his cheek. "In the next week or two we will defeat those bastards. There is no room for inhuman creatures in this world!"

"Let's get back Sly! We will get to it in the morning and also when Frank Junior is here on Friday. But for now, we deserve a drink in the hotel bar. And, thank you so much for walking with me. I think you and I have a really special supernatural connection. I have sensed it from the moment we first met. And today has proved it. Sitting next to me on the wall, my thoughts came to me in quick succession and were quickly cast together in my brain's foundry. So thank you so much!"

Both now very happy people, they strolled back, in a glorious sunset, to the hotel. A couple of drinks in the bar, then Anneliese excused herself, saying she needed to sleep.

Sly spent the rest of the evening with Csenge. They chatted mostly about the PRP's disgusting plans, but then how Anneliese was such a fabulously intelligent boss. Penny, now recovered, knew Anneliese would get things fixed. Louis continued, with Michel in tow, to flirt with Penny!

Chapter 28

Coup Planned

The penthouse suite had magical views across the Amsterdam skyline. Penny, standing alone in the middle of the working space she had prepared, glanced around, checking every detail.

A knock on the door heralded the first arrivals. It was dead on 8am. Penny closed one eye as she peered through the peephole. It was Anneliese, Csenge and Sly. Penny took a step back and opened the door to its full width. As she uttered a polite "good morning" two more faces appeared. Louis and Michel were now a very solid part of the Amsterdam EAI team.

Another knock, a couple of minutes later, announced the arrival of the coffee and pastries breakfast trolley.

All were polite, courteous and reserved, ambling to the coffee and selecting delicious croissants and Danish pastries. After a few minutes, Anneliese strode to the centre of the seating area. Scanning her team, she said, "Please carry on enjoying breakfast whilst I begin. I am not going to recount all that stuff that Tibbs built a fantasy around. I have checked, and the economy is healthy. The black picture he painted about his Chancellor's ability to pay benefits, fund national services, support the defence industry, is all a mound of manure. The opposition know this, but have been intimidated, warned off, and are scared to speak out. These so-called Emergency Powers, have prevented Parliamentary debate. No bills are being allowed to be entered in the Chamber. No Acts are being passed. The House of Lords has been dissolved. He has replicated the tactics that Henry VIII adopted and the grip that Oliver Cromwell applied to the Parliamentarians before they figured out a workable Parliamentary process!"

"Before I reach the key element of Tibbs' horrendous plans, I will advise you of some events. Norman will be with us around midday. He, very bravely, has lived in the midst of Tibbs and his cronies, so will be able to update us. Frank Junior and Rashi will be with us midday tomorrow. When we are all together, we will develop and agree plans for something that has not happened in the UK since Oliver Cromwell and the Civil War. We will plan a Coup! If you are not comfortable with this, please leave the room now. I trust every one of you, and know you would not leak our thinking. And we won't think bad of you. I understand; this is a massive task. So please, take a minute to think. If you cannot be part of this, just get up and leave."

Not one single person moved, blinked or twitched. The room fell silent as everyone stared at Anneliese with belief beaming from their eyes. Anneliese inhaled a long deep breath. Her smile grew as she began to pace around.

"The hideous barbaric sections of Tibbs speech firstly involved his plans for old people, the disabled and mentally disturbed. I'm not telling you anything you didn't hear already. And you saw the impact it had on Penny! Everyone across the whole of the UK will feel the same. It's unimaginable that families will watch grandparents, brothers, sisters, even children, dragged out of their homes, to be executed. In the name of building an economy for the future! But really, an economy to fill the wallets of these heathens, and the Russians and Iranians."

Anneliese, overcome with emotion, stopped for a moment and sat in her seat. Glancing around, she uttered, "I am one of those over 70's they want to put to death!" She stood. Her face developed excruciating anger. "That will never happen. I will never let it happen to anyone, none of the UK families and friends. None of you, my friends!"

"The one thing I will never forget and will take with me to the grave are those last few sadistic words that Tibbs spoke. 'It's your duty to die' His expression and tone were as if he could get us to believe we should capitulate and do this happily for our country. Those words 'IT'S YOUR DUTY TO DIE,' are borne out of depraved evil!"

Penny had waited for that break. "Anneliese, I have a secure line from Rashi." "Hi you guys, first, just to let you know I haven't been able to contact Norm for over 12 hours. It's not like him. Also, to let you know, I am with Junior and we are on our way to the airport. We should be with you midday tomorrow. Junior asked me to inform you that Ankenbauer was visiting Washington. They met and you have their full and complete support. NATO will initially provide American troops. It was discussed with President Newman who agreed to sanction SBS support. He said to give you his regards, and knew that the SBS would be all you would need! But if you require more, just ask!"

They clearly heard Rashi inhale sharply. "One last thing you guys. A deep learning programme that I integrated with a listening multimodal AI system has listened in, via satellite, to a conversation between Tibbs and his Home Office minister. They were feeling secure as they strolled out of number 10 and stretched their legs in Downing Street."

"Those motherfuckers are going to initiate the DTD onslaught immediately. Tibbs broadcast had announced that "Duty to Die" would commence at the end of the month. They have the first computer runs of people to be selected, and will instead, begin tomorrow to haul them out of their homes. They will be taken to board cruise liners at Tilbury and Southampton. The ships have been staffed by paid illegal migrants. They plan to murder these elderly citizens once out in the Atlantic, and dispose of the bodies overboard into the sea." Rashi's voice crackled with emotion. After a minute's quiet, recovering her speech, she said that Tibbs had commented that the assisted dying camps that he had set up in ex-army sites were overflowing and throughput was fantastic!

Anneliese shouted, "Rashi, that's enough! We need to reconcile our minds to this brutality. I don't mean to be sharp, but we need some time. Just get here with Junior as quickly as possible!"

Stunned silence engulfed the room. Penny, once again began to sob. Anneliese rose from her chair. "Penny, calm yourself! We will not let them inflict this wickedness on any of our people."

Chapter 29

Body Found

"Penny, Csenge, anyone! Get Frank on a secure line to me....now!" One minute and Frank was talking with Anneliese. She paced to the far end of the penthouse. "Frank, their holocaust...." Frank, his tone serious, broke in. "I know Anneliese, but turn the news on. They have found a body, close to Parliament Square. Let's listen to that, then call me back."

Anneliese screamed out, "Louis, turn the TV on to the BBC news." She rushed back and they all sat, watched and listened.

The TV news was already covering the scene. A body had been found, early morning, in the Temple area of the embankment. Less than a mile from Parliament Square. The whole embankment had come to a standstill as Police cordoned off the scene, and began to investigate. Forensic police vans were parked around the area and the BBC reporter stated that the body had been lying slumped at the rear of Cleopatra's Needle.

A young male civil servant had found the body, as he walked along the Embankment to work in the Parliamentary offices. He had gone with Police to West End Central Police Station, to assist their enquiries. He was not, in any way, a suspect. But he had been heard to say he recognised the person.

As the news item finished, the phone rang. Csenge answered and passed the phone to Anneliese. "It's Frank." Csenge's head dropped as anguish leaked into her mind.

This time, Anneliese stayed in the midst of her team. She wanted them to hear every word she spoke. "Frank, we must act with lightning speed, otherwise people will be dying. I desperately need you to muster and instruct the military. The SAS, the American SBS, and whoever else we need. More importantly, I need you and Matthew here with me to direct operations. Frank Junior will arrive tomorrow, and I believe we need to consider an immediate attack."

Just then, Louis shouted, "listen, ecoute cette est important." Anneliese dropped the phone line and scooted back to the TV. The police had determined the name of the victim from identification on his body. He was Norman Simpson. He worked directly for the Prime Minister, providing legal advice. Until now, Sly had silently listened. This news inflicted a numbness. He stood staring at the Amsterdam skyline!

The worst of the day was not over. They had all been exposed in the past, to violence, death and treachery. But this was one of their own! Anneliese then asked them all to take a break for a couple of hours. Then they would get together again late in the afternoon.

Penny began bustling around, tidying. Csenge, the last to leave, was hovering at the door when Anneliese's secure mobile rang. Csenge stopped and stared as Anneliese answered. As she listened, she gestured to Csenge to return to her side. Hands clasped between her knees, Csenge anxiously peered at Anneliese's ponderous expression. As the caller completed the message, Anneliese's face transitioned to one of disbelief. Then turning to grasp Csenge's arm, Anneliese screeched with anger!

"Who is it Anneliese, what is it?" Csenge shuddered under the tension. Penny rushed across the room, her expression now tormented and fearful. Anneliese tossed her mobile at a settee, then stood and paced up and down!

"That was Frank. He's heading with Matthew to Blackwall, for safety. Jerome was summoned to Downing Street. While he was there, some CID officers arrived and arrested him!"

"Frank has a mole in the Met who will give him more information as soon as the picture gets clearer. What he did explain was that Tibbs is claiming there is evidence that Jerome is a subversive who has been working for a foreign power."

"That insidious depraved freak of a tyrant will get his just desserts. I swear I will make sure his fall from power ends in the Tower!"

Anneliese's nostrils flared. Her deep breathing brought some calmness. "Csenge, Penny, let's have a drink in the bar whilst I think through how to proceed. Frank will phone again, once he's at Blackwall." Sly, Louis and Michel were already in the bar. They ordered the ladies drinks and then all headed to a corner table. Anneliese calmly and quietly explained the latest events and information.

Sly now appeared composed. Leaning forward, his elbows on the table, his eyes drifted to Anneliese's. "Mam, when we organise the Apocalypse for these bastards, I want to be at the front of the charge. I want to cauterise the world of them. I am absolutely certain they killed Norm and I want to be at the front of the team sealing their fate!"

Anneliese's response had a strong but quiet emphasis in her tone. "Sly, I understand how you feel. We will meet tomorrow when Junior and Frank are here to plan the incursion and attack. And I will ensure you get a sympathetic hearing and are prominent in toppling these evil bastards!"

After arranging for food to be sent to the Penthouse, they all, with burdened minds, headed back to the room.

In a tense atmosphere, a God-given break of around 15 minutes allowed them some sustenance. Anneliese's mobile rang at the point she was munching on a salmon and cucumber sandwich. She passed the phone to Penny, who answered in her usual polite and welcoming voice. "It's Frank," she said, passing the mobile back to Anneliese.

"Frank, I'm going to put you on loudspeaker." Another voice interjected. "Anneliese, it's me, Matthew. Darling, I know this is a difficult one, but you have dealt with worse. So keep your beautiful chin up." Anneliese began a stuttering reply, then realised it was now Frank on the line.

"Anneliese, I'm here with, not just Matthew, but Major Fite and a few of our SAS buddies." Anneliese squeezed in a hello, as Frank continued talking.

"Major Fite asserts that he needs to get Matthew and me out to Amsterdam. His view is that London is now totally insecure for us. He goes further. He wants to be with us in Amsterdam. He will bring his best planners and logistics personnel. And we can plan the whole operation from Holland."

A quiet period followed as Anneliese thought it through. "Frank, I agree with Major Fite, but not in Amsterdam. I have secure offices, generously provided by the Dutch Government, in the Hague Parliament Buildings. Your ideas all fit nicely together. Frank Junior is flying in to Amsterdam tomorrow. This can be our nerve centre!"

Major Fite now began to speak. "We, in that case, will join you tomorrow. Then I would propose we spend the weekend planning the coup. Our thinking is the attack should commence as Parliament is sitting on Monday." Frank came back on the line. "Rashi has kept me up to date. I know NATO and the Americans have agreed to provide support. A key to this operation is the SAS.... and the American Special Boat Service. But for them to operate effectively, they need a Corvette, in the Thames, as their base. What we need to clarify is if we can get a ship anchored in the Thames by Sunday night. I have tried contacting Rashi, but they are in the air, and the signal keeps breaking. Anneliese, would you please continue trying. If that doesn't work, please ask the question as soon as they arrive in Amsterdam!"

Csenge, Penny, Sly and Anneliese were somewhat relieved. For all of them, adrenaline and excitement were building. Friday and the weekend were, without doubt, going to be monstrously hectic.

Chapter 30

Meet in the Hague

About half an hour later, Anneliese said, "Listen you guys, go and get yourselves something to eat. I'm not hungry yet so I'm going to begin to think about, and work, on the plans." As she finished those words, her mobile rang again. It was Frank.... Again! "Anneliese, we will be with you in a few hours. Major Fite and I re-considered. There are so many different elements to this, we think we need to begin kicking it around tonight. Is that OK with you?" "Yes, of course," replied Anneliese. "I was thinking the same thing! But Frank, fly into the Hague and we will meet you there." "We will be in the SAS Blue Thunder helicopter. In fact, two!" As Frank finished speaking, Anneliese's mind moved up a gear. "There is a playing field adjacent to the Parliament. Aim to land there."

"Frank, I am going to get off the line and prepare. See you in a few hours." Looking around the team, she said, "Sorry you guys, we will have to eat later. Penny, please get Josef Kalkwarf on the line." Penny loved being needed!

Penny passed the phone. "Good evening, Josef. We are now needing to proceed with urgency. I would ask a favour. We want a secure meeting in those offices you offered, for the next few days. It will be our command centre. We wish to begin as soon as we can get there. Is that OK?" "So that is tonight, Madame?" "Yes, Josef, and it will mean a lot to me if you could join our team. We will arrive approximately 9pm. And just one more thing. There are two SAS helicopters landing on the adjacent playing fields. Could you arrange for your Dutch Police to provide security for them through the night, and possibly tomorrow." "Madame, no problem, we have Government and NATO instructions to provide full support!"

Approximately 10.15pm, European time, the choppers arrived. Anneliese and her team were already in situ. Frank led Major Fite, Matthew and several uniformed military personnel into the room.

First, Anneliese introduced Josef Kalkwarf and the EAI team. Now Frank proudly stood to make introductions. Staring at Anneliese, Frank grinned. "The first person I must introduce is Matthew, Anneliese's husband. They haven't seen one another for a while. Business has taken priority."

Matthew stood and saluted as his eyes moved from face to face. Matthew then, unusual for this somewhat introverted character, strode across the room, to Anneliese. With everyone watching, he clasped her cheeks and softly delivered a long, lingering kiss. Anneliese's eyes smiled with her heart!

Frank continued, "Major Fite of the SAS, Captain Luke Donovan of the Commando Raiders 47 Special Operations Force, and Commodore Jason Englehardt of the Royal Navy." They were supported by several ranked officers, important to the operation. And Frank went out of his way to introduce each individually.

The room silenced as Anneliese stood and strode into the centre of the conference room. She, with a glorious smile that always got attention, asked, "Do you mind if I use a flip chart? I know we are in a computerised world, but this is my world. I find it easier to work with!"

"So, and to be fair I am already ahead of you, but what do you feel is the most urgent thing we need to tackle?" One of the troopers stood. "Your name Sir?" "Mam, I am Lennie. And I have heard from family today that lots of our old folks have been dragged away to what are called DTD ships. But really, they are just murder ships. My Aunt and Uncle were taken today!" He stopped, as Penny began sobbing!

Anneliese, with a glum expression walked to Penny and stroked her back. "Penny, we are here to fix this, and we will."

"Lennie, thank you so much. I am in total agreement. So, this is the only thing we will fix tonight and then we will make more progress tomorrow, when we will receive more help. The American contingent will be here midday!"

"So now we will attempt to get some action on this, Lennie. And also, for my Penny who is worried this will happen to her parents."

"Louis and Michel, we need you to work on this. I gave it some thought earlier. Please approach French Government Ministers responsible for Fishery and President Delacoix, if possible. We need tens, hundreds, thousands of French fishing boats blockading Southampton and Tilbury Docks. The French Government should inform the media that the fishermen are protesting at PRP's recent reduction in their fishing quotas."

"Louis, Michel, please get all this on the move today! We must ensure none of these cruise ships are allowed to set sail. They cannot let even one ship implement their insane evil intentions."

Anneliese's eyes turned to Commodore Englehardt. "Sir, would you mind helping with this part of the operation? I am certain Naval Intelligence could rapidly determine which cruise liners have been seized by PRP to act as DTD vessels, and scheduled times for departure!" The Commodore smiled. "Of course, Mam!"

Now Anneliese strolled across to the flip chart in the corner of the room. She dragged it around to face the assembled company. The first three bullet points summarised the elements of the plan they had just discussed. The fishing boat blockade, identification of the cruise ships and scheduled sailing times.

"I worked these three points through earlier. I needed to tackle the most urgent actions in relation to our crucial timeline. But now I'm going to offer you all an apology. I had said that after we settled on the plan for these, we would leave everything else until the American contingent arrives tomorrow."

"But there is another extremely critical feature. I was planning to talk with the US Director General of EAI tomorrow to agree the provision of his SBS troops, to be stationed on a Corvette moored in the Thames. But now, as the timeline has shortened, I realise two things. They probably would not be able to get here in time. The Americans may have a Corvette somewhere around European waters but I'm doubtful. However, we can get the SBS troops here in time if we fly them in. That just leaves us with needing to find a Corvette."

Anneliese, with appealing eyes, peered in the direction of the Commodore. "Jason.... Sorry, I should have asked. Do you mind if I call you Jason?" Smiling he also dumped formality. "No Anneliese, of course not." Taking a deep breath, he prepared to speak. But a mobile phone started to bleep. It was sitting on Penny's lap. It was Anneliese's. Penny arose and scuttled across to Anneliese.

Looking around the room, Anneliese remarked, "I have to take this." "Hello Junior, I've been trying to reach you.

Things have become very urgent. I am desperate for you to get your Special Boat Service lads on a plane to arrive here in the next 24 to 36 hours. They should fly into England, RAF Mildenhall. We can tie up all the loose ends tomorrow. Goodbye Darling!"

Commodore Englehardt began to chuckle. "Well Anneliese, that sounded a novel call.... So who the hell is Junior?" Anneliese's giggle, in a nanosecond, turned into a belly laugh. "Oh, I'm so sorry. I suppose it did seem very personal. And it was, because he means so much to me!" The Commodore's eyebrows raised, so now all the EAI team chuckled.

"Jason, don't' let your imagination run riot." Anneliese rounded on Frank. "Who is Junior, Frank?" "He's my Godson and ....your son!" The Commodore developed a knowing smile, "Yes, and I can see you are all very proud of him." Frank and Anneliese both nodded. "Yes" replied Anneliese, "and he's very important to this operation. He is Director General of EAI in the States." Frank couldn't resist his next sentence, "Yes, Sir, and for his sins he is named after me. He is known as Frank Junior."

The Commodore uttered, "Well, I think it's fabulous that you have managed to keep this secret work in the family, and I look forward to meeting Frank Junior tomorrow. We have all enjoyed the light relief Anneliese, but now I will attempt to answer your question. Yes, we have two Corvettes off Finland, on a reconnaissance mission to prevent the Russians attacking our pipelines and seabed cables. I will get one in position, in the Thames, and I think we should anchor it about two miles downriver from Parliament. Just one question Anneliese, how and why did you select a Corvette?"

Her smile broadened. "When I started on the flipchart, it came to me to do some homework. I had originally thought a frigate, but the internet informed me that the passage up or down the Thames, with the bridges, depth of water and the Thames Barrier would be very difficult for a vessel as large as a frigate, so I worked through the vessels that could be quick and agile."

The Commodore slowly stood and applauded. "My God Anneliese, you know your stuff. It's going to be an absolute pleasure to work with a lady of your knowledge and intellect!"

Anneliese, never easily embarrassed, just returned an enigmatic smile. Looking around the faces in the room, she said, "It's late, nearly 1.00am, so would you like to continue or wait for the morning. But before you answer, remember we need a meticulously crafted plan that is 100% successful to avoid death and destruction. And if we can get almost everything completed, it will be so much easier tomorrow with the American contingent. Don't think because their leader is my son it will be a pushover. He will want to be certain that our plans are totally and completely sound. Anybody here wish to retire?" Nobody spoke.

"Right now, then, I suggest we take a one hour break. The things we have agreed so far must get on the road. Louis and Michel, you have time now to contact France. Jason, Commodore Englehardt, your efforts are crucial. We need that Corvette in the Thames by Sunday night. And in the morning, I will clarify with Junior that the SBS troops are informed and will arrive in time to board the Corvette."

Csenge approached Anneliese as those with assignments left the room. Penny wasn't far behind. "Excuse me, Csenge, but I think everyone needs some coffee, sandwiches, sustenance and I've not done it before in this building." Csenge searched the room for Josef Kalfwarf. He was in the corner on the phone. "Penny, go see if Josef can help, because

I agree. If we are going to continue, we need something to keep us going."

Ten minutes later, three waitresses appeared carrying plates of food. Another lady arrived pushing a coffee trolley. The second and third shelves were adorned with a beautiful selection of pastries and cakes. Everything was placed on and by a table in the corner. Josef approached Anneliese and Csenge as they were deep in conversation. "Madame, does the buffet meet your needs?" "Oh Josef, yes fabulous. But please stay with us because there may be more important things, other than cuisine to deal with."

They reconvened at 2.15am. Anneliese had added all elements of the plan to the flip chart summary. Frank was now about to be brought back onto the field of play. Anneliese, her expression reflecting her deep thinking, asked Frank, "What other military personnel are with you? I've heard from the SAS, the Royal Navy and Lennie, but," and she smiled at them, "There are several more guys and one lady we haven't spoken with yet. Frank, would you introduce them?"

Frank eased himself out of his seat. Pointing along the line, Frank said, "These guys are all Royal Marines, except the lady at the end who is with the Metropolitan Police."

Anneliese sauntered across the room and stood directly in front of their group. "You look so young!" As she was about to continue, a blond-haired guy stood and saluted. "I am my troop's Captain. I am Adam, and we have been instructed to do whatever we can to help you on this mission."

"Thank you, Adam, but I've just thought of something. Can I come back to you in a few minutes?" Looking at her wristwatch, Anneliese said, "It's now 2.50am. I am going to halt this meeting at 3.30am. We need some sleep before we get to work with the Americans." Her eyes now singled out

Josef Kalkwarf. "Josef, would you organise some bedrooms or dormitories, hopefully with sufficient comfort for all our guests." Josef strode to the door, "I will do it immediately, Madame, and also arrange breakfast." Penny, as if Josef's shadow, followed as he exited.

Returning to Adam, Anneliese took a few seconds to gather her thoughts. Her cheeks bulged as she pressured her breath against her taught lips. Her wide-eyed gaze settled on Adam and the troopers. "You, the military, are absolutely key to success. And your involvement is going to be complex. Therefore, we will give it the highest priority tomorrow.... when Frank Junior and the Americans are here. So, if you don't mind, I will move to our colleague from the Met. Police."

"I suppose the first thing we would like to know is your name."

A very confident response underlined a level of authority. "Yes, sure, I am Deputy Assistant Commissioner Bright, and I report to the Counter-Terrorism Senior National Co-ordinator." She leaned back in her chair, and after a short intake of breath said, "I'm sorry, it's such a long label! Just to add, as well as National, we have an international role, which my bosses thought may prove important"

"Well, I have to say I like their thinking. But another question about your name tag. May we call you by your first name, and of course, please call me Anneliese."

Miss Bright clenched her teeth. "I knew that would be your next question. I always attempt to avoid this part." Anneliese's expression became quizzical. "Well, as I said, my surname is Bright".... Her voice hovered two or three seconds. A deep breath then, looking down, she continued. "My first name is Summer! And before you begin to laugh, my colleagues refer to me with a more laughable nickname.... Happy Daze!"

There were a few respectful smiles around the room, but Anneliese broke in. "Well Summer, you have managed to lift the spirits in this room, which I thank you for. It's a beautiful name, and appropriate for the operation we are on. Your name will motivate us to success. Once we defeat these lethalists, we can all enjoy the brightest summer ever. And so will the whole country! Now to some things to get your teeth into. I will scribble them up on the flip chart."

- A key member of EAI was arrested. He is Jerome Janowski, Director General of GCHQ. Where is he being held and on what charge?

- Another key member of EAI, Norman Simpson, was found dead on the Embankment. How did he die? Was it murder? What caused his death? Where is his body?

- Just prior to our incursion and coup in the Houses of Parliament, we need the Met Police Officers providing security around Parliament to be advised there will be a military security exercise. They must not, under any circumstances, impede the military personnel or get involved in any way. It must be emphasized to them that this exercise is classified as TOP SECRET!

At 3.30am, Josef and Penny escorted everyone to their sleeping quarters. Now on her own, Anneliese flipped to a clean page, ready for the morning. As she moved toward the door, she stopped, spun around and, with strong conviction in her stride, returned to the flip chart.

Gripping the felt tip, she, with an artistic flourish, wrote some big bold words at the top of the page. Taking two steps back, she read the words out loud. OPERATION – "AGE OF WISDOM".

Slowly, elegantly, but with a poignant expression, she slipped off to join Matthew for well-earned slumber.

Three hours later, as Anneliese and Matthew were almost ready to find breakfast, Josef rang, "Madame, hope I am not too early. When you are ready, just come to the ground floor reception and I will escort you to breakfast." Anneliese replied, "We'll be down in a few minutes. Thank you, Josef. I'm ravenous!"

They were the first. By 7.30am all had arrived and were enjoying a sumptuous buffet selection, both hot and cold. Anneliese sipped her dark roast coffee, Commodore Englehardt stood behind her and leaned down to speak. "Anneliese, good morning." Surprised, she turned and their eyes met. "Jason, morning." The Commodore lowered further. "The Corvette will shortly be on its way. The captain is one of my best. Hearing he would be supporting SBS troops from the USA he will be well prepared for them. He has stored 3 RIBs on the Corvette."

Anneliese turned another 20 degrees. Her eyes tightened almost to a squint. "Jason, what is a RIB? Are you talking food stores or what?" "No Anneliese!" Matthew now leaned to listen in. "My dear Anneliese, I should have given you more information." The Commodore straightened and smiled at Matthew. Bending down again, Jason said, "My Captain knows the work of these American special service guys. They operate very swiftly. And most of their operations are conducted in fast inflatable boats. A RIB is a Rigid hull Inflatable Boat. This piece of equipment is their business card, their signature tune."

Anneliese, wide-eyed, stared into the Commodore's eyes. "Jason, that's fabulous, amazing! You are lucky to have self-starters like your Captain, thinking for themselves. Please give him my thanks, and say I hope we meet after we conclude this."

Chapter 31

Operation "Age of Wisdom"

Half an hour later they all began to settle in the conference room. Anneliese stepped in front of the flip-chart. "Please everyone, burn this name into your memories. This operation will be called…. "AGE OF WISDOM" As leader of this operation, I have chosen the name without consultation with anyone. Do any of you have any issues?"

Matthew stood. "No, I don't have an issue, but think it would be good to explain your thinking." Anneliese nodded. "I'm not sure I have much I can explain. It is more a feeling. Every one of us have elderly people in our families. And with every day that passes, we are all getting older. But now think about the most important things you have learned, and who was your teacher. It was your mother, father, grandmother, grandfather or even a close uncle or aunt. As people get older, they gain experience and their wisdom grows."

"We cannot, and we will not, lose our elderly people. They are the ones that have helped bring us up, and imparted their wisdom to us. It's much the same with our disabled brothers, sisters, cousins and our sons and daughters. We love them! They are part of us and our families. They should never, in a civilised world, be a target to just save money!"

"Is that enough of an explanation for you all. Once this is all over, we will celebrate elderly people, the disabled and people suffering mental health issues. They are our families. Not Governments. Not Companies. Us; the people of a glorious God-given world!"

Anneliese took a breath and strolled to the coffee pot. The room was quiet, overcome by the words she had spoken. But today, she was unstoppable. She lurched back, coffee in hand, to the flip-chart.

"Adam, I'm so sorry, this is the second time I have relegated our planned discussion. But I won't take more than a few minutes."

"Josef Kalkwarf, you are my next target!" Josef approached. Anneliese walked across to meet him. Her arm outstretched, she gave Josef his second introduction. "Josef made us all comfortable in the night and laid on a fantastic breakfast." Josef nodded to everyone. Anneliese turned to face him. "But now Josef, I need more, much more! I dreamt about this in the night." Josef's face developed a questioning gaze. "Josef, this was my work brain preventing deep sleep. I believe we need physical, as well as moral support from Europe. I want to ask you to talk with your government. I am requesting that the Netherlands provide a detachment of KCT to take part in this operation." Anneliese peered at Frank and Matthew. "What do you two think?"

Matthew spoke first. "Anneliese, that's a great idea. Every corner of the globe would perceive this as the Western World, as a whole, agreeing to indict the PRP. It would give credence to the charges the PRP will face for their atrocious, wicked acts."

"We only have a couple of hours before my son and Rashi arrive. So, I would like to return to the question of military involvement. That should give us an almost complete outline plan to review with the Americans."

"Captain Adam of the Royal Marines. We never got your surname." Adam stood and gave a mini-salute. "Anneliese, I'm sorry, we are taught from the beginning not to bandy our surnames about. I am Adam Lister. My team rank from Lieutenant Sebastian, through 2nd Lieutenant Arthur, and my two very experienced sergeants, Bruce and Nicholas."

Anneliese returned a cute female salute to all of them. Just then, Summer Bright's phone rang. With a strained expression, she apologised saying she needed to take the call. As Summer left the room, Anneliese now beamed a smile at the Marines. "I'm going to use the flip chart! I will begin by listing the different military brigades." First on the list were the American Special Boat Service. Next were the SAS. Frank, for a giggle, now made it competitive. He screamed out, "No Anneliese, SAS must be at the top of any military list." Laughter, boos and cheers caused a growth of infectious laughter throughout the room.

Anneliese, enjoying the moment continued. "I am assuming we will gain acceptance from the Dutch to deploy a KCT detachment in this operation."

The Royal Marine 2nd Lieutenant, Arthur, raised his hand, then stood. "Anneliese Mam, this question will probably indicate stupidity. If so, I am willing to accept that I am." Captain Lister spoke before Arthur could continue. "No Arthur, we all wanted to ask that question. We've never worked with the Dutch before, so it's an important point! So who are KCT?"

Strolling back and forth in front of the Marines, both Anneliese's hands grasped her shining locks and her fingers brushed strands off her face.

Emotional nostalgia was about to invade her thoughts. "Do you know, Adam, and the rest of you brave Marines."

She stopped to swivel, to search all the faces. "Do you know, I lived most of my early life in Holland. Then my career in Counter Espionage and Criminal Deterrent, or the acronym CECD began. And guess where the first couple of years took me. Holland, predominantly Amsterdam! It was only then that I became associated with the work of KCT."

"In Holland, they are known as Korps Commande Troepen. They are an elite Commando Troop. When not on assignment, they spend every hour training, both physically and mentally. They are superb. And I have worked with them several times. Hopefully, Josef will confirm, in the next few hours, that KCT will join our operation."

"Time is getting short so I want us to move on. The next team to note is the EAI team. But before I list them, I'm sure we all appreciate we have the Royal Navy as support. They will not be in the attack formation, but they are essential to the SBS, and depending on how things work out, may need to attack from the River."

"Ok, so now to EAI." Now came an immediate question from Major Fite of the SAS. "Anneliese Mam, so far you have listed and talked about trained and experienced military personnel. Does that really apply to EAI?"

Anneliese's chuckle was full of sarcasm. "You are sitting with Frank. Do you know of his career history, especially with the SAS?" "Yes Mam. But that's Frank!"

"Yes, that's Frank. And he will be with you in the thick of it. Then there is Csenge. She's spent the last few years fighting the Russians out in Eastern Europe, mostly in Ukraine. Her undercover work has been astounding. Then we have my son, Frank Junior. I know he will want to be with you." She stared at Major Fite. "That scares me shitless! I won't be able to stop him. He spent years in Pakistan and Afghanistan fighting the

Taliban, ISIS, the Mujahideen. These people's credentials are solid. So please, Major Fite, embrace them. They are only a few, but they are worth an army. And if I know my son, he will be bringing more with him!"

Chapter 32

Summer Brings Answers

Major Fite smiled at Anneliese and nodded complete acceptance. Just then, the door opened, and a smiling, proud looking Summer Bright took her seat. Anneliese's perceptive instinct surfaced. "Summer, the sparkle in your eyes tells me you have some news."

"Yes Mam, I have answers to all your questions. I will take them in no particular order. Senior Met officers will communicate with all Met security officers assigned to the Parliamentary Force. Both around and inside the building. In turn, they will alert Parliamentary workers, employed on elements such as visitor supervision, hospitality and maintenance. Our Seniors propose this should occur no sooner than 10 minutes before the incursion. Furthermore, they request that you concur with me and five of my counter terrorism specialists being deployed among the usual Met Security police."

Anneliese's lips became taught as she gave it thought. "Summer, of course, I know you will be an asset to our team." Her lips now widened into a smile.

Summer Bright returned the smile, then continued. "I am now going to refer to Mr Janowski. For the time being he has been placed in Wandsworth Prison. I say for the time being because the informed word on the street is that he will be moved on Monday, to the Tower of London. Prime Minister Tibbs is, apparently, wanting to make an example of him. He is accused of treason and will probably be subjected to false and corrupt evidence. That last statement was prevalent among GCHQ Intelligence Analysts. They believe Tibbs and the PRP are intent on a 'Show Trial', that depicts Mr Janowski as a traitor, to be compared with the worst in the countries' history."

Anneliese inhaled deeply as she controlled her anger. Pacing into the middle of the room, with a daunting expression, her eyes moved slowly to each individual. "This operation will commence on Monday, and will include the rescue of Jerome Janowski. It will also be the day where Premier Tibbs is incarcerated in the Tower of London. It is a date that, just as Eleven Eleven is celebrated, will be an exalted day of freedom. Monday is 10th October. Ten/Ten will be remembered forever!"

A knock on the door and Josef entered. "Sorry if I am interrupting." He stood with his back leaning on the door to keep it open. "Lunch is served!" Three ladies pushing trollies, laden with mouth-watering dishes, entered then left. Josef stepped in front of the glorious array of tempting dishes. "One thing more. Our Parliament have granted involvement of a KCT platoon in the operation. They have also agreed to commit any further military resources you may require!"

Anneliese, jumped out of her chair. "Thank you so much. That means so much to all of us, and the whole of the UK." Josef, a little embarrassed said, "Ladies and gentlemen, please enjoy the lunch!"

Bodies began scurrying around the trollies, Anneliese, Csenge and Matthew moved close together, taking a few minutes to relax. But not for long! Another knock on the door, and as it partially opened, Frank pulled it wide. A slow nonchalant entrance by Frank Junior was met by his namesake, Frank. Manly hugs were only allowed to last a few seconds. Csenge was out of her seat, faster than a greyhound in the greyhound Derby.

Initially Csenge's embrace was emotionally passionate. As she realised all eyes were on them, she eased into a reserved embrace. Sensing Anneliese behind her, she stepped back, and the loving emotion burst through again.

Anneliese whispered in Junior's ear. "Frank, I need every ounce of you with me on this. Thank you for getting here so quickly." But as she whispered, she noticed the long queue behind Junior. Stepping back, they all began to enter.

The first behind Frank Junior was Denton. As he clasped Anneliese, more bodies edged in. First it was Asha and Kainaat. Csenge couldn't believe her eyes. A triangular format of emotion took charge. Behind them Amos, Donald and Hana. Hugs, backslaps, some kisses, chuckles and giggles. But that was not the end. The cast continued! Ece sauntered in and stood by Denton, grasping his reduced waistline!

Calm and collected, the rest of the American contingent strolled in. Enrique, Ben and Adam, went around the room, shaking hands and introducing themselves.

Rashi arrived a few minutes later, squeezing in beside Sly. Break time lasted another ten minutes. Anneliese, with an assertive tone, called everyone to order. "It may seem as if we have plenty of time, but we don't! All of Sunday will be taken up with final preparations and, several hours briefing the SBS unit. So we should kick on and let summer Bright of the Metropolitan Police continue her report."

Summer referred immediately to the question concerning the death of Norman Simpson. Rashi's arm wrapped around Sly's shoulders. His expression hardened as Summer began to give answers.

"Mr Simpson died from respiratory restrictions and subsequent cardiac arrest. These occurred about ten minutes after he had left the House of Commons. The causal factor was a nerve agent, Novichok, which had been applied to his personal umbrella. It had been raining all morning, and the moment he grasped the handle, Novichok began to take effect. Depending on the victim's health, an amount as tiny as one-sixth of a grain of salt can be lethal. For several years, Novichok has been the signature of Russian bio-aggression. This information was established and verified by the Defence, Science and Technology laboratory at Porton Down."

Summer Bright slowly looked up from her papers. Sly, his eyes welling up, shrieked! But then drew breath to calm himself. His anger eased and his voice softened. "Norman was my best friend for years. Ever since we joined the service. He was kind, understanding and did his best with everything. He was incredible, my best mate, and I know I will never find anyone to replace him. But I know, and you know, these sadistic cruel bastards, working with the Russians, ended his life. I will take my revenge for him. But, like all our EAI assignments, I will do it in a planned, controlled and team-executed way!"

Sly's voice began to crackle again as he stood and nodded at Summer Bright. "Thank you Mam. Thank you for your hard work. You have given me and all of us an understanding of what happened!"

Anneliese said, "Thank you, Sly." She moved back to the flip chart. "I am going to spend a few moments listing the EAI resources we now have. Whilst I do this, please take the chance to grab a coffee or tea!"

As everyone sat, grasping their drinks, Anneliese, perusing her previous pages, eyeballed first Frank and then

Junior. "This gets complicated from here, so please keep an eye on me and let me know if I get it wrong or you disagree."

"Our priority is logistics. The timeline! The where and when! Tomorrow is the easiest. We will go over the plan time and again. Sunday is more complex. My thinking is that the Corvette, with SBS troops aboard should, by midnight, be anchored just prior to Tower Bridge." The room silenced as everyone gave this thought.

Junior, with a strong voice, said "No Mum, I disagree. Sorry I mean Anneliese! All the French fishing vessels will be blocking their way up the Thames from Tilbury. Why not warn the French the Corvette will anchor amongst them, and they should let the RIBs through during the morning. Anneliese, what time do the SBS need to be at the Houses of Parliament?"

Chapter 33

Coup – 2.50pm

Anneliese's answer was fast and assured. "I think our incursion should occur at 2.50pm. After question time has begun."

Frank Junior turned to Frank. "What time do you think they need to get from Tilbury?" Frank, without delay, answered, "About 30 minutes."

Frank Junior smiled, and leaned back as his mind walked up the steps. "Ok, so they should leave Tilbury at 2.20pm." Denton, the thinking Walrus, put his oar in the water. "Junior, give them ten minutes breathing space. They can always adjust their speed up the Thames!" Anneliese peered at Junior. "Are we all agreed?" Everybody nodded. Anneliese, now in an excited mode, continued. "So, the SBS will arrive at the Parliament Building, then enter from the Thames, climbing the walls into the Pavilion Terrace. That is on the lower ground floor; then up the stairs and straight through into the Commons Chamber."

Anneliese's eyes tracked to meet Junior's "Your observation and thinking will provide camouflage for the Corvette; keeping it down river until the last minute will help with secrecy. I would suggest the Corvette arrives at Tilbury around midday. So do we have agreement on the SBS plan?" After a few seconds, everyone was nodding.

"Next on the list is the frontal attack from Parliament Square. My vision for this is that it will involve the SAS and the 47 Commando Raiders Platoon. Their convoy will travel from East London, along the Embankment, turning into Parliament Square. Using their vehicles, they should then blockade the Square to prevent traffic entering or leaving. Summer; the Met Police should help with this part of the exercise." Summer Bright's head bowed as she scribbled a note on her pad.

"Now it's time to put some stakes in the ground. The reason I said the convoy would travel from East London is this. Saturday, after dark, all you military people should head to the muster point. I am proposing the secret and secure GCHQ satellite in East India Dock at Blackwall. I believe this is far enough away from the target to avoid raising suspicion. And there is plenty of room to bivouac your troops"

Peering around, Anneliese's first comment was to the Commodore. "I assume, Commodore, you will wish to make your way to the Admiralty to review the plans with your Royal Navy Hierarchy and the Corvette's Captain!" "Yes, you are correct, Anneliese. Thank you!"

Summer Bright was next to be singled out. "Summer, my thinking is exactly the same for you. I expect you will head to Scotland Yard to brief your seniors. Just one thing. Please do your very best to keep this Operation watertight. Only inform Senior Ranks that 'need to know' and that you believe are completely trustworthy."

"I will continue with the detailed plans for Operation 'AGE OF WISDOM'. But before I do, are there any questions or observations?" One hand went up. "Yes, Junior, go ahead." The smile from his eyes was captivating. "Anneliese, so far you are destined to win the puck at the end of this ice-hockey game! Although this operation is like skating on thin ice, your leadership is incredible!" Frank and Sly loudly shouted 'here, here'.

Striding across the room, Anneliese stood directly in front of Captain Adam Lister. "Adam, in my mind the assignment for the Royal Marines is the most complex. There are four cruise ships sitting in Southampton Docks. Probably, by now they are full of terrified Senior Citizens waiting to meet their maker. Those ships are not going anywhere due to the efforts of the French Fishermen. But the timescale to prevent them being taken into open water is severely limited. And they must not be allowed to suffer that mental torture longer than necessary. I visualise your troops boarding those ships on Monday to mount a rescue. It must be simultaneous with the coup at Parliament. They are guarded by migrants; forced by the PRP to do that wicked job. So there may be some resistance, but I am hoping it will be minimal. I am asking you to be their saviour. They will need transport, and every ounce of tender loving care from your Marines. Medical support also is essential."

"But the question is this, Adam. I had assumed that your troops would wish to be part of the main military contingent in Blackwall. However, there is an alternative. You and your people could operate out of your HQ in Taunton. It's not too far away from Southampton, and you may wish to return there to select troopers that are best qualified for this type of assignment. Either way, the journey to Southampton will require helicopter transport for a significant number of Marines, I think you need 100+. Blackwall can accommodate these troops and choppers. I assume your HQ at Taunton could also."

"So, Adam, it's your choice." Frank interjected as Adam took a deep breath. "Adam, for my money Taunton has to be the correct option. It gives you the chance to apply a selection perspective, rather than just requesting 100 troops to be transported to Blackwall!"

Adam's eyes met Frank's. "Thank you Sir, on balance, I agree. So I am opting for Taunton!" Anneliese uttered, "Thank you, Adam, and you also, Frank. I think you have made the right choice. This part of the assignment deserves special care and attention!"

"Now we have to consider the second area of relief and rescue for our beloved Senior Citizens. Tilbury! There are three cruise ships docked in Tilbury, that, like Southampton, are by now, full of the UK's most valuable citizens. Josef, I need you and your Dutch troops to do the same job that we have just discussed with Adam. One critical thing; because they will be dealing with elderly citizens, it would be a great help if your troops, or at least most of them, had good English skills."

"I guess you will fly them in to Tilbury by helicopter. There are many green field areas around, but we can discuss that and be selective. Josef, are you ok with what needs to happen?" Josef nodded. Then proudly stood and answered. "Yes, Madame Anneliese. It will be a proud moment for Holland to help the UK!"

Just as Anneliese was preparing to continue, a knock on the door was followed by the refreshments trolley. Within ten minutes, everyone had drinks and pastries and the room prepared to begin again.

The first words came from Penny. "Anneliese, I have contacted Blackwall. They think they can accommodate everything you throw at them. And if not they can overspill into Millwall Docks. It has also been left vacant, but has private properties, mainly high rise flats overlooking it. But the area is excellent for landing helicopters!"

"Thank you, Penny. Thanks for checking it out." Anneliese swivelled, then with delight in her eyes, she approached Summer Bright. "Summer, you and your team are so important to this operation. You have heard the complexity of it in terms of saving the lives of thousands of our elderly people. Those murdering sites at Southampton and Tilbury may need your support. Once again, I want to ask you to be ready to provide backup to the Marines and the Dutch. I know you will get that organised. But the other part of the equation that we must not forget is the elderly citizens, all over the country, that may sincerely wish to join their maker. The issue is that the PRP have been putting the frighteners on elderly people to get them to voluntarily join the queues at the various ex-army camps."

"Summer, I need you to help me to put a stop to this, until we have a code of practice in place that is sincere in seeking out their truthful beliefs and wishes. And, that has professionals providing a check and balance on the whole thing for every individual."

⚜

Chapter 34

Assisted Dying Will End

"Summer, the bottom line is that from midday, Monday, the assisted dying process must come to an end. Police must access every establishment and put an end to it, until it has the full support of the House of Commons!"

Summer Bright screwed up her cheeks. "My God, Anneliese, that's an enormous assignment!" Sweeping her dark brunette locks from her face, she started to place her face in her hands; but stopped and looked up!

"Yes, yes, Anneliese, it's wrong. We will stop it. I will do it!" She slowly calmed. "I will find all those sites and get them closed down."

"I will plan and prepare my staff. I will network with Chief Constables in every region. Police officers, with some riot police back-up, will get into position on Monday, and arrive at the various sites at 2.30pm."

"That's a great plan, Summer. But don't forget these are our elderly, and most valued citizens. Some may have severe health conditions. So you will also need medics and the Ambulance Services in support."

"Anneliese, you can be assured I will make this happen. It will go like clockwork! Anneliese, may I take my leave for an hour or two to get this underway?" Anneliese gave a grateful smile! "But, Summer, when you return we must plan the rescue of Jerome Janowski."

Anneliese sat and relaxed for a few minutes. Junior strode round the table and leaned on the back of her chair. "Are you ok, Mum?" "Yes. Of course dear. This business keeps me alive and kicking!" Junior bent and whispered in Anneliese's ear. "Mum, you are looking tired. Don't overdo it, would you like me to take over?" A wry grin stormed across Anneliese's gorgeous lips." Junior, yes, of course, one day, but not yet! I must see this through to the end!" Her eyes flicked adoration into Junior's as she grasped and gently massaged his forearm. He leaned over and softly kissed her forehead. Her eyes followed his path back to his seat, between Rashi and Csenge. Anneliese studied Csenge as she moved her chair closer to Junior, and watched intently as she whispered in his ear. "I need you to show me love and affection like that!" Anneliese lip-read every word!

Josef Kalkwarf walked in the room just as Anneliese was going to bring everyone back to business. Anneliese asked, "Josef, what time should we be ready for dinner?" "Madame Anneliese, you can carry on for another hour. Food will be on the table at 7.30pm. And Madame, I need to take up some of that hour. I have met with my superiors and they have asked me to talk with you about transporting the KCT Platoon to Tilbury. My masters, for many and varied reasons, would prefer them to travel in a Netherlands Navy Corvette. They think a second Corvette would add strength to the assault from the Thames, if it is required. The KCT platoon would leave the Hook of Holland midnight Sunday. That gives the Officers time for in-depth selection, planning and training. They would arrive in Tilbury between 10 and 11am on Monday. They would anchor behind the fishing fleet, which would make them less obtrusive! However, my superiors believe the key advantage involves the cruise ships. If any of them decide to barge through the fishermen, they will be ready to intercept. They would not attempt to ram a Corvette!"

Anneliese arose and turned toward the window. She stood looking across the Plein. Beautiful gardens and historic buildings, statues commemorating hundreds of years of Dutch history. She slowly reversed, trying not to show her face. Reaching into her handbag, she once again turned away, dabbing her eyes with some tissues found there.

Facing them, she inhaled an enormous breath. With glistening eyes, her courage overcame her emotion. "Josef, all of you. Every one of you. I've never ever worked with a team that have put so much clever thought and ingenuity into an operation. And I have worked with many. So you have my love and my thanks. Josef, that proposition is one I cannot refuse. So please, thank your superiors, your Government and, indeed, the people of the Netherlands."

The door opened; it was Summer Bright. "Anneliese, everything is arranged. I am totally confident we will succeed!" Now Josef alerted everyone. "Dinner is ready, and I am certain you will enjoy our chef's specialities."

Surprisingly, the chef was Greek, so the dinner began with many hors-d'oevres, mainly dips, but with a favourite, prawn saganaki. The main course comprised souviaki, and gyros, followed by baklavan sweet treats. The dinner complete, they all returned, with full bellies, to the conference room, wondering how they would stay awake!

As always, Anneliese was unstoppable. She immediately engaged Summer Bright. "I now want us to tackle the incarceration of Jerome Janowski."

"I remember, you advised that Jerome was being held in Wandsworth Prison, but would be transferred, on Monday, to the Tower of London. It will be a story that Jerome will thrive on at dinner parties, for the rest of his life."

Although attempting to appear jocular, Anneliese's eyes had visiting teardrops. Her voice crackled as she moved to stand in front of Captain Lister. "Adam, your participation in his rescue is absolutely essential! Whatever the final plan, you and your Marines must locate Jerome and get him out of that cell. EAI operatives will be there to assist."

"My guess is that Jerome will be shifted, early morning, to the Tower. Probably, before they would experience the quagmire of work traffic congestion. They will, no doubt, have a noticeably strong security presence, police cars front and rear. The PRP will want to make a show of the transfer to the Tower, and will have alerted the TV stations to film and record in time for the 8am news!"

"I can imagine the blood curdling things the TV presenters will have been prepared with; to put out over the airways to the nation. This man, Jerome Janowski, sitting at the head of our own countries' Secret Service, is charged with treason. His family, after WWII, were welcomed into this country as displaced immigrants. The accused is said by the PRP to have, with Russia, been planning and orchestrating the existential overthrow of your Government, the PRP!"

Anneliese, her anger building, squinted and gritted her teeth. "Summer and Adam. We must decide how we can rescue this innocent, paramount pinnacle of this country's security. I will sincerely tell you, here and now, that I would give my life for Jerome. In fact, I know him so well, I know he would be the first to give his life for everyone in this room, and his country."

The silence was deafening. The passion in Anneliese's words struck the hearts of everyone in the room! Frank Junior, then Frank stood. Everyone followed. Applause started slowly, then reached a crescendo.

With a quiver in his vocal chords, Captain Lister spoke. "Anneliese, I think we should be patient. It's too dangerous to the public to attempt an interception as they travel through London. My vote goes to waiting until they arrive at the Tower."

Anneliese's eyes moved first to Summer then back to Adam. "I am in total agreement with you. And from what I see in Summer's face, I believe she agrees also!"

Summer nodded, then pushed further on. "Anneliese and Adam. The Tower is not an easy place to access. The prison van will arrive at the entrance. No doubt, visitors will be mingling around. The place will be saturated with media, photographers, cameras and so forth. The barrier will be lifted and the van allowed in. That, I think, is the time to rescue Jerome. The Tower wardens will be inside the barrier, ready to accept the prisoner and assist the security guards."

Anneliese's eyes shuttled back and forth, between Frank Junior and Rashi. "Do you both agree with Summer?" Rashi's lips tightened. "Well no, I believe it leaves us with an issue." Junior had been pondering the alternatives. Now, immediately Rashi finished speaking, he jumped in, feet first! "It creates a massive issue!"

All the assembled company peered at Junior, waiting for his explanation. Junior stood and paced into the middle of the room. His hand moved up to his forehead; his eyes closed as he massaged his brow. "It's like this, you guys! It's pretty simple really. If we, early morning, initiate a military style rescue, with the whole country watching on TV and commentators describing the whole episode, it may turn out to be like a red rag to a bull. The PRP will become suspicious about what may follow, and pull the shutters down."

"We definitely can't afford that. Our coup is not scheduled to happen until after 2.50 in the afternoon. It will be as if we have given them notice that something monumental will occur. We cannot give the PRP that much time to build a defence! And, don't forget, we can't change the time because we need the full Government in the Chamber. That can only be guaranteed in question time…. After 2.50pm."

Anneliese, coffee in hand, sauntered out to join Junior in the centre of the room. Her right arm reached across Junior's shoulders. Now almost on tiptoe, her eyes scanned around every person in the room. "Thank you, Summer and you, Rashi. I think we are close to a final plan." Her lips moved close to Junior's ear. She whispered, but loud enough for everyone to hear. "Frank, if this all works out, you are definitely, absolutely, the one!"

Rashi, now acknowledging they were all on the front foot, asked, "Anneliese, may I inject some more thoughts. I have to be honest, Junior and I have discussed the possible plan for Jerome. I know Junior has immense feelings and respect for Jerome, which go back to his days as a toddler. So I want to be his mouthpiece on this. I am not anywhere near as attached, so I can help plan this without emotion getting in the way!"

"Of course, Rashi, go ahead." Anneliese and Junior both stepped back to their seats. "Our ideas go something like this. The SBS will, at 2.50pm lead the charge into Parliament. We will have two Corvettes sitting at Tilbury. The one provided by Holland will commence the rescue of the elderly. The other Corvette, could speed up to Parliament. If the incursion has been successful, Prime Minister Tibbs and the PRP would have been ousted and arrested. The SBS troops could get him onto the Corvette. At an agreed time, the SBS troops could take Tibbs, in a RIB, to the Tower. The remaining SBS troops could, if necessary, follow in the other two RIBs. I know there are many details to be worked on with this but the SBS could enter the Tower, rescue Jerome and place Tibbs in the Tower prison. I know that's a lot to take in, but, assuming the coup is successful, I don't think there would be any resistance anywhere!"

Anneliese stood. "I need to go to powder my nose. That proposal is outstanding. It's so good I'm almost wetting myself! Rashi, you have painted a picture that I must see before me, at end of day tomorrow. In the meantime, shall we all meet in the bar for a very well earned drink! Then, we should re-convene to agree the details, and finalise the most important plan of our lives!"

Chapter 35

Coup Detail

An hour or so later, they dug deep into the detail. Three RIBs would transport a total of 45 SBS troopers up the Thames to the Parliament Buildings. Fifteen fully laden troopers in each RIB! Their attack would begin at precisely 2.50pm. Their incursion into the House of Commons Chamber would be consolidated with a frontal attack by the SAS. The SBS would arrest Premier Tibbs and evacuate him to a RIB which would then power across the Thames to the anchored Corvette. The other two RIBs would depart to the Tower to lay the groundwork for the arrival of Tibbs. The Corvette would remain at anchor opposite until it was safe to take him to the Tower in the third RIB.

In the meantime the SAS, Met Police and EAI Agents would arrest and detain all PRP Cabinet members. The Met Police would have the same instructions regarding all remaining PRP MPs and Party Members. Their destination would be West End Central Police Station, to be charged.

"One question. How will our EAI Agents get secret access into Parliament?" Anneliese peered around the room, waiting for an answer. She didn't wait more than three seconds. Rashi said, "I think I have the solution, Anneliese. I have used one of my AI perfect imaging and replicating programmes to prepare visitor security passes for all of us. We are all depicted as a group of visiting tourists. The facial recognition programme is perfection itself, and will be accepted by the security camera check. Each and every security pass photo will contain a strong disguise. I have arranged for an expert Movie Company disguise team to help with this, midday tomorrow. We can't afford all our faces to be clear and distinguishable on TV. Our future work would be shot to pieces!"

Anneliese looked across the room at the smiling face of Frank Junior. "She is pretty good, isn't she?" Rashi ignored the compliment and added, "This programme is counterfeiting perfection." "Anneliese, with these security passes, our EAI Agents will be able to access the building, even the Visitor's Gallery. Historically, it's known as the Strangers Gallery. We must remain strangers! That is why I have arranged for disguises!"

They now were allowed a short break for dinner. But after a while, Anneliese urged them to finish, and get back to work.

"Ok, let's get going again. This is starting to look like a meticulous, cohesive plan! I think the next thing I should do is list the EAI team on the flip chart and plan their roles. I am going to apologise to Major Fite, and the rest of you military guys." Questioning frowns appeared on all their faces!

Anneliese, noticing this, began to smile. "I told you guys there wouldn't be more than a few EAI operatives invading your military space during this operation. But I did warn that Frank Junior's arrival may add to the numbers. Well it has, and quite substantially. I believe we have the equivalent of a platoon." As she was speaking, she was listing their names on the flip chart. "Yes, I believe EAI will comprise 16 personnel!"

Next came sarcasm! With a wry smile she added, "It's not as disastrous as it sounds!" Major Fite stood. "Anneliese, I wasn't...." Anneliese interrupted! "Major, I know! I believe the American expression is, I was pulling your Dick!" Laughter exploded all around! A wide-eyed Anneliese wondered why the use of an expression she didn't quite understand, had attracted such a reaction.

In her French influenced Dutch accent, she ploughed on. "This is how I see our EAI team being organised. I, with my Intelligence team, will be stationed at Blackwall. We will watch the banks of screens, with constant AI picture-feed and commentary, on both inside and outside the Commons. That team will be Denton, and Rashi; supported by Penny. And, of course, myself!"

"The Strangers Gallery team will be led by Csenge. I have written the rest of her team on the flip chart, for you all to see. I will now move onto the tactical on-the-spot supervision. That will be led by Frank, working with Matthew and Amos." They all looked at one another and gave genuine smiles of appreciation.

"If EAI is required to support the military in combat, these are the people I have selected. They should play the part of tourists, visiting the Houses of Parliament. They will be armed and stay around the entrance pretending to admire the architecture, statues and generally watching proceedings as they develop. As they will be armed, they must not attempt entrance through security, into the building. This team will include Frank Junior, Kainaat, Asha, Hana, Ece and Sly."

Frank Junior quickly moved around the table to Anneliese. Before he reached her, Anneliese spoke again. "Those of you outside the building must maintain contact with everyone, including my team at Blackwall. Rashi will ensure you are provided with the most up-to-date sophisticated communication devices. Please don't lose contact. It could cost lives!"

Anneliese strutted into the middle once again. With the figure of a 25 year old, all the men's eyes followed her every movement. "Ok, so now I am prepared to listen to you! Have I got anything wrong? Does anyone wish to move teams?"

Frank Junior had been left standing behind her chair. He stepped out and approached Anneliese. Her heart strings tugged to widen her smile.

Putting his arm around her shoulders, his eyes moved around every person. "I am not too proud to say this, but Anneliese, my Mum, must have fought, long and hard, with an emotionally difficult decision. None of us want our loved ones to be put in jeopardy. To be put in the firing line! However, her decision and planning today has proved to me that her love for the world, this country, and all democracies has surmounted her affection and love for me. This is an assignment that is clearly in her vision, Afghanistan was not! She just hoped and prayed I would be alright."

Frank Junior grasped Anneliese's cheeks and gently kissed her. "Mum, I thank you in front of everyone. I am not embarrassed to talk like this in front of everyone! I am proud of you, and want them all to see the fabulous, brave, superb person that brought me into this world."

Junior, once again, held her face and stared lovingly into her eyes. She placed her hand over his lips. "Thank you darling, but please indulge me. We have lots to get through. So let's get back to the planning for Monday."

Junior grinned, recognising Anneliese's embarrassment and need to step back into her favourite world of intrigue.

"Today, we together, have constructed a very strong plan. Tomorrow, we will revisit it, time and time again! By tomorrow evening, you will all probably see me as your worst enemy. But that is when you will all escape to your bolt-holes to plan and prepare for Monday."

"I will also escape down to Blackwall with my team. And even then, you won't escape me. I will be with every one of you throughout this operation. Sometimes, it will seem I am your best friend and ally. If you don't do your jobs and allow things to go wrong, I will be your worst enemy. But now I have spent time with each and every one of you, I know, I am totally confident, that this negative aspect will never happen!"

Chapter 36

Disguises and French Fishing Fleet

Saturday was spent reviewing the whole plan, several times. Roles, responsibilities, timelines and equipment. Anneliese invested a lengthy period in training regarding everyone's knowledge of their colleagues' roles and whereabouts, and also Rashi's communication devices.

Early afternoon, the Movie Company make-up artists and disguise experts worked on all of them, three at a time! They were trained to apply the cosmetics and disguises. But they would not be left to their own devices. Two of their staff would appear early Monday morning to provide support.

This aspect of the planning finished around 6pm. Lots of banter and laughter regarding the photographs that had been taken. The military, naval and police personnel were now heading off to their respective locations.

Everyone, as they were leaving, made it a priority to thank Josef Kalkwarf. Summer Bright had found the whole experience exhilarating. It had been intensified by a strong attraction to Josef. He had helped her throughout, because he felt the same! As they embraced, she whispered, "Josef, I would love to meet with you once this is all over." "Summer, I would love that!" He passed her a card with his phone number. She giggled as she gave him hers. As she began to ease away, Josef's eyes were twinkling. He did not want to let go of her hand. "Summer, I must see you again soon!" He let go and she slowly edged toward the door, glancing a wishful smile over her shoulder.

The whole EAI team had breakfast together. They were now feeling relaxed as Josef switched the television on to the Sunday morning breakfast news. The report began with coverage of the French fishing fleet embargo. Initially, the article focused on the reasons. The reduction in fishing quotas imposed by the PRP Government! The numbers of fishing vessels was growing all the time. Tilbury was suffering the worst, but the embargo around Southampton was growing by the minute.

The EAI team watched with intense interest. Next came interviews with two ministers. The first, the Minister for Agriculture and Fisheries. His attitude, like the rest of the PRP was aggressive. "I am working with the Navy to arrange to shift these French floating match boxes!" The report moved on to the Minister for Trade and Industry. He did not pull any punches, and his language surpassed the worst in TV's archives. "If these French bastards don't move soon, we will send hundreds of drones to fucking blast them out of the water. And if that doesn't work, I am sure Premier Tibbs will announce that we, Great Britain, are at war with France. Those frogs will stand no chance, and maybe we will invade them and take France for ourselves! Our land army is now massive. The immigrants will fight for us and we have close to half a million of them."

Chapter 37

Josef's Romance

Josef Kalkwarf had been buzzing around the breakfast room, checking everyone was completely satisfied. With a delighted, whimsical expression, but with his thoughts elsewhere, he bumped into Frank, ricocheted off and fell sideways into the chair next to Anneliese. Blurting out an apology to Frank, he swivelled to Anneliese and was just about to apologise to her. But Frank spoke first. "Josef, you look like the cat that got the cream! Or is it that you know we will be going soon." "No, no, not at all Frank, indeed we will miss you all." Frank nodded politely, and went on his way.

Anneliese reached for Josef's hand, then knowingly peered into his eyes. "I have seen that look many times before. It's the look of the plant that's growing in your mind. The plant that distracts and unsettles one's equilibrium. The name of this beautiful flower is…. Infatuation."

Josef, with a wide-eyed surprised stare, developed a glowing smile. "Anneliese, you are so perceptive, but may I ask you a question. Would you allow me to come back to the UK with you? I have asked permission of my superiors and they think it's a great idea. I will do any work you require, I can keep my Government informed, and perhaps even help with our KCT troops!"

"Josef, certainly, we would be pleased to have you in our team." She inhaled a deep breath. A widening smile developed as she added a comment based on intuition. "And Josef, someone else will be overjoyed to see you, and I pray you and Summer will make some time for romance!"

Josef blushed and uttered a sigh of relief. "Anneliese, what time should I be prepared to leave with you? Major Fite said he would be returning today to fly you all, in two helicopters to the UK. But I didn't get a time." "It will be around 9pm tonight, Josef, as darkness falls. Two Dauphin, Blue Thunder helicopters will arrive on the adjacent playing fields. We have plenty of room for you as those choppers can carry 12 people in each. Now get on your phone and make Summer deliriously happy!" Still holding Anneliese's hand, Josef stood, bowed and kissed her hand. "Madame, I thank you, with all my heart!"

Mid-afternoon, Anneliese had her team back together again. "Is anyone unsure of the plans for the operation tomorrow?" Nobody made a noise or moved a muscle. Anneliese grasped the arms of her chair, stood, then wheeled around behind it. Leaning on the back of the chair, she slowly glanced around the room. "Does anyone have any concerns or questions? I want to know you all have belief in our plan!" Strained expressions stared back at Anneliese. "So, I'll ask one more time. Are you confident in the plan and fully understand the part you will play. Please, everyone give me a loud, convincing reply. Now!!!"

"Yes" was the word screamed from every wide-open mouth! Anneliese slowly edged around the whole team, shaking their hands and thanking them individually.

"I have just two more questions before I reach complete satisfaction. The first is simple. Are you all ready to leave? Major Fite will arrive just prior to 9pm to transport us all to Blackwall. So if you are not prepared, once we finish you have plenty of time to get yourselves organised. My next question is to the combat team, led by Frank Junior. Have you all accessed your preferred weaponry? If not, please see Josef. He will escort you to the armaments store, which I understand is in the basement. Now a reminder. You have all had training in how to apply your disguises. The experts will be with us in Blackwall at 7am. That gives you all a massive amount of time to get it right. There will be lots more photos taken. But please keep working at it until you and they are convinced it is perfect. We cannot afford any slip-ups."

"I will get together with Major Fite in the morning. I believe we will leave Blackwall around 1.00pm. We must not be early, or late! But I will handle the timing with Major Fite, and give you plenty of notice."

The whirring sound of helicopter rotors were heard in the distance. It was 8.50pm. As the rotor and engine noise increased, it alerted them all. At 9.00pm the whole team were ready in the entrance hall. Josef included. His eyes sparkling with anticipation!

Chapter 38

Josef – Many Answers

A nneliese sat at the front of the fuselage with Josef sitting next to her. They chatted about everything, and nothing, for a while. Then Josef admitted he was excited. He'd only been out of Holland twice before. Two package holidays to the Costa Del Sol. Anneliese always had a way of prising out information! Her gentle technique gained several important personal facts. Josef was 26 years old. Beyond all else, he loved his country and the UK. Grandparents had instilled in him how brave and wonderful the UK had been in WWII, defending and then rescuing their country from German domination. He had never been married and had never had a real girlfriend. There was one at school, but it only got as far as holding hands, as they walked to school.

Anneliese, now intent on gently finding out more, began with an explanation. "Josef, men of your age, are constantly intimidated by the need to find a woman to love." Josef stared into Anneliese's eyes with embarrassment. "Josef, please don't be embarrassed. Do you know, in my twenties I lived in Amsterdam. At the time I was on assignment for the CECD but, to be frank, they had placed me there as a sex worker. I was a Red Light girl. So nothing you ever tell me will surprise me. And nothing you tell me will ever go any further!"

"Josef, please believe me. I am an expert in romance, relationships and how to enjoy and develop sex with your partner. It's important, if you want to meet someone and stay with them forever. So now, I'm going to ask you a difficult personal question. how many women have you had sex with?" Josef, looking into Anneliese's eyes, realised this was the moment his shame would surface. "Anneliese;" his head dropped as he took a breath. "Anneliese, none. I am a virgin, at the age of 26, here in the centre of the sex world, Amsterdam!"

Anneliese's expression transformed from enigmatic to strong endearment. Her voice lowered and softened. "Josef, you are a very attractive, intelligent young man." Josef offered a rapid response. "Yes, Anneliese, intelligence has helped me in my work life, to the point where I have romanced my career, rather than searching for female love and affection!"

"Well, my Josef, that will stop right now! I have seen the tenderness in the eyes of both of you. Believe me, I know this time you will find your soul mate. Let's get this operation out of the way, then I will mentor you through the early romantic phases with Summer. I can assure you, it will be the most spectacular time of your life! I will make it perfect, because I can. Always remember, I wrote the book of love!"

After a very soft careful landing, Anneliese quietly led the way into the small, dimly lit Blackwall reception area. Once everyone had congregated together, Anneliese with a soft, but assertive tone addressed them all. "I don't often do this, or even need to do it. But I'm going to give you all an order!" Looking at Major Fite, she grinned as she said, "that includes your SAS troopers." "If you want, you may have one drink in the bar. Then, you are all ordered to bed. I need you all with very clear heads tomorrow. There are only four exceptions. Frank, Major Fite, Matthew, and of course, myself. I need to go over a few things with them just one more time."

A queue formed in front of Anneliese. First Denton and Ece. "Goodnight, we need slumber!" Next Hana and Donald, same reason, more embraces. No surprise in the next couple; Frank Junior and Csenge received strong loving kisses from Anneliese.

But now came the surprise! Anneliese was confronted by the tall Frenchman, Louis. Her brow furrowed as she wondered why he was in line with the other couples. Two small arms became visible as they slid around his waist, and a sublime expression stealthily appeared. Yes, it was an embarrassed but intent Penny! "Anneliese, we are tired and need our sleep. Is that OK with you?" Anneliese who already had suspicions, grasped them both. "Yes, please head up those stairs. I am expecting a lot from both of you tomorrow!"

That first drink was like frequenting a singles bar. Anneliese and Matthew collared Frank and Major Fite. The rest sat at the bar, enjoying conversation that led, most times, to hilarity. Slow lingering sips replaced the usual gulps, but eventually, the singles drifted off to their rooms.

Frank asked first, then ordered a second drink for them all. They had, during the first drink, worked through a few last pygmy concerns. But now, all feeling completely at ease with the planning, started to relax.

Frank chuckled as he mentioned the growth in romances. Adam Fite sipped a large Brandy, then inhaled. "I've ordered my guys to stay well away! They are all fit, healthy and on the point of exploding with testosterone. I've heard them talking. They have mentioned almost every female. But their fantasies seem to centre on Kainaat and Asha. I've given them a severe talking to and warned them off. I just need it to hold until the operation is over!"

Anneliese had been thoughtful all the way through Major Fite's comments. But now her expression was overcome by laughter. She wobbled on the bar stool as her mind wandered back through the myriad of times she had seen and experienced this part of life. Matthew steadied her.

As she calmed, Major Fite, with a pleasurable look in his eyes, asked the question. "Anneliese, what was it I said that had such an impact." Frank sat with a knowing look on his face!

"Adam, it's purely nature. I shouldn't need to be saying this to you three. You are men, so will have experienced it. However, this is my dissertation. From the age of around 12 to as late as 90, men's brains are overwhelmed by the female form. I believe that up to 90% of their thinking power is devoted to their attraction to females." In other words, sex. They can't help it! Some clever men fight their way through it by becoming absorbed with something else. Indeed, I have come across that today. I have a good friend who has been so absorbed in his work, he has not allowed himself to look beyond it! But now the attraction is too strong. He is infatuated with someone!"

"This is all part of the natural, healthy process that God has given us. You saw all the romantic couples saying goodnight to me. I am pleased for them! It's what a peaceful, natural world is meant to do! However, that early romantic period is physically demanding. While we are at war, like tomorrow, we need our guys to be at peak physical fitness. So I am glad, Major Fite, that you have kept your guys minds on the job."

Frank began to chuckle. "Here we are on a life and death mission, and they've got us discussing their romantic inclinations. We just have to believe it will lift their spirits and stiffen their resolve!"

A naughty grin spread across Anneliese's face. She replied, "Stiffening resolve is the least of our worries!" Their laughter could still be heard as they stepped out into the passageway and headed for their beds.

⁕

Chapter 39

Russian Spills the Beans

The make-up and disguise geniuses were in their allocated room at 7am on the dot. By 7.30am they had worked on three of the EAI team for almost 30 minutes.

Rashi sped into the room then stopped to look at the faces. She was finding it difficult to recognise any of them. So she decided, the best course of action was to shout her question. "Has anyone seen Anneliese?" A face turned to speak. She closely resembled a young Jennifer Lopez! "She went for a walk outside with Matthew. She said she needed to nourish her brain with oxygen before our performance." The scintillating features of this young lady turned away and the make-up artist resumed her work.

Rashi, as if standing in no-man's land, stamped her foot, turned and waltzed out toward reception. As if by magic, the entrance door opened and Anneliese and Matthew appeared!

"Anneliese, Anneliese! I've got some good important news. Please, both of you, can we go to a quiet corner of the lounge?" They sat together; Anneliese and Matthew both peering at Rashi. "So Rashi, what's got you so excited?" As she prepared to speak, courtesy gained a foothold. "Would you both like a drink? Tea, coffee, water perhaps?"

Anneliese leaned forward and clasped Rashi's hand. "We can see you are excited, and so you've got both of us excited!

For pity's sake, Rashi, spill the beans. If your information is worth it, we will celebrate with a coffee afterwards."

Rashi, breathed deeply for several seconds. "Anneliese, I've had Tiny Tim feeding me information and talking to me almost the whole night." Anneliese and Matthew turned to stare at one another, their eyes squinting under furrowed brows. "Rashi, please go on, you are getting us both close to orgasm!"

Rashi's lips gripped tight together, as she attempted to stifle laughter. "Ok, I'm sorry." She inhaled again and opened her eyes wide. "I will take you slowly through the whole thing!"

"The Americans, and by that I mean our EAI team in America, have a Russian in custody. He just surrendered to us. Denton's people have been interrogating him now for over 36 hours. Tiny Tim has led the investigation. He believes this Russian is sincere and willing to give us valuable, indeed, crucial information, concerning Russia's involvement with the PRP in the UK."

Anneliese's hand moved to Rashi's lips. "Rashi stop there! That is absolutely fantastic. For days and weeks now my mind has been intimidated and terrorised by one question. How do we prove the PRP's subversive work with Russia? Rashi, I know your AI systems have captured snippets of conversation and elements of communication, but I've never been sure it would be enough to convince a court that it was sufficiently incriminating."

Rashi's eyes, now wildly excited, begged Anneliese to stop and let her deliver the sucker punch. "Anneliese, there's more, much more!" "This Russian would only impart a certain amount of knowledge, firstly to get us on the hook and believing in him. And, of course, his second objective was to get agreement to his demands." Once again, Anneliese's brow furrowed. "What Rashi, are his demands?" "Well, Anneliese, it's as simple as this! The leads he gave Tim were relatively innocuous, but I have worked on them. He is being absolutely honest with us. And all he wants is to be allowed to live in freedom, with his family, away from the tyranny in Russia. A new life, initially protection, and a new identity for him, his wife and two children. He is a very brave man!"

"Anyway, let me move on. He gave Tim a limited amount of detail concerning the secure systems used by the Russian FSB, the Federal Security Service, and the SVR, their Foreign Intelligence Service."

"Tiny Tim sent what he had to me. I poked it into my supreme AI information Processing programme. It independently worked on it for two hours. Now I have every communication, every word spoken, between Russia and the PRP. My birthday came early when it showed me a video of a meeting between Premier Tibbs and President Sokolov discussing and planning the execution of Norman! Even to the point Sokolov explained how they would get the Novichok into the UK, for Tibbs cronies to use on Norman Simpson!"

Rashi's despondent expression gradually arrived as her heart and soul surfaced above her waves of excitement. At that moment, the realisation that a colleague and friend had died, and that her work was miniscule by comparison, hit home.

Anneliese and Matthew sat quietly holding hands. Rashi's eyes began to flood. Anneliese reached for Rashi's hand. The tears were infectious! As Anneliese's eyes began to glisten, she put all her effort into the brave world that would be essential today.

"Rashi, you, Tiny Tim and Denton's team back in the US have given us the evidence we need at the end of today. But now I must proceed to take this whole operation through to conclusion. One last question. Have you brought Frank Junior up to speed on this?"

Rashi's smile and her answer explained the negative. "No, Anneliese. I was nervous to disturb him. He was with Csenge!" Anneliese smiled. "Rashi, please do, and tell him I am so proud of him, you, and all his fabulous staff. You have given me the end of the story. Now, all I need is for everything to go to plan to reach that ending!"

Rashi wanted to say a few last words. "Anneliese, I have shown my work to Tiny Tim. He's not tiny, he's enormous! He has committed himself saying that any court would see this evidence as incontrovertible, absolutely conclusive. So, press ahead today! You will seal the fate of those morons, as I always knew you would!"

An hour or so later, Matthew, at Anneliese's request, went around everyone asking them to assemble in the breakfast room. Anneliese sauntered in. "I would like us all to get together again at midday. By then the disguise applications will be finished." Most began to chuckle, pointing at Sly, Csenge, Junior and a few others. Anneliese, smiling, continued. "In between times, please, all eat a hearty breakfast. This may be a very long day and we will all need tons of protein in our bellies."

Frank and Matthew joined Anneliese and their trio tripped down the corridor into the fresh air.

At midday, disguises finished, they were beginning to feel comfortable. Photographs had been taken and Rashi's AI 3D programme had worked wonders on the security passes. Her little machine had given birth to the passes, a few seconds at a time. Rashi now sat attaching lanyards with various country's emblems emblazoned along them.

Anneliese, Frank and Matthew strolled in to join their team. Denton, only a few steps behind, stopped to watch as Frank meandered into the middle of the room. Frank, always the one to thoroughly enjoy lifting spirits before a battle, gritted his teeth and glared at the assembled company.

As his eyes scrolled around the room, his twinkling eyes turned to Anneliese. "Hey Matthew, you have brought us to the wrong room!" He bent over and took a deep breath. With smiling eyes, he began to point at the individuals before him. "This is the movie stars room. Look, we have Jennifer Lopez. Now I'm getting excited! And Johnny Depp." Pointing at Frank Junior; "Look it's Orlando Bloom. Fuck, you don't look anywhere near as tall in the movies." Now, Ece was his target. "I saw you in that film "Fifty Shades of Grey! You were fabulous. Can't remember your name, but I'll always remember your body!" Ece's face blushed through her make-up!

Spirits lifted into the stratosphere. Laughter continued for several minutes. Frank bowed out! Applause followed him!

Anneliese took Frank's place. Standing in the middle of that room, her elegance and gracious smile captured everyone.

Her nostrils flared as she inhaled to bring her love for these people to the forefront of her mind. "You all look fabulous. So I wish to begin by thanking Rashi for her planning, and the Pretenders Movie Company Artists for their work. I have seen your security passes and they deserve an accolade. Rashi prepared them and they are more than precise. Absolutely no one will question them!"

"Pressing on, a coach emblazoned with tourist advertising will be here for you at precisely 13.20. You will be driven through the East End to the embankment and disembark about half a mile past Temple Station. You will then walk, as if a tourist group, the last half a mile to the Houses of Parliament. You all know your roles from that point. The SBS will arrive in the Thames at 14.50. The question and answer time will be five minutes in by then. Those of you that will be inside in the Strangers Gallery must be in your seats no later than 14.35. I am going over those names once again. Csenge, Ben, Enrique and Donald." A wry smile gradually appeared on Anneliese's face. "If you guys get locked in at any point, I am confident Donald will work his magic on the locks, and get you out!"

Chapter 40

The Coup Begins

The Commando 47 Troop and SAS teams' helicopters landed just after 12.25 hours. They quietly scrambled into the Blackwall facility. Anneliese was there to meet them. Each trooper, loaded with equipment, grasped Anneliese's hand, politely nodded, and thanked her; then headed into the restaurant.

The EAI team's coach arrived on time. Other than glancing cheek kisses for both Matthew and Frank Junior, no time was given to fuss or emotion. Anneliese, Rashi and Denton's small group uttered good luck as the team stepped up into the coach. At 13.35 they were waved through the barrier and accelerated onto the A13.

Josef had been standing alone, but now shuffled across to Anneliese. "Madame, I desire to help in any way I can!"

Anneliese took Josef's hand and led him in. The rest followed. As they strolled along, she uttered, "We should go to the Command room to watch for developments. Rashi has linked every CCTV camera in London to our screens, so we should watch the team's progress along the Embankment and into Parliament Square. Just another thing, Josef, please stick close to me for the rest of the day. I'm feeling my age and not too great!" Josef squeezed her hand and whispered "Of course Madame, I will stay with you as long as you want me to!"

The three of them, Anneliese, Rashi and Denton, sat in a row, watching blank screens. Josef had wandered out, but was back in two minutes, carrying a large water jug and several glasses. He bent over Anneliese and whispered, "Madam Anneliese, please drink lots of water to avoid dehydration." Then he sat on her left side. Anneliese smiled a thank you, just as Rashi brought the screens to life.

At 14.00 a single screen focused on their coach as it pulled into the kerbside, 400 metres past Temple Tube Station. The team assembled under a tree, then followed behind Matthew, holding high a paddle; performing as the tourist group leader. They nonchalantly strolled toward Big Ben, with Matthew checking his wristwatch every few minutes. They were aiming to be outside the entrance to the House of Commons at precisely 14.20. The planning allowed 2 minutes each for the four agents to pass through security, and a further 3 minutes to reach their seats in the Strangers Gallery.

The minutes, ticking by, seemed like decades. The strain was also impacting those in Blackwall. But now, on that same screen, the camera moved to the river. The Thames was like a millpond, and the camera picked out the three RIB's leisurely moving toward the Parliament Buildings.

As the camera turned and captured the RIB's approaching Westminster Bridge, smiles broke out across the Blackwall faces. People walking across the Bridge and on the Embankment were frantically waving.

Once again, the EAI team featured on screen. Matthew was seem shepherding everyone past Cleopatra's Needle. They were allowed to glance at the flowers that had been placed beside it.

Anneliese giggled when Denton picked out Sly, he had an uncanny resemblance to Johnny Depp! As the RIB's slowed under the bridge and steered toward the Parliament

Building Wall, the crowds on the bridge grew. Cheering, whistling, even singing, broke out.

It was now 14.40. The SBS troops having enjoyed the moment, began their work in a serious professional manner. Grappling hooks were tossed upwards onto the Pavilion Terrace. Eight minutes later, most of the troopers were together, helping the last few over the wall.

Loud cheering from the crowd on the Westminster Bridge had drawn several of the Parliament Wardens into the Pavilion. They had received notice that an army exercise would take place, and began enjoying the spectacle.

Just as the SBS were about to batter their way into the Pavilion Terrace, one of the Wardens, with a huge smile, stepped forward and released the door bolts. Led by their platoon Commander, the SBS troopers snuck in. The Commander, his finger up to his lips, indicated they needed silence.

The Wardens stood back, as the SBS platoon sprinted into the House of Commons, and up the stairs to the ground floor. Their lieutenant edged stealthily up to the top stairs to the ground floor and peered around. Several people were milling around in the vast entrance hall. His eyes followed the last few MP's walking towards the Chamber of the House of Commons. As the last MP entered, the Chambers vast dark oak doors slammed shut.

The lieutenant stared at his Omega wristwatch, his eyes followed the rotating second hand for 120 seconds. His platoon crouched on the stairs behind him. It was now 14.53.

With a flexing of his arm and wrist, the lieutenant gave the order to move across the entrance hall to the debating Chamber. At the same time, Frank was watching from the entrance, and moving forward toward security, his pass dangling on his midriff.

Chapter 41

Anneliese in the Thick of It

Back in Blackwall there was no longer much to see on the screens. Anneliese stood and stared out of a window. With a strong determined tone, she shouted "Josef, get us a car…. Right away! Denton, come with me and bring me a pistol. Rashi, man the command centre. We are going to Parliament!" Within 3 minutes, one of the Blackwall guards arrived in an EAI car. Anneliese ran to the car and jumped in the driver's seat. As both rear doors clunked shut, Anneliese sped toward the main gate. As the barrier opened, she reached forward and switched on the blues and twos.

Anneliese opened up the throttle. Within 5 seconds they were travelling at 60mph. Cars and trucks on the A13 were scuttling every which way. Now she tried to ease the fear showing in her passengers' eyes. "All those high speed training courses they sent me on are paying dividends. And this Ford Capri EV is sensational. So responsive!" Just at that moment a van pulled out of a side street. Anneliese, still with sirens blaring, swerved inside it, mounted the kerb and continued, at high speed for about 70 metres; straight through the next set of traffic lights and into the Limehouse Link tunnel, on the wrong side of the road, swerving back and forth to avoid oncoming drivers.

Anneliese kept her foot on the pedal, as they exited the tunnel onto the embankment. "This is great fun. I'd forgotten how much fun you could have behind the wheel. I don't think I'll go back to being chauffeured any time soon. This is amazing!"

In Parliament, the SBS lieutenant standing at the door to the Commons Chamber, with a sig P226 pistol in his right hand, waved his sergeant forward. "Use the butt of your Carbine to bang on the door three times." The sergeant nodded and pounded his Colt Canada Carbine on the door.... Three times!

Chapter 42

Tibbs and the PRP Overcome

The door slowly opened. At the halfway point, the SBS troopers burst into the Chamber, closely followed by Frank and the SAS troops. They stationed themselves facing the MP's benches, up and down the small corridor that runs between the banks of benches. Guns pointing at both the PRP Government and Opposition. Slowly and carefully, the EAI team positioned themselves in the middle of the troops. Captain Luke Donovan and the Commando 47 Special Forces troop settled around the doorway blocking any attempted exit. Kainaat and Asha stood by the entrance to the Parliament building; Beretta revolvers in hand, securing and preventing entrance to the main building.

For once, despite being as full as the Ganges on a holy purification day, the Chamber was silent for 30 seconds.

The silence was broken by Prime Minister Tibbs. He stood, pushed his way through the SBS troops and marched to the ballot box, as if to make a speech. His dominant, intensely vicious stare, searched the room.

"Who the fuck are you? What are you doing in my country's Parliament? My police and my troops will be here any moment. And you are being televised, we will have a record of all your faces!"

Major Fite stepped forward. "Mr Tibbs, we are your troops!" At that moment the door to the Chamber opened. The Metropolitan Police Commissioner marched towards the ballot box. "Yes Mr Tibbs, Major Fite represents the British Army. I represent the British Police Force, and I am placing you under arrest. You are charged with treason, sedition, money laundering and there will be a million other charges. The most heinous charge is multiple murders. You don't have to say anything now, but if you..." the Commissioner never had the chance to finish his arrest warning!

A man in the Strangers Gallery, stood and fired a pistol shot at the Commissioner. It missed but the person behind him, his Police aide, collapsed and fell to the floor. It was Summer Bright!

As troopers fell on their knees to attend to Summer, a second shot was heard. The guy that had shot Summer, fell forward out of the Strangers Gallery crashing into the Opposition benches below. An accurate fast shot from Frank Junior's snub-nosed Colt had finished him.

Next, another guy in the Strangers Gallery, pulled a gun and fired. But before he could take aim, Donald smashed an accurate punch into his face that sent him hurtling into the people sitting beside him. Those people just happened to be Ben, Enrique and Csenge. As Ben and Enrique beat and restrained him, Csenge's karate training took control.

Her right arm wheeled back behind her shoulder. The blow to his throat was so ferocious, his eyes reeled backwards in their sockets. His breathing faltered, and he was out for the count! Both attackers were PRP personal security mercenaries.

Once again, the room fell silent. People at home watching could not believe what was happening and wondered what would come next.

They didn't have to wait too long. The door opened. The troops made way for.... Anneliese. As she stood in the middle of the Parliamentary benches, Josef, walking just behind her, saw Summer. Still lying on the floor with SBS troopers attempting to stem the bleeding.

Josef knelt beside her, holding her hand. Looking into his eyes, she said, "Please, Josef, don't be concerned. It's just a shoulder wound. And an ambulance is on the way."

Tibbs began to screech again. With intimidating eyes he shouted, "Who the hell are you? Why are you here?" Anneliese sidled into the middle of the Commons Chamber. Her glare at Tibbs would have melted icebergs. "My name is Anneliese Teer! If you had done your homework you would know who I am. But no, you are an evil person that spends his time cultivating insurrection, subversion and murder. Do you know Mr Tibbs, I have spent my whole life dealing with wicked, evil people. But you are the worst I have ever come up against. So, who am I? I'm a wife, a mother and a person with values. You do not have any morality; any ethics, any values! And because you are so evil you can't live in normal society. You will spend the rest of your life in prison, in order to protect the rest of us. The reason I can be sure of this, is that I am the Director General of EuroAm Intelligence, EAI. The Western World Security Agency. And this operation has the full consent and support of NATO."

"Do you know Mr Tibbs, you are going down in history. You will be taken from this place to be incarcerated in the Tower of London. The last people to be imprisoned there were the Kray Brothers. And they had nothing on you!"

Anneliese wheeled around to look at the Government PRP benches. "All of the PRP Government and party members will also be arrested. You will stand trial for your involvement in the crimes that have been committed. At the very least you will be charged with collusion in treason against the UK."

Sly couldn't keep his emotion in check. He strode out from behind the troopers, and over to Premier Tibbs. Pulling Tibbs hands behind his back, he quickly applied handcuffs. Leaning forward he whispered in Tibbs ear. "You fuucker, you killed my best friend. If it was up to me, right now, I would carve open your stomach and slowly pull out your intestines. But I am learning to be civilised, so I will go along with the law. Just don't upset me!"

As Tibbs was being taken out, Anneliese faced the TV cameras. "Hello people of Great Britain. Under normal circumstances I would not be allowed to talk to you. But these are exceptional circumstances. And to crown it all, I am retiring today! So, this is the last operation I will be involved in, under the constraints of the Official Secrets Act."

"You have suffered a nightmare with a Government intent on destroying families, treating our senior citizens as garbage, and embezzling tax payers' money. We have evidence they have colluded with Russia and Iran in these despicable crimes."

"The Democracies of the Western World, NATO, decided they had to act. So here and now, I am announcing that this is a bloodless coup, to reinstate democracy in the United Kingdom."

Ten feet from the door, Tibbs shouted "So which countries do you represent? Which countries gave you the authority? You are full of shit!" Anneliese snarled, "Mr Tibbs, you really must learn to listen!"

Several EAI Agents moved to the front and shuffled through the crowds. Standing beside Anneliese, their disguised faces stared at the TV cameras.

Anneliese peered around the Chamber then proudly proclaimed, "My team are here with me; here and now they will tell the whole of Great Britain the countries they work for. Countries that could no longer stand by and watch this callous, deranged PRP Government commit genocide and continue their subversive activities. Indeed, the whole of NATO voted to depose the PRP!"

Anneliese's face swivelled back and forth across her team. Then with a commanding voice she shouted, "Please loudly shout your country!" Csenge, still in the Strangers Gallery was first; she stood and shouted HUNGARY. Ece screamed TURKEY. The shout UNITED STATES of AMERICA came from several of them. Next CZECH REPUBLIC. Frank screamed SOUTHERN IRELAND. Anneliese proudly announced CANADA. The loudest voice of all came from next to Tibbs. It was Sly! He screamed at the top of his voice LIVERPOOL! Several Conservative MP's applauded. Josef, kneeling by Summer was another voice. NEDERLAND! Last in this long list was Louis and Michel. Jointly they proclaimed FRANCE!

Everyone thought the violence was at an end, and the Operation over. Paramedics pushed the door open, and led by Denton were soon putting Summer on a stretcher. Denton moved to Anneliese and quietly, had a word in her ear.

Chapter 43

Senior Citizens Rescued

Anneliese turned to face the TV cameras again. "I am to give the people of the UK some good news. I have just been informed that your Senior Citizens on the Death Ships at Tilbury and Southampton are safe and well. Over 80% have been evacuated and have been placed in safe havens. The remainder are being rescued as we speak. However, I am extremely sad to tell you that six of your elderly on the Tilbury ship have passed away. It seems the death workers had already begun to apply lethal injections, thinking the ship was close to sailing."

Screams and groans from around the Chamber preceded further news. "The Assisted Dying Centres throughout the country have been closed down? Your old folks will be brought home to you within the next 24 hours. Your new Parliament will decide if and when they will re-open."

Staring into the cameras, Anneliese continued. "I am informed that almost the whole country has come to a standstill and is watching us on TV. So to give you some more pieces of information on this historic day. We, your Secret Service people, named today's operation "THE AGE OF WISDOM." Today your old folk, who are our age of wisdom, are safe. So let's all hope and pray we, as a world, will enter an age of wisdom. Also today's date is 10 October. It is a day of rescue and re-birth. Ten Ten should be celebrated every year, just as Eleven Eleven is, to remind us to always defend against evil."

"Two last pieces of news. The Death Ship at Tilbury was evacuated, and its old people rescued, by the Dutch military. We all owe the Dutch Government and their military a massive vote of thanks and gratitude that will last forever! And for that matter, the French for their fishing fleet blockades!"

"The only thing left for me to do is to request the Leader of the Conservative Party, Mr Holderness, to take on the job of Interim Prime Minister until democratic elections can be organised. Thank you and God Bless every one of you!"

Tibbs, being led by Sly, and surrounded by SBS troopers and Met Police, was taken down the stairs to the Pavilion Terrace. Summer, with Josef, was now on her way to St Thomas's Hospital.

Sly and SBS troopers dragged Tibbs to the Pavilion wall. Two troopers grabbed hold of the ropes, sat on the wall, turned and clambered down. Two others tossed Tibbs down into the RIB. The Thames was clear as they powered across to the Corvette anchored on the south side of the river.

Now, 30 more troopers dropped down the wall, and, in 2 RIBs, accelerated up to 30 knots, toward the Tower of London.

Chapter 44

Jerome – Back in the Fold

nneliese standing with Junior in the Parliament entrance, was greeted by a regiment of photographers and journalists. Frank and Frank Junior brushed the media aside and ran to Anneliese's Ford Capri EV, parked and protected by the two military coaches. Anneliese now made a run for it. As Frank Junior heard the clunk of the door locks, he turned in his seat and asked "Where to, Mum?" "Frank, we must go to the Tower to release Jerome!"

"OK, Mum, five minutes." What a driver Junior was! Almost equal to Anneliese. With blues and twos blasting out, Frank Junior, looking in his mirror, joked, "Mum, we have two police cars as company. Their sirens are on. Do you think they are chasing us? I'll try and lose them!" Frank sat with hands covering his eyes. The speedo reached 90mph at the end of the Embankment and through the whole of the Link Tunnel. Just three minutes later, they scorched down the slope to the Tower of London entrance. The media were everywhere. TV cameras, reporters holding microphones, photographers and journalists.

Still in the Capri, they could see a group walking up from the river wall. As they neared, they became visible. It was Sly, still leading; pushing and shoving Tibbs. Surrounded by SBS troopers and a platoon of Royal Marines.

Frank Junior, looking in the rear-view mirror, said, "Oh, oh, the Police are heading towards us." Two officers plodded up to the Capri and rapped on the window. Junior turned to Anneliese. "Mum, I don't want points on my clean licence." She giggled as he pressed the button and the window dropped.

The officer had a wide smile for Anneliese. "Mrs Teer, please go in. The Yeoman Beefeaters are expecting you. We will look after your car." The policemen opened the doors for Anneliese, Frank Junior and Frank, and as they stepped out, a very smart salute followed.

The group led by Sly disappeared into the Tower. Another group walking towards the entrance now came into focus. Four marines with three Beefeaters, surrounding and assisting another individual. Anneliese ducked under the barrier as it began to open. Frank and Frank Junior followed.

Anneliese's eyes fixed on the group. As they came closer, she recognised the small individual in the middle of the group. It was Jerome. Anneliese began to walk towards them. She broke into a run, then an Olympic sprint for the last 50 yards. Frank Junior trying to keep up with her, shouted, "Mum, please slow down, be careful!"

Anneliese burst through the group, grasped Jerome's face and kissed it. "Jerome, are you ok!" "I am now Anneliese, thank you so much!" Next came embraces from Frank and Frank Junior. Anneliese stood back and perused Jerome. "My God Jerome, you look thin. Are you unwell? Were you treated ok?"

Jerome's head fell on Anneliese's shoulder. "The first 36 hours were horrific. But let's get back into the world that I love, and I will tell you all."

The walk to the car was beyond belief. The SBS, the police, the Marines and even the media put everything into reviving Jerome from the nightmare he had been through.

Blues and twos rushed them back to Blackwall. The whole EAI team were there on the steps ready to greet them.

Once in the Blackwall building, Frank and Anneliese sat with Jerome in the lounge. After a coffee, but a tea for Jerome, Anneliese asked, "Would you like to go and have a shower, then join us all for dinner?"

Jerome's face saddened. "Anneliese, I find this difficult to say. I am embarrassed! Unless it's a disabled shower with a seat and hand rails, I don't think I could manage it. Under Tibbs instructions, I was locked in what is known as the Little Ease Cell." Tears began to fill his eyes, "Tibbs had instructed that I should be in there for 36 hours, then he would re-consider. The cell was just over a metre square. I could not bend, sit and was not fed." He managed a smile. You don't want to hear about toilets."

Anneliese screamed! Tears flooded down her cheeks. "That evil, wicked fucking bastard. In this day and age we are still facing mediaeval torture!"

Frank took hold of Jerome's hand. "Come on my old mate. I will help you with everything and we'll have you back on your feet in a couple of days." Anneliese, with a sympathetic expression said, "We are all meeting in the bar at 8.0'clock. We will all understand if you feel you can't make it. But it would be great if you could. You are the star of the show!"

The evening, as it began, had a difficult, tense feeling. Emotion abounded! Anneliese had announced her retirement and Jerome had been severely mistreated, to the point of sadistic torture!

But spirits lifted when Josef came in and stood by the door. With a massive grin building above his bearded chin, Josef proudly announced, "May I introduce one of the celebrated heroines of today." He pushed the door wide open and shouted, "An English Summer has arrived!"

With an embarrassed expression, Summer stepped in. Everyone applauded with most taking turns to carefully embrace her. Her torso was bandaged from the shoulder joint, across her chest and down her left arm.

Peering around, she asked, "Where is Jerome. I was told he was with you." Anneliese and Frank stood back pointing at Jerome.

Sitting in a large comfortable armchair, Jerome's eyes began to sparkle as Summer approached. Then she said, "Jerome, it's a privilege to meet you," as she dropped to her knees in front of him. "I am so relieved you are ok! I've heard from my bosses that you suffered nightmares in there, but we will get your engine revs back to normal in just a couple of days!"

At that moment, the background music got Summer's attention. She screamed to the bar, "Please barman, turn it up....loud!" Holding Jerome's hand, she stood, swaying from side to side. She began to sing along with the music. "We can't give you anything but love, baby." She had changed the words slightly, but everyone joined in.

As their voices combined, and the volume of the track was increased, even the bar staff joined in, as the song reached fever pitch.

In the last few stanzas, Jerome's eyes livened with pure pleasure. His seated dancing, holding Summer's hand, as she swayed, had worked miracles. When the end came, the room erupted. And as it did so, Jerome's love for his friends flooded energy into his mind and body. He stood, then with one hand on Summer's hip, swayed through the last few bars.

The music ended, but Jerome continued to sway with Summer. "I can never thank you enough. You have brought my spirit back. I am an East End lad, and now I feel ashamed that I let myself get so low. You found the key to open the lock that's pulled me out of my melancholy. I will never forget you for that!" Summer returned a smile. "Jerome, I have read of your work. You have so much to be proud of. Is there anything else I can do to help you on the road to recovery?"

"Yes, but first I need to thank another person." Jerome's eyes moved to Josef, "This wonderful lady has just asked if I need anything more. Josef, yes I do. First I want a very large scotch. It's not really my drink but it will bring back important memories. Second, I want you to dance with Summer this night and every night for the rest of your lives!"

Fatigue, all around, was becoming evident. Noticing the pale skin of tiredness gradually overcoming Jerome's face, Anneliese called Josef over. As she prepared to speak, Summer sidled alongside Josef. "Hello you two, I want to ask for some help with something."

Anneliese edged slowly out of her chair, and with her arm gently placed across Josef's shoulders, eased him away to the centre of the bar. Summer stuck to Josef like superglue. Anneliese's eyes softly appealed to Josef. As the three huddled, Anneliese quietly explained, "Jerome has had an horrendous ordeal. You both will have gathered how much we all love him. Josef, would you get with the Blackwall staff to see if an exceptionally comfortable room can be found and prepared for him. All the rooms here are acceptable, but I want him to be pampered. It needs to be available in about 30 minutes. Would you try?"

Summer spoke first. "Anneliese, Josef and I will find something special." Josef nodded vigorously! "And while we are on that subject Summer, what are you proposing to do for the night hours?" "Oh, Anneliese, I will head back to the Tower Hotel. A police car will take me."

Anneliese smiled. "Summer, there are rooms here if you wish, but if you need to return to the Tower Hotel, I will arrange a car to get Josef to meet you for breakfast." Josef grasped Summer's arm, saying to Anneliese, "We will get Jerome's room organised first, then discuss it."

They returned in 20 minutes. A glorious super-king room, with pure white bed linen, a shower with a comfortable seat, and even an umbrella hanging on the closet door, was available immediately.

Summer, having spoken with Anneliese, approached Frank. The two of them escorted Jerome to bed. Summer returned with a glorious smile. Frank was helping Jerome, who was so appreciative of the luxurious appointments and facilities.

⁕

Chapter 45

Going Home?

Early morning, Anneliese and Matthew were bustling around, excited, arranging their flight back to Toronto and beginning to pack. There were several loud knocks on their door. Anneliese's brow strained, annoyed at being disturbed on her crusade to return home.

It was Frank; seeing cases and clothes strewn across the bed, he said, "Anneliese, sorry! But I don't think you will want to leave yet." Anneliese and Matthew both developed a questioning gaze. "Why Frank? We're not in a hurry and were planning to see everyone before we leave. But I would like to get to the airport early to do some shopping in duty free. It would be nice to do something normal for a change!"

Frank grinned as he pulled out his pocket handkerchief to wipe his brow. "I probably need to say sorry 3 or 4 times, before I explain." But before he could, there was another knock on the door. Frank strode forward and answered it.

Jerome was standing in a stream of sunlight, looking healthy and immaculate. Sauntering in, he lavished embraces on Anneliese and Matthew. "You two have resurrected me. I'm almost back to normal and so can never thank you enough!" He glanced around the three of them. "We have loved one another for almost a lifetime and I want that to continue forever. Once you are back in Canada, I would like regular visits, if you can put up with me?"

"Absolutely, Jerome, we insist you have at least one holiday a year with us!" Frank now interjected. "I need to explain because things will shortly start to happen. Jerome knows what I am about to tell you, so I will just blister through it."

"At 10:00am Summer and Josef will arrive. Also Major Tony Fite and Mr Holderness, the Interim Prime Minister."

Frank ushered them all down to the Blackwall reception area. Just before 10:00am, Summer and Josef walked in. Josef thanked Anneliese, saying her car had taken him to breakfast with Summer, not in the hotel, but at a fabulous little restaurant, across Tower Bridge, on the South Side of the river. They were both overjoyed with the breakfast and views across the river to the Tower of London.

The interim Prime Minister, Mr Holderness, arrived with Major Fite. The sound of the chopper landing announced their arrival.

As the Prime Minister began to speak, the EAI team sneaked in behind them. Then the numbers grew. All the Blackwall staff joined the throng.

Premier Holderness made a short speech. "You, Anneliese, and your EAI team, have saved the UK from an insidious attempt to install a foreign power's tyranny on our shores. It has never happened in modern history. Your work has taught us all, every person in the UK, to be very careful in the selection of a Government. So from the bottom of my heart, and on behalf of every one of our citizens, I give you our thanks."

⊶⊷⟨⟩⊶⊷

Chapter 46

NATO Invitation

Next, Josef and Major Fite stepped forward. Tony Fite nodded at Josef, who spoke first. "Major Fite and I have been requested to give you NATO's warmest thanks and congratulations on such a long and illustrious career." Josef's eyes were sparkling. "I have also been asked to say how proud the whole of the Netherlands is to have been involved with you, in such a successful operation."

After a short pause, Major Fite moved forward. "It has fallen to me to ask if you would mind changing your plans. Everyone understands how much you want your family life back. But it would be greatly appreciated if you would accept an invitation from NATO." Both Premier Holderness and Josef joined Major Fite, to give moral support. "It is our privilege to inform you that NATO have organised a meeting, two days hence, to review, discuss and establish, lessons learned from those dangerous events in the UK. They are not asking for your input, although it would, probably, be at the top of their wish list."

"Their priority is this! All countries in NATO wish to express their gratitude. You, your husband and your son, Frank Junior, are invited into the auditorium on the first morning of the meeting. Then you could probably, with some relief, return to your normal family life in Toronto."

Premier Holderness, the UK interim Prime Minister, took the baton. "The meeting will take place in the White House. President Newman is inviting you and your family to travel to Washington in Air Force One. It will land at Gatwick shortly. The President's White House Staff have made arrangements for you to stay at one of the most luxurious hotels in Washington.... The Ritz Carlton, and all transport throughout the trip will be provided by the President's own motorcade."

Prime Minister Holderness took Anneliese's hand. "Mrs Teer, if you accept this invitation, I would find it a privilege if I could travel with you! If my interim position only lasts long enough to fill the gap in the country's leadership, nothing would give me greater pleasure than to tell my family and grandchildren, that I have been with you in those final days of your history-making career!"

Anneliese's gracious smile and loving eyes glanced around the room. Smiling eyes, and a few nods seemed to seal the deal. Anneliese lifted the Premier's hand and gently kissed it. "I gratefully accept, but with a single condition. I must take all my senior people with me. And that includes Josef Kalkwarf, Summer Bright and the military leaders." She peered at Major Fite as she spoke those words. "This complete team deserve the utmost recognition! Not for prowess in combat, not for fighting the enemy, not for killing people on the battlefield. But for something way beyond aggression. Simply put, working in a team, that, every step of the way, understood that the best way to win in this conflict, was to avoid casualties. These guys held that objective sacrosanct from the very moment we began to plan each and every treasured step. I have a sneaking suspicion that love for their old folks was the catalyst. This goes to prove that money, reward, uninformed politics, and the lack of careful judgement, should never be allowed to let any form of evil take our most valued elderly citizens away from us."

Anneliese's eyes glimpsed a smile on the face of Premier Holderness. "Mrs Teer, I will call the President and repeat those historic words you have spoken. I am sure he will agree for your whole team to be welcomed into Washington. The flight leaves at 4:00pm. If there are any issues I will get back to you. Otherwise, be ready for a 4:00pm flight!"

"Mrs Teer, I will never forget the words you have spoken today. Eventually, I will get round to writing my memoirs. The story of this historic day, your leadership, your diplomacy, your bravery, will take pride of place! On behalf of humanity, I thank you with all my heart!"

Chapter 47

Washington D.C. Farewell

The camaraderie, attendant luxury, drinks and cuisine, lifted everyone's spirits into rapturous joy. Anneliese, sitting alongside Matthew, Junior and Csenge, could only peer around at the close company and feel overwhelmed by the euphoria that they were now feeling. Romance, love, pride, friendships and solidarity surrounded her. It brought a strong realisation! Her career had injected some good into the world! Her mind was now in Utopia, and later in that comforting bed, she drifted into peaceful sleep.

The arrival in Washington was slick. The President's motorcade had them in the hotel lobby by 11:00am. Even then, they had nothing to do. Luggage, check-in, maps of the hotel, all happened in the blink of an eye!

On their way to the rooms, Junior and Csenge caught up with Anneliese and Matthew. "Mum, shall we meet for dinner, around 8pm?" Matthew nodded at Anneliese. "Darling, that sounds wonderful. Let's have a last day fabulous meal together!"

The rest of the day was spent enjoying luxury; some ventured into the swimming pools, or the spa, for a dose of pampering. They all met sporadically as they milled around enjoying the delights of the hotel, and generally chilling out. The exception was Summer and Josef.

On arrival they had been persuaded to attend an appointment with the President's personal physician to examine Summer's shoulder wound, apply new dressings, and undergo a complete health check. They were back in the hotel late afternoon, having been given a clean bill of health and told that healing would only require a couple more days.

Almost all the team were in the hotel restaurant for dinner. Anneliese noticed that Penny was not to be seen. Frank Junior explained that Sly had asked for a pass for him, Penny, Louis and Marcel. They wanted to visit the sites of Washington, not having been before.

Anneliese scowled as she asked Junior, "Did you tell them to get back at a reasonable hour? We have an early start in the morning and respect for our hosts must be paramount." Like a typical son, Junior chuckled. "Mum, you have retired! They are no longer your responsibility. They are adults, and after all they've been through, deserve a few hours enjoying themselves. Even if, in the morning, they are wide-eyed and legless, I promise you here and now, I will get them to the White House."

Matthew clasped Anneliese's hand. "Darling, please relax. We have years of enjoyment and relaxation ahead of us, so now would be a good time to ease into it!"

At that point, Frank arrived at their table. After ruffling Junior's head of hair, he got straight to the point. "I have arranged for us to fly out to Toronto tomorrow at 2pm." Junior interrupted as he looked sideways at Anneliese and Matthew. "Mum, Dad, would it be OK if Csenge and I came with you and had a couple of week's holiday at your place?" Anneliese immediately responded, "Frank, we would love that." Now Frank Senior interrupted. "OK, so now I need to get back on the internet and add two passengers. I don't mind, but I wish Penny was not French smitten. She's believed all that voulez vous couchez avec moi ce soir stuff, and left me to be the secretary!"

Frank grinned as he stopped to ponder. "Now I think back, it was just the same when I first met Lucia. So I take it all back! My God, it's been months. I can't wait to see her. I love that girl so much! It's right what they say, absence makes the heart grow fonder. I just pray she feels the same!"

Next morning, they all experienced a five star breakfast. Junior, good as his word, had Sly, Penny, Louis and Michel, up and in the restaurant. They looked a little worse for wear, but constant coffee seemed to be working.

The President's motorcade arrived dead on the dot of 8:30am. The NATO meeting was scheduled to start at 9.00am. The UK Acting Premier had left earlier, probably to have discussions with his NATO counterparts.

On arrival at the White House, they were met by the music of a US Marines band, playing the British National Anthem, which transitioned into a loud, proud, Star Spangled Banner!

As they stepped out of the cars, several Marines shepherded them toward the East Room, on the edge of the White House. This was the largest room in the Executive Residence of the White House and was being used this day to accommodate the NATO meetings. This was a fantastic room that had undergone recent substantial redecoration. The First Lady, Marianne, had been the driving force!

Anneliese stepped in first, followed by Matthew, and Frank Junior. The US President, President Newman, accompanied by the Acting UK Prime Minister strode across to meet them. As he embraced Anneliese, he said "Please bring your whole team in. I want them to hear every word spoken today." They entered, grouped behind the key players, Anneliese, Matthew, Frank Junior and Csenge.

As President Newman strolled to the podium, Anneliese perused this very large conference room. Rows of seats, in front of the podium, were filled with representatives of all the NATO countries. However, she was not quite sure what was going on in the corner where a stage had been recently erected. Some people were setting up what looked like a band or an orchestra.

President Newman began to speak. "I wish to offer a warm welcome to all my NATO comrades, and a very special welcome to the EAI team that have, only in the last few days, rescued the United Kingdom from the clutches of subversists, traitors and foreign powers. We, in America, must learn from this. So to my NATO allies, I say, that is why we are here today. To review the events in the UK and pay close attention to the lessons learned!"

Chapter 48

Farewell from NATO

"But before anything else, there is a much more important thing that we must do." Anneliese stood ready to be called forward. But no! President Newman proudly proclaimed, "I wish to invite a very special Senior Citizen to speak. Please, welcome US President Hayden into the forum!"

It was a delightful surprise for everyone. He had been a fabulous anti-racist, humanitarian and egalitarian throughout his term of office. He stood erect on the podium, still appearing much younger than his true years. "This is the most pleasurable experience of my life," he declared.

"On behalf of all NATO countries I have been honoured with the duty to offer you, Anneliese, our sincerest appreciation and respect for your long service to humanity." The representatives stood, cheered and whistled! It took a while for the room to settle. President Hayden continued. "Some of the younger folk in this room are not aware of the strong relationship between us and Anneliese's family. Also, my wife and I have several close friends amongst the EAI Agents. Indeed, we are very proud to have been guests at some of their weddings!"

"Eleanor, please come and stand with me." The First Lady, with delight showing on her face, strode to President

Hayden's side. President Hayden grinned as he introduced a new subject. "Do you know that since my retirement, one of my daily pleasures is to listen to 20th century rock and pop music. And you are going to hear some now. Possibly too early an era for some of you, but I'm hoping you find it memorable, enough to act as a book mark for this amazing triumphant day."

"A very good friend of ours has practiced these old songs, and I am certain she will capture your hearts with her renditions. She and her band have become pop icons in our country and many countries around the world. So I would ask you all to give a big hand to Guapa and her Guys."

The wide double doors opened. The band, led by Guapa, rushed onto the stage. Anneliese, initially appeared bemused, but then her applause almost matched the speed of her widening smile.

President Hayden grasped the mike again and strolled toward Guapa. "I did not go too far back in history for this song, which was a hit for a British band. And I believe its title and lyrics will reinforce the meaning of today. So Guapa, please do your stuff!"

Several of the EAI team could not contain themselves. Jerome, Denton, Ece, Hana, Frank and several others broke into applause, cheers and whistles. The most vocal of all was....Frank Junior! The song was "Memories." The room quietened as the words "toasts to the ones that we lost on the way" were sung with emotion and sincerity. But then everybody joined in as the whole verse was repeated!

At the end, the applause was deafening. President Hayden and Junior marched forward to the stage. Guapa leaned forward to hold their hands and kiss their cheeks!

President Hayden, once again took up the mike. "Well I can see you all enjoyed that, so now we are going back farther. Back to the Beatles era, the 1960's." Sly jumped out of his seat, screamed at the top of his voice…. "Liverpool!" President Hayden, trying to contain a giggle, said, "Sorry Sly, it's not a Beatles number."

The band began the intro. Softly, and carefully, to match Guapa's gentle, tender tone. As she began to sing the lyrics, Jerome burst to the front of the EAI team and sung along, His voice surprised everyone. Completely note perfect and in perfect harmony with Guapa. She could not resist. She jumped from the stage, grasped Jerome's hand and they shared the mike. Jerome knew every word of the song, and as the lyrics were repeated, the whole audience joined in, singing at the top of their voices.

The song, a classic 1960's pop song was…. "Listen, do you want to know a secret!"

Guapa and her guys applauded Jerome as he sauntered back to the EAI group. A torrent of embraces flooded over Jerome as he joined his colleagues. President Hayden, picking up the mike once more, said, "My job as compere for this part of the proceedings is nearly over. It's amazing that we have found another fantastic singer amongst our EAI team!" Turning to the seated audience, he said, "Let's give it up for Jerome, Director General of the UK's GCHQ." The whole auditorium stood to applaud for close to a minute!

With the microphone close to his lips, President Hayden moved towards Guapa and her Guys. "Guapa, you and your Guys have been sensational. But now, for reasons of national security I must ask you to leave the room. As explained earlier, it's the usual protocol when NATO are about to get back to business. But please take with you, our love and blessings."

As the band were gathering up their belongings and valued instruments, Frank Junior strode across to Guapa. As he got close, she jumped from the stage, clasped around his neck and kissed him. As she stared into his eyes, she asked, "Why didn't you ring me?" Junior, totally surprised, whispered his answer, "Guapa, you were a famous celebrity. I was a nobody 15 year old!" With a wry smile, she chuckled. "I understand, you are forgiven. We are both older now, and I am always around for you. So please don't forget me!"

Once Guapa and her band had left the room, President Newman took up the mike and profusely thanked President Hayden for a very enjoyable last hour.

Chapter 49

Junior's Appointment

Strolling into the middle of the auditorium, with all NATO representatives hanging on every word, he slowly explained, "Anneliese has retired, and my God, we will miss her! But one thing we did earlier was to vote on her replacement. The last Guapa song may have provided a clue. With a vote of over 90% it is my duty to tell you the secret!"

"Frank Teer is installed as the Director General of Western World Intelligence and Security. Frank Junior please join me!"

As Junior strode confidently toward President Newman, he stopped, wheeled around and took a couple of steps to Anneliese, kissing both her cheeks. Then a strong handshake and hug for Matthew. The EAI team, as a whole, stepped forward as their cheers erupted.

All delegates stood and continued the cheering and applause as Junior took the last few steps forward to shake President Newman's hand. Junior's eyes studied President Newman, who was smiling at President Hayden and his first lady, Eleanor. President Newman's chuckles into the microphone were heard by everyone. "I have to tell you all this wonderful story given to me by President Hayden."

"Apparently Junior, you were four years old when you first met President Hayden, at the wedding of Hana and

Donald." The President waved at them as they stood amongst the EAI team. "Since that time, Junior, I am told you have always called President Hayden, Uncle Bruce."

"During your first meeting you referred to Eleanor as the President's beautiful girlfriend! Although she was a beautiful mature lady, you already knew the way to her heart! President Hayden tells me that it was then that he knew you were destined for greatness. He told me more; that day, several of the EAI folks here today saved his life, and in the aftermath, it was your concern, your eloquence, your comical childish quips, that quickly healed his mind and the wounds that had been inflicted during the wedding celebrations."

Hana, Donald and the whole EAI team were emotional and showed their pleasure in this speech with cheers and loud applause.

President Newman passed the mike to Junior. "Would you like to say a few words?" "Well Sir...., you Presidents certainly know how to embarrass someone!"

Chapter 50

Will She, Won't She?

Junior, mike in hand, wandered across the auditorium to the EAI group, grasped Csenge's hand and led her across to President Hayden and Eleanor. "Sir, Uncle Bruce and Eleanor, may I introduce my beautiful girlfriend, Csenge! She is a very accomplished EAI Agent with the strongest of beliefs in democracy and her desire for a peaceful humanity!"

"I love her more than I can explain, and want her beside me when I speak. Today is my Mum's day, Anneliese's day! She and my Dad, Matthew, had a really hard time bringing me into this world. But earlier, it was mentioned that I was destined for greatness. That may be true, but only God knows the truth! It is my belief, and I have felt this since that age of 4, I do have a destiny! I know, in my heart, in my soul, I am on this earth to fight evil, defend against evil, and I will, I have to, fulfil my obligations. And it is the marvellous legacy I have from my Mother and Father which confirms that, one day, I will reach my destiny!"

The whole room was silent. Canada's representative stood to break the silence. He began to applaud, slowly at first, then other delegates joined. The EAI team's applause engulfed the room. The rapturous applause ebbed away as President Newman climbed back on the podium. Looking around, he thanked everyone. "Do you know, this has been the best NATO meeting I've ever attended. And like most of you, I am convinced we now have a continuance of excellence in our Western Security and intelligence. Thank you all; we will take a short break, then continue with the NATO agenda, in 30 minutes."

As the EAI team exited, Frank, standing at the door, was exuberant. As their team passed, all Frank could say was, "That was fabulous, fantastic, better than I ever imagined!" The EAI team assembled on the lawn; waiting for the motorcade to arrive. Frank Junior, Csenge, Matthew and Anneliese were last out, but closely followed by President Hayden and his First lady, Eleanor.

Embraces and handshakes were humongous. Junior leaned in the middle of the group and grasped Anneliese's arm. "Mum, could I have a word." He took a really deep breath, then looked up to the bright blue sky. He inhaled, then took a few seconds to peer, tenderly, into Anneliese's eyes.

"Mum, I have just asked Csenge to marry me!" "Oh my God, my wonderful boy" Anneliese turned to glance at Csenge. "Mum, she said she needed a few hours to absorb the day and everything."

Just at that point, a collared dove fluttered down and strutted on the lawn, just in front of them. Junior smiled, "Mum that's a sign! She will accept, I know she will.

I pray she will!"